Praise for
The Trouble with Hating You

"With witty banter and fascinating characters, Sajni Patel takes the classic enemies-to-lovers trope to a deliciously charming level. I loved everything about this book."
—Farrah Rochon, *USA Today* bestselling author

"Liya and Jay are a couple I've been waiting forever to meet in a romance novel. *The Trouble with Hating You* has delicious banter, deep wounds, heartwarming friendships, and a path to love that often feels impossibly hard, and the payoff is satisfying enough to give you a book hangover the size of Texas."
—Sonali Dev, *USA Today* bestselling author

"The enemies-to-lovers arc is classic, but the cultural specificity [Sajni] Patel brings makes this rom-com feel fun and fresh."
—*Publishers Weekly*

"Sajni Patel bursts onto the scene with a debut that will make you laugh!"   —Jenny Holiday, *USA Today* bestselling author

"*The Trouble with Hating You* was everything I needed—witty banter, explosive chemistry, and a hard won HEA that still has me smiling long after reading the last page. I can't wait for Sajni's next book!"   —A.J. Pine, *USA Today* bestselling author

"An enjoyable debut! The chemistry between Liya and Jay is off the charts. You'll be rooting for these two from their first meeting!"
—Farah Heron, author of *The Chai Factor*

FIRST
LOVE,
TAKE
TWO

ALSO BY SAJNI PATEL

The Trouble with Hating You

FIRST LOVE, TAKE TWO

SAJNI PATEL

FOREVER

New York   Boston

Copyright © 2021 by Sajni Patel
Reading group guide copyright © 2021 by Sajni Patel and Hachette Book Group, Inc.

Cover design by Sudeepti Tucker. Cover copyright © 2021 by Hachette Book Group, Inc.

Forever
Hachette Book Group
1290 Avenue of the Americas, New York, NY 10104
read-forever.com
twitter.com/readforeverpub

First Edition: September 2021

Forever is an imprint of Grand Central Publishing. The Forever name and logo are trademarks of Hachette Book Group, Inc.

The publisher is not responsible for websites (or their content) that are not owned by the publisher.

Library of Congress Control Number: 2021939249

ISBNs: 978-1-5387-3336-3 (trade paperback), 978-1-5387-3338-7 (ebook)

Printed in the United States of America

LSC-C

Printing 1, 2021

To my husband.
You're basically Daniel and Jay put together.

Author's Note

Dear Reader,

Thank you so much for picking up *First Love, Take Two* and joining Preeti and Daniel as they navigate family and society to find their truth again in sometimes funny, sometimes heart-breaking ways.

Although *First Love, Take Two* is a tale of second-chance romance with lots of flirty banter and food cameos, the story also deals with mental illness, racism, and a brief fetal demise scene.

Preeti is finally ready to share her journey with y'all, brimming with friends, family, food…and, of course, a hefty dose of Daniel! He might be just what the doctor ordered.

I sincerely hope you enjoy!

Many thanks and so much love,
Sajni Patel

Chapter One

Some things that I found fascinating: the geometric designs of flowers, the way rectal polyps reminded me of raspberries, the number of penises I saw in a day, and lacerating this infected lesion so that the swollen cocoon of skin around it deflated like a saggy balloon. Oddly mesmerizing.

As I finished the debridement and meticulously applied a padded wound VAC and sterile dressing around it, I nodded proudly at my work, as if saying: *Fine job*. Another beautiful fix, and another infection case to add to my research project.

As a fourth-year medical resident, I saw patients on my own and treated them, with a physician's sign-off. As chief resident, I'd just gotten off night call but had to cover for a sick colleague, since no one else could; I still had the holiday schedule to work out for fellow residents, plus their final assignments; and I was a million days behind in my work presentation on infectious diseases. But thanks to this new patient, I met the minimum requirements for case studies. This presentation queen was on her way, giddy with the thought of color-coordinated cards. First came prep, then wowing my boss enough to land the one coveted open position at this practice.

I'd interviewed two weeks ago and was slowly crumpling from the suspense. However! Every day that passed without a decision meant I was still in the running, and every day that I was in the running was another chance to show my worth.

I went over care instructions with the patient and called in the receptionist to set him up with a visit to the wound care clinic for further treatment.

"Thank you. Thank you so much, Doctor," he said effusively, offering his hand for a shake after I removed my gown and gloves.

I glanced at his outstretched palm, a request for something so common, for reasons beyond me. Not wanting him to feel that my response to reject his handshake had anything to do with him, but rather everything to do with my touch aversion, I smiled. "So glad to help. It's what we're here for," I said as I went to the sink to wash my hands.

Family practice wasn't always a walk in the park, but the rewards were immense. Helping people, breaking symptoms down to find diagnoses, prognosis, and treatment, was the most fulfilling job in existence. Developing lifelong relationships with patients was a major bonus. I couldn't imagine doing anything else with the rest of my life.

I scrubbed my hands to death in the patient's room before leaving. Then again in the locker room for good measure before changing into my dress pants. Life hack: pull-on pants are as comfortable as scrubs, which are in fact as comfy as pajamas. I declined an invitation to go out for drinks with the other residents and hurried out the door, checking my watch, on the way to my tenth interview in the past three months.

Traffic had nefarious plans to thwart my punctuality, causing me to be fifteen minutes late. Which, in turn, diverted my focus. I stuttered, shook, and tripped over answers...no wonder the interviewing doctors seemed eager to get me out of their space.

Every day had its ups and downs, but this down felt deeper than it had been in weeks. My residency was up in two months, and not having a permanent job yet had my stress skyrocketing.

My chest ached. There was no worse feeling than the anxiety that came from not acing something so important. My headache started before I reached my car and then worsened into a stabbing pain.

"Crap," I muttered. I turned on my calming app to help alleviate some stress before heading to the apartment.

My roommate, Reema, was due to return this weekend from her honeymoon, with a new husband attached, and three made for an awkward crowd.

Rohan had given up his place to move in with Reema, seeing that our apartment was bigger and conveniently located for both of their jobs. That left me in search of a new place. Something I should've found by now, but as it turned out, there was such a thing as losing an apartment if you didn't sign the lease in time.

By the time I parked and pried my fists off the steering wheel, they were aching from the death grip. My heart pounded and a dizzy spell bore down on my thoughts, my head crowded with haunting missteps from interviews past and trying to figure out where to live. The hospital might not approve of me utilizing the on-call room as a permanent residence.

I could move back home with my parents, since they kept offering, but the drive from their place to the hospital and clinic was too far.

Reema and Rohan weren't heartless, though. They would let me stay a bit longer. Things were okay. No need to panic. *Calm down.* Reema was like the mom in our tight circle of friends. She kept us all in line and brought profound wisdom. And a mom wouldn't just kick a roomie out if they didn't have a place to stay.

I walked up the open staircase to the third floor, my backpack full of textbooks and a laptop, while responding to texts and managing to trip only twice.

> **Reema**: Hi! Sorry to bother you, hon, but do you mind bringing in the delivery Rohan received, if you're going to be there? We got a notification it arrived earlier today. It's his new desk!

> **Me**: *OfC! Hope you're having a fantastic time!*

> **Reema**: It's perfect! We're so ready to jumpstart all of our plans when we get home. But first honeymoon calls. ;)

They had lots of plans, all right. Rohan worked from home twice a week and his first goal was to have an office ready to go. AKA my room.

I felt like a college kid who realized their parents had turned their bedroom into the hobby room they'd always wanted. There was *no* moving back home after that. There was no staying for me.

Time to woman up and live on my own. Just until my own wedding, which seemed to be nipping at my heels. My body wanted to shut down at the thought. Marriage wasn't always about love and connection. Sometimes it was about fulfilling happiness in other ways: duty and honor and moving forward with life. But in my case, moving forward meant having to scale a massive wall studded with the jagged edges of my emotions.

A giant box at the door glared at me as if it had won a battle. It had. It was taking my room from me.

After unlocking the front door and depositing my backpack on the couch, I lugged in the box. It was so wide I could barely get my scrawny arms around it. I channeled all of my effort into my legs, grunting the whole time. Ugh. I should've done more weight training and less cardio.

With a final pant, I pushed the box into the center of the living room, between the back of the couch and the hallway. It wasn't the best place, but neither was my still-intact bedroom.

Exhausted, I showered, slipped into my favorite pair of pink sweatpants and a T-shirt, and heated up dinner. There was just enough space beside the box to ease onto a barstool.

I called Liya as I ate generous wedding-food leftovers. Couldn't let it go to waste! And not just reception dishes, but snacks from the actual wedding and food from the events leading up to it. Cake was next. There was this thing, apparently, where couples froze the top tier of their wedding cake to eat on their first anniversary, but Reema and Rohan wouldn't have any left at this rate.

"Hello, love!" Liya said in an unexpectedly affectionate and energetic voice. She was the wild, fearless one in our group of four, and hearing this unusual sweetness from her had me wondering what she was up to.

"Um. Hello. Love?"

"I'm trying it out. What are you doing?"

"Eating wedding food."

"What is it?"

My mind went blank as I pushed a fork through the vegetarian dish. "Um. Curried chickpeas."

Liya asked dryly, "You mean chana masala, chole? Anything but *curried chickpeas.*"

"Couldn't think of the word. Sorry. Sheesh. Do you want to take my Indian card?"

"Um, yes. I think I have to."

"Fine. I don't have many cards left anyway."

She laughed. "You don't. But you at least like Indian food. Eat your chole in peace."

"You know, I'm a doctor. I can't remember everything at all times. Anyway...are you feeling better?" I asked, my gut twisting as I remembered the night of Reema's wedding. Going after Liya that evening had meant being the only one there for her when her prick of a father and an elder in the community had tried to destroy her. It was the final straw that pushed my dear childhood friend out of town.

Her tone seemed relaxed, calm when she replied, "Yeah. Actually. Moving to Dallas was the best decision for me, you know? Don't get me wrong, I miss you girls the way I'd miss cheese if I had to go vegan, but Houston is too toxic for me. I feel like I can breathe here. It's a new start, but not too far. I make more money with this job and it's not nearly as stressful as the last. Jay is moving here, helping me cope."

"I wish I had known. Liya, all this time you'd been suffering at the hands of a man who everyone else respected."

She scoffed. "Except you."

"Well, he did spread vicious lies about me when it came out that I was dating Daniel," I said, skipping a breath from having said his name aloud, both a soothing balm for the burnt remnants of our past relationship and a tormenting memory of how things had ended.

"We all know your fois lit those fires. But let's be real. A lot of folks here were racist to begin with, not just your aunts. That crap doesn't rear its head just because one of their own is *sullied*."

"I hate him for what he did to you."

"Me too. But things are good, Preeti. They really are now. The only way they could be better is if you moved here," she said, hopeful.

I laughed. "The only thing I can promise is that I'm looking for work in Dallas. But who knows?"

"You haven't heard back from any interviews?"

My shoulders slumped. A panic attack brewed at the edges of my thoughts, creeping closer and closer as my unease turned physical. Anxiety was like soft, annoying fingers pressing down on my brain. If I didn't take care of myself now, that soft but unnerving stroke would turn into a harsh, suffocating grip. "No. I'm so tired of interviewing and wonder if I'll ever get a job at this rate."

"You'll get the one you want. Look at everything you do, Miss Chief Resident!"

"I really hope so. All those hours doing side projects and scheduling and filling in for sick call at the drop of a hat and mentoring new residents better be worth it."

"Don't worry. They will be. Reema and Rohan are back this Saturday night, right? I'm driving down. We'll get your mind off job hunting."

I beamed. "That would be fantastic!"

"By the way, did you find a new place? In all my drama, I don't think I asked where you'll be living."

"It slipped my mind to turn in my lease for the new apartment with all the chief resident duties. In the chaos of the wedding and you leaving and work and seeing Daniel..." I muttered.

"Oh? Did you speak to him at the reception?"

"No. I managed not to."

"Did you run? Like, literally, run?"

I was an expert at running from Daniel: dodging calls and texts, ignoring his knocks on my door, making my friends evade his questions, and, more times than I could count, literally just walking away. Avoiding confrontation wasn't my best feature. Quite possibly one of the worst things about me, actually. If I had better conflict management skills, I would've shut down my aunts at the first accusation and maybe I'd still be with Daniel.

I admitted, "I ran as fast as I could in my chaniya choli."

"Ah. Since I took up my new job's offer of living arrangements, I still have two months left on my Houston lease. Why don't you stay there?"

I gasped. "Are you serious?" Liya's apartment was the perfect location for work, and when else would I ever get a chance to live in such a posh place? Oodles of stress immediately drained out of me at the knowledge that I would have a temporary place to live and more time to find a permanent residence, and could get my butt out of this apartment before Reema and Rohan returned. It was perfect timing, too. Her apartment lease would be up when my residency ended, so no long-term commitment if I didn't secure a job nearby.

"Yes! And my new company provides a furnished apartment because they wanted me here on short notice. I won't need my furniture for a while. It's just sitting there."

"You'd be saving me! I would pay rent, of course."

"Oh my god, Preeti. No. You're not paying rent. But for full disclosure, someone else just asked me about it, too."

My shoulders slumped. "If you gave it to someone, then no worries."

She quickly rebutted, "Do you have another place to live?"

"No…" I bit my lip.

"Then maybe you two can share the place? You take the bedroom, he can take the couch?"

"*He* who?" I sat up pin straight. I couldn't believe Liya would seriously suggest I share an apartment with a stranger, much less a man.

"Um. Daniel," she replied, sounding a little like a kid saying *oopsie*—but more like a giddy woman executing a setup.

I nearly choked on my water and almost fell off the barstool. *Please, lord, tell me she's joking.* "How is that a good idea?"

"It's temporary. He needs a place for three weeks. That's all. He can take the couch. You can have the entire bedroom. And if y'all work it out and get a little busy, then hey, icing on a very delicious cake."

"Liya!" My skin heated at the thought of all the very intriguing, sexy things that could, but would not under any circumstances, happen. "I'm dating Yuvan! Our parents are expecting us to get engaged."

"Do you even love Yuvan? Or rather, don't you still love Daniel?"

I opened my mouth to protest the validity of that question, but she quickly went on, "And don't even try to deny. You are the worst liar in Houston. You've been in love with him since college, and I don't know who Yuvan is, but he's not Daniel. And that's all anyone needs to know."

I groaned into the phone, but there was no argument to have. No one compared to Daniel.

"You could live with Reema. But Rohan will be there. And when your parents find out, they're going to make you move all the way to their house in the suburbs. And you can't live with Sana because she's living in a full house with her family."

I pressed my lips into a tight line. Liya was right. Even if I wanted to squeeze into a bunk bed with the fourth member of our girl group, Sana was already losing her crap from the lack of privacy.

"What's the worst that could happen, anyway?" she asked.

I guffawed. "Ruining my relationship with Yuvan? My parents finding out and their utter disappointment? Any auntie at mandir finding out and going through the exact same thing that happened years ago? A lot is on the line, Liya."

"I know that. But I think you also know that you've got some sorting to do. You're an adult," she reminded me. "And if you can't stand to be near Daniel without ripping his clothes off, then you'd best rethink this whole Yuvan business."

Dang it. "I hate when you're right."

"You love when I'm right," she teased.

I gnawed on my lower lip as anxiety descended again. I closed my eyes and made a snap decision, based on logic and current needs and the most efficient way to do things, just as I would with an emergency at work. "Okay, fine!"

"*Yes!*" Liya whooped.

"But just so you know, I'm going to move forward with dating Yuvan, and eventually engagement, because it's the right course of action."

"Engagement? Ugh. I can't believe you never told us you'd been dating some guy."

"I had to be certain about him before you started a debate," I muttered.

Yuvan and I had been chatting for months, so when the time would come to say yes to engagement, I could be one hundred percent sure without the pressure from friends and family. But in my family and in our community, going public about dating was basically an announcement that we were considering marriage. My stomach sank at the thought. Marriage felt so...permanent. "My parents have their hearts set on him."

"I still think you need to work things out with Daniel."

"Not possible."

"Tell me that after you spend some time with him. One night alone with Daniel and you wouldn't be entertaining this ridiculous idea of being with anyone else. You saw him for part of a night at the reception. You need to finish that night."

I wished she could see the scowl on my face.

"I mean...what would you do if you were stuck alone with him?" she asked almost whimsically.

"Probably hide."

"Preeti! He deserves the truth. First love always deserves a second chance. All right. I'm going to give him a heads-up about you staying there."

Maybe Daniel would decline the offer to stay if he knew I came with the apartment. Hope fluttered through me.

"Well, you better get to packing! I'll be in town Saturday to welcome Reema back to good ol' Houston. I'll get some things from my place, but I'll be staying with Jay, so feel free to start sleeping there right away," she said almost too eagerly. "I can help you move."

"That would be great. I want this place clean and ready for their return."

"I don't think I volunteered for cleaning duties."

"What are best friends for, though?" I grinned into the phone.

She sighed. "Fine. See you then!"

As soon as I got off the phone with Liya, I called Sana to see if she could help me move over the weekend. She, of course, was eager to spend time with me and Liya.

I giddily packed blouses and slacks. I'd never lived by myself before, much less in a luxury apartment. And seeing that my singlehood could come to an end faster than the onset of lidocaine, I suddenly felt the need to live it up—after Daniel moved out, of course, because until then, I would be a master of hiding.

Maybe it was cold feet.

Maybe it was the constraints of marriage to a person I didn't feel a connection with.

Maybe it was leaving the days of roommates and fully embarking on my own.

Whatever it was, I had a couple of months to be wholly free.

But that was the problem, wasn't it? Singleness equated to freedom while marriage meant binding myself to a guy whom I didn't love in hopes of developing those feelings later. It wasn't unheard of—marrying out of pragmatism and falling in love at some point afterward. My parents had done it. My aunts and uncles and several cousins and countless others from mandir and literally millions across the Indian diaspora and beyond had done it. Our culture wasn't the first or the last to encourage marriages according to carefully laid-out plans.

My brain, full of intelligent reasons and conceptual propositions, bluntly declared that marrying Yuvan was the practical, correct course of action. He was patient, successful, and adored by my parents. But my heart, or rather the chemical impulses raging uncontrollably across my system, blasted off that it was still, and always would be, a die-hard lover of Daniel Thompson.

Well, too freaking bad, oh treacherous heart. The brain must win this one. I had come too far in my personal journey to be swayed by a few encounters with Daniel.

I took in a couple of shaky breaths. *Get a hold of yourself! You are a doctor, for goodness' sake!* How was it that I could deftly use a scalpel to cut open body parts and reapproximate everything without being a nervous wreck, yet I couldn't manage to see my ex without imploding? One look at Daniel and I was five steps back.

All right. I could work past this.

Living with Daniel for three weeks? No big deal.

Calm down, body. No need to get all revved up.

Chapter Two

Thursday was typically family dinner night with my parents, but moving and overworking had me breaking the tradition this week. On the bright side, I could dodge questions about Yuvan. Circumventing questions was my specialty. I had at least three gold medals to show for it and might hit a fourth one for this week alone (crossing all fingers).

"Come to the house for dinner with Yuvan and his family. We can discuss dates. What do you think?" Mummie said over the phone that morning.

"Lots of work. Can't this week. Besides, I need to take care of Liya."

"Oh my! Poor, poor girl," Mummie replied, and sent our conversation toward holding one of our elders accountable for assaulting my best friend. It was not easy. We lived in a society where a victim had to fight to prove her story while every skeptical doubt was thrown at her. She was villainized more than the actual villain.

I clenched my eyes, feeling the pain Liya had endured.

Mummie had a sudden fire in her that I lived for, though. I was content listening to her updates from the auntie squad. She'd banded with Liya's and Jay's and Reema's moms and a bunch of other moms and orchestrated a plan to hold Mukesh accountable while Jay worked on the legal case. It made my heart swell with pride. Liya was strong and loyal and loving, and she'd found a match in Jay, who never left her side. It was a weird feeling to be elated for her and yet sick to my stomach for her.

I blinked and stared at my bedroom wall. *Don't think it.* But ghostly whispers formed in the depths of my mind and curled to the surface.

Why hadn't my mom spoken up for me when the fois raged with seething gossip bathed in inherent racism about my dating Daniel? Where was this band of aunties then? I *knew* my situation wasn't as horrific as Liya's, but still... where was the community to support me?

When we hung up a short while later, I sat on the bed and lost the battle to scroll through my contacts list.

I lingered on Daniel's number, wondering aloud, "Is it still the same?" as my fingers hovered over the cell phone screen.

Great seeing you. Sorry that I ran off at Reema's wedding. Just wanted to say that you looked nice. It's been so long. How long are you in town for?

I groaned, deleting the text as quickly as I'd typed it. What would I say if he responded? *Hey, we should grab dinner? Let me explain why I left you the way I did and broke your heart?*

Ugh. It was best to leave him alone. He probably didn't want to hear from me, probably would ditch the apartment knowing I would be there, too. How could he ever forgive me? He likely thought that I had no problem taking four amazing years of dating, of being in love, and throwing it away like it meant nothing. He probably thought I was callous, even six years later. If he knew the reasons why I'd left him, there was no way that he would look kindly at me again. He'd have so much hate. And well... I wouldn't blame him. I was a coward. Gold medal for that, too.

Why couldn't I commit to deleting his number?

There was a profile picture next to it in my contacts, taken years ago, a masterful selfie of me beaming down at him while he lay on his back in the park. My sun-drenched hair fell over my shoulders as I leaned over him. We'd had the biggest, cheesiest grins. He wore a muted gray button-down shirt and I had on this bright pink blouse. I hadn't thought much of the top, but Daniel had thought the combination of it all created an ethereal glow. Together we looked... *perfect*.

I couldn't even delete this picture. In this frozen snapshot, all I could see was love and all I could feel was pain.

I remembered the day Daniel walked the stage for his master's degree, when I'd met up with his parents before the ceremony. They'd never liked the fact that we dated, which was why Daniel and I hadn't spent much time with them. His mother had been kind, although the quiet disapproval in her features wasn't.

Daniel's father had looked down on me the moment he realized Daniel and I were still together.

"That's my boy, my firstborn, my legacy," he'd said beside me in the stadium as we located Daniel among the other graduates. Daniel's mother sat to Mr. Thompson's left, while Daniel's sister, Brandy, and her grandparents sat to my right. I didn't understand why Mr. Thompson wanted to sit next to me until his words came. "Our family fought hard to get to where we are so that Daniel could have a better life and fewer battles. I don't blame him for thinking things like choosing a future wife are simple. Just love. Treat each other well and all's good."

He'd turned to me then, amid applause for another graduate who walked the stage. He studied the stunned look on my face and went on, "You have no idea what you'd have to learn and sacrifice, being with him in the real world. Our world. All the business and leadership required."

"I don't understand," I'd said.

"Of course you don't. Do you realize he's worth millions?"

My jaw had dropped. Not just because of the sheer amount of money but also because Daniel had told me otherwise. I'd never asked Brandy about their family's wealth, as that seemed too personal and unnecessary to our friendship. But Daniel? I would've never expected him to lie.

"He never told you? Interesting. I wonder why. Was he afraid you're a gold digger? Unworthy of the respect and responsibility that knowledge brings? You come from a traditional family, don't you?"

I'd nodded, dumbfounded and queasy knowing where he was going next.

"Then you understand how a relationship like yours is doomed. Different cultures, different religions, different societies. We don't live for ourselves because we're not selfish. We have family and community to consider. Daniel needs a woman who knows our life, who's better suited for it. I'm sure your parents want the same for you."

He harrumphed. "You also understand how pursuing passion can destroy generations' worth of hard work. You've been taught to value logic above anything else. So know that when I say you're not prepared to be in his future, I'm right. To help carry our empire on your back, to support him as he uncovers his greatness, you'd have to be strong. And you, Preeti, are not strong enough for my son. You're not adding value to him. You're hindering his potential. If you love him and want what's best for him, then you need to end things. Save both of yourselves."

Even to this day, his words stuck with me. Logic over passion. Not being strong enough. He was right.

I'd never told Daniel, would never want to be the reason he hated his father when their relationship had already been strained.

The name Thompson flashed across my screen as it lit up with a phone call. I almost dropped my phone, thinking it was Daniel.

Brandy Thompson. Oh, lord! She almost gave me a heart attack.

"Hi, Brandy," I said, trying to sound as relaxed as possible.

"Preeti! What happened to you at the reception? You disappeared. We didn't get one picture together. Even Reema and Rohan were looking for you."

"I know. I'm sorry. An emergency came up and I had to deal with it."

"Was it my brother?"

"No. Much worse."

"I hope everything is okay?"

"I hope it will be." I twirled the end of my ponytail, desperate to tell her Liya's story. We'd all been friends through college, and Brandy and Liya had clicked on a personal, fashion-passion level. But it was not my place or my story to tell.

"Um, how's Daniel?" I asked, my throat suddenly dry. Did I even have a right to ask?

Brandy paused before replying, "He's as expected."

"What does that mean?"

"You know what that means. You know he's messed up from seeing you."

"No way. He can't possibly be after this long."

Her voice turned stern. "You did break his heart."

"How are we even friends?"

"Y'all's business is not my business, as much as I'd love to know why you left my brother. Like, the real reason, because him lying about his financial status wasn't it, and don't even try to convince me that it was."

"He was angry seeing me?" I asked nervously, turning the conversation back and tugging my hair even harder.

"Angry that you ran off. Really, Preeti? You walked away. Not even a hello."

"What am I supposed to say? How I left him was horrible."

"I dunno. Woman the hell up. We all want to know the reason," she prodded. "My grandparents maybe even more than Daniel."

"Is that why you're calling?" I stood and one-handedly packed medical books into a box.

"Actually, my grandparents are having a dinner and they invited you."

"Aw. They're so sweet." I practically drooled at the thought of Grandpa Thompson's marinated chicken and Grandma Thompson's family-recipe Southern pies.

"It's tomorrow night. Sort of dressy."

"Lots of people?"

"Some business people, probably, and family."

"Wait. Will Daniel and your parents be there?"

"I can't confirm they will or will not be there."

I groaned and dropped the last book into the box. "Not a good idea."

"Just come early, grab some food, and head out. Grandpa will make you a to-go bag."

"You know that your grandparents aren't going to let me just slip in and out without sitting down to eat."

"Grandpa's insisting, really. Actually, they're right here, and if you say you're not coming, they're going to grab this phone, and you know they will *not* take no for an answer."

"Oh, lord."

"Listen. It starts at five. Come by, maybe, four thirty? The food will be ready, people might arrive a little after five."

In the background, Grandma Thompson called out, "Pie!"

Brandy laughed. "Yes, Grandma. She's making you your own pie, Preeti."

"How can I say no to that?" I asked.

What was the worst that could happen, anyway?

Chapter Three

The party was *not* at Grandpa Thompson's house, but at Brandy's parents' house. Which meant that despite my leaving early for the anticipated twenty-minute drive, it took forty minutes to get there, and Brandy sending out the address last-minute didn't help.

Brandy and Daniel's childhood home was a large house on a massive lot, pushed back from the street for added privacy and space for more than a dozen cars along the wide and generous driveway. There were plenty of cars here already, and I didn't want to get trapped between any, since my plan was to get in and get out. I parked farther down the winding drive in exchange for a longer walk.

The gravel walkway crunched beneath my steps and a slight breeze swept through. Japanese maple trees with the most gorgeous shade of maroon-purple-tinted leaves mixed dramatically with oaks on a manicured lawn.

I texted Brandy to let her know I'd arrived, just now seeing her earlier text telling me to let myself in. I took a few breaths to steel myself in preparation for seeing her parents and Daniel.

I opened the opaque-window-paned front door to a hum of

conversations, light classical music, and a banquet of scents, some delicately floral, some luxurious perfumes, some decadent food.

The living room appeared to the right, speckled with oil paintings and a floor vase of silk flowers.

I maneuvered through chattering groups, feeling more and more out of place. Women in cocktail dresses and pearls and men in suits and watches that caught every glint of light like diamonds made me feel plain and simple in my blouse and slacks. But this was the norm for the Thompson family. They were Southern royalty, and I had no idea what was going on, nor an ounce of belonging, as I searched for Brandy and her grandparents.

"So good to have Daniel back," I heard someone say.

"Wonder if he's taking over the business now?" another asked.

Others chuckled. "Think his dad is going to hand things over like that?"

"What are we thinking? He's much too possessive to let go of control."

"This'll all be…so interesting."

Was Daniel back for good? Not just for a few weeks while we shared an apartment? Had Brandy lured me into a homecoming dinner for the brother I'd *dumped*?

The hairs on my arms stood up, warning me it was best to hurry.

Daniel's family didn't play it small and quiet. The backyard, visible through large windows covering the entire back side of the house, was set up with tables underneath blue and gold tablecloths for catered appetizers. A bartender was making all sorts of drinks. The living room and yard were decorated with vases of flowers and ribbons wrapped around pillars.

"Everything is an opportunity for the future," a man said.

I would have recognized Daniel's father's voice anywhere. It was deep, like Daniel's, but stern and level, whereas Daniel's was more soothing. Mr. Thompson was an intimidating man, to say the least. Tall, handsome, commanding, poised, intelligent, and capable of speaking his mind with just a glance.

Could I slip by without his noticing? Should I say hello? No. Of course not. He wouldn't want to see me after having told me to leave Daniel alone all those years ago.

"Right. Because a quiet meal with the family was too much to ask for," Daniel replied.

My heart fluttered. My chest filled with rampaging zombie butterflies gnashing around. Daniel had his back to me, but there was no denying exactly who he was from the mere sound of his voice, throaty and sexy.

I couldn't help but eavesdrop from the other side of these tall plants, drinking in his voice. My legs wouldn't move.

Mr. Thompson was decked out in a finely tailored tan suit while Mrs. Thompson stood nearby with another woman.

"It's time to work hard, Daniel," his father said.

"Harder, you mean?" Daniel retorted. Then he eased out of the conversation with an "Excuse me, Dad."

"Trying to make a quick getaway?" a tall, beautiful woman asked as he walked off. "Welcome home, Daniel," she said with a bright smile.

As I watched her lean in to kiss his cheek, I felt a nasty stab in my guts, like someone had prodded my insides with a red-hot poker.

After all this time, of course Daniel would've moved on.

I nearly jumped out of my skin when someone tapped my shoulder. I spun around to face Jackson, Daniel's best friend and Brandy's boyfriend. He grinned. "Preeti! You made it!" He gave me a side hug that lasted the entire two seconds he was allotted by my touch aversion.

"Jackson! You scared me." I put a hand to my chest.

"Were you eavesdropping?"

"Uh, oh," I stuttered. "I didn't mean to. Seeing Mr. Thompson is usually cause for freezing up."

"I'm just joking with ya."

"Who are they?" I cocked my head toward the small crowd around Daniel.

"Frank Peterson. Best friends with Daniel's dad. Future business partner. Owner of a real estate empire. Alisha Peterson, his daughter, following in her mother's footsteps. Part of the next generation of board members of local charities and the organization founded by Daniel's grandmother. Powerhouse businesswoman. Set to take over the Peterson legacy."

So she was even more formidable than she appeared.

"Let me introduce you around. Brandy is taking care of some things out back." He led me to a few small groups, making introductions and joking and being his charming self. All the while, Daniel moved from Alisha to others and passed us from behind. I could detect him the way bees detected flowers, alluring and delectable. I called it the Daniel Effect.

Jackson led me down the hall. "Grandma's in the kitchen. I'll be back. Just need to check on a few things. You okay?"

"Yes. Thanks."

I turned from him and emerged into a room with a kitchen big enough to feed a school to the left and a dining table for eight to the right. I sidestepped to stand behind a dining chair as I searched past the small group of caterers in black-and-navy uniforms.

Grandma Thompson spotted! Her perfect crown of salt-and-pepper hair was twisted into a bun and locked in place with a subdued purple hair pin. She tossed her head back and laughed, her cheeks dotted plum with joy as she nudged Daniel with an elbow.

He chuckled and reached around her, hugging her as he rocked back and forth.

Oh. My. Lord.

I knew I'd have to face him sooner or later, but being in front of Daniel was always a jolt to my system. As if I'd been walking around half-dead and his closeness was the lightning bolt that brought me back to life. Exhilarating. Dangerous.

Six years. *Six* years since I'd left him, since I'd last loved him with all of my being, and yet the reaction to him was as immediate and strong as if it'd been just yesterday.

My breath hitched and my gut sank.

There he was. The smoothness of dark brown skin glowing like the sun itself. Those perfect lips that had once devoured me. Thick black hair grown out just a little into short twists, shorter and clean-cut closer to his neck. Sparkling brown eyes as rich as honey. A firm, square jawline like brushstrokes from a master painter. Six feet, one inch of delightful, powerful height. One could tell from the way his clothes hugged every contour that he probably didn't skip the gym for three months at a time like I did.

He was as immaculately and demurely dressed as his parents. He wore dark blue slacks, a black dress shirt, and a tie with speckles the color of bluebonnets.

I loved bluebonnets. He knew that, because I'd forced him to take bluebonnet pictures with me when we were both in Houston. He'd grumbled like he hadn't wanted to, but it was a Texas spring tradition. He'd asked me to get dressed up, so I'd worn this little dark-blue-and-purple outfit that I'd thought was so cute. Then he'd shown up, decked out to the nines in a suit very similar to what he wore now. We'd driven out to some seemingly random place off a highway, when in fact he'd scoped out the best places to get a picture packed with wildflowers, without a bunch of people or traffic. And he'd found the perfect spot beneath a lone, towering oak tree. He'd put out a blanket and a full picnic and taken lots of pictures of us in a sea of bluebonnets mixed with red-and-yellow wildflowers below the setting Texas sun. It had been magical.

Daniel stabbed a fork into one of five pies and shoveled a bite into his mouth.

"Daniel!" Grandma Thompson rebuked him, but then smiled and rubbed remnants of crust from his chin.

"That one's mine now," he declared.

"Son, you're going to waste your appetite," Grandpa Thompson playfully scolded, but then he got sidetracked by a glance at three pitchers filled with amber liquid that seemed to glow in the fading sunlight.

Grandma Thompson had made her world-famous iced tea, as sweet as honey with a certain kick at the end that was sure to leave anyone feeling good and heady. She carried a pitcher out but didn't see me.

Grandpa Thompson tore away from this nectar of the gods, as Brandy called it, to pile food on a platter. The kitchen smelled of sweet baked fruits, aromatic spiced meats, and buttery breads.

My mouth watered. Hard. My stomach growled as if I'd neglected my body for weeks with starvation.

"You didn't have to go to all this trouble," Daniel said to his grandfather. "Dad catered."

"He can keep that fancy food for his business associates, son. My grandchild deserves some home-cooked food," he replied.

"Mm! Can't wait to eat!" Daniel rubbed his hands together and glanced up, his chin a little high, his gaze finally meeting mine. His smile slipped and his lips parted like he wanted to say something. But then he pressed his mouth into a tight line, flashing that dimple, and I knew he was less than happy to see me.

My heart pounded out of control and my breathing turned

erratic, harsh. It was like my lungs had forgotten what they were made for, and my skin flared hotter than ever. Thoughts careened through my head, making me all sorts of antsy, bombarding me with memories, flashbacks, raw emotions.

All signs of an oncoming anxiety attack. I was too close to the edge.

There was a sense of urgency and betrayal in Daniel's features, a reaction that fragmented my insides and reminded me of what a terrible coward I'd been, running off the way I had. His jaw hardened and his body tensed for the quickest of moments. I expected him to rush toward me and demand answers.

When Grandpa Thompson finally saw me standing off to the side, his gaze following Daniel's, he gave me a wink. We met partway across the grand kitchen, his arms extended. He hugged me. "Oh, baby girl. You made it. Let me take a look at you."

Grandpa and Grandma Thompson, much like my inner circle, didn't aggravate my touch aversion. Their hugs felt like sunshine.

He pulled back, his hands still gently on my shoulders as he took in my face. "As pretty as ever. Been too long, though."

I tried not to look at Daniel, because the truth was that I saw his grandparents every couple of months. Despite the breakup, they had insisted on having me over for brunch regularly.

"You're too sweet, Grandpa Thompson," I said, relaxing in his presence.

He batted away my words. "You can call me just Grandpa, you know? Thought I told you that."

He had. But that felt weird, considering the situation.

"Come sit. We're ready to eat."

I shook my head. "Oh, no. I couldn't intrude. I was supposed to take something to go?"

"You're never intruding," he insisted. "And you still have a bag to take with you. Don't worry. Did you honestly think we'd invite you and *not* insist on you joining us?"

"This sounds like a homecoming, and I had no idea." I finally glanced at Daniel apologetically. The edge to his features had gradually softened. The rigidity of his jaw, shoulders, and hands relaxed. Even more so when his grandfather nodded at him with his notorious, infectious grin.

"Nonsense! We have plenty of food and seats, and you can still go home with a bag of goodies. Daniel, son, do you mind?" Grandpa Thompson asked him.

Daniel stuffed his hands into his pockets, casting a cold and silent, albeit fleeting, look at me. He shrugged at his grandfather and shook his head, adding a slight, soft curve of the lips like he had no choice.

Chapter Four

Grandpa Thompson slipped into the backyard carrying a platter of food while Daniel inched toward me until he stood two feet away, his arms crossed. His biceps tugged at the fabric of his tailored shirt. My insides did all sorts of somersaults. I shivered down to my bones.

"What are you doing here?" he asked, his tone level.

"Your grandparents insisted that I drop by and get some food. I'd planned on getting here earlier and leaving before…"

"Running into me?"

"Yeah."

"Still avoiding, huh?" he asked sharply.

"I, um, can leave." I pointed at the hallway behind me like an idiot.

He swallowed, contemplating an answer, which should've been an answer in itself. "It might be best."

Dang if words weren't sharper than daggers, but what did I expect?

"Unless you want to tell me why you've been running from me for six years."

My body went slack. The truth burned on the tip of my

tongue. He deserved to know. It wasn't fair that he didn't. But I should've spoken up years ago. Let me loose in medical school and residency to tackle the top spot, and I was a bulldog. But leave me to confess why I couldn't handle things back then, and I was far from tenacious.

How could I tell him? How could I see the hurt and pain unfurl in his eyes?

Oh, gee, Daniel, your father loathes me because you're too rich for my lower-middle-class, unrefined, immigrant blood. You needed a woman who could fit into your world of business empires and galas and elegant Black society. I could and would never understand your family's struggles and ambitions and was told that I was a hindrance to your full potential.

Even now my heart ached at his father's words.

More importantly, had Daniel felt that way? Was that why he never spoke to me about his parents or leading empires or how his family made more in one year than I ever would in my entire life?

Or *Gee, Daniel, my aunts are so passively racist that the toxic fumes curled over my family and strangled us? That it sent my mother to the hospital with a heart attack and shoved my father out of the good graces of the one community he felt he fit into?* How could I tell Daniel that I chose my parents over him, not because they asked me to but because I couldn't withstand watching society batter them to pieces? I couldn't hold his hand and shield my parents at the same time, and the guilt added to the gnawing monster in my head known as anxiety.

Back then, these had seemed like giant, valid, crushing reasons, because I was young and scared and—although it was hard to admit—easily manipulated to cower into myself instead of standing up for myself. But now? I just sounded like a coward, and no coward deserved Daniel Thompson. His father had been right. I wasn't strong enough for him.

He cocked an eyebrow and waited for an answer.

I frowned. "Now's not the time."

"Right. But I heard that a certain person comes with Liya's apartment, so expect to give an answer soon."

I swallowed hard, my throat aching. I wished that I could just tell him and get it over with, but not here. "I should've given you an answer back then, but let's not act like you didn't have something to hide."

He groaned and rolled his eyes. "Now wait a damn minute. What do you mean by that?"

My gaze followed a couple of caterers passing by, my voice quieting until they were gone so as not to make our argument a spectacle. "You didn't tell me about...all this." I waved a hand at everything around us. The lavish food and drinks, the granite and wrought iron, the expensive china plates and heirloom silver, the extravagance.

"My parents' house?" he asked dryly.

"Don't play that, Daniel. You lied."

He let out an exasperated breath. "It was a small lie."

"It's the fact that you lied to my face. Several times. And you did it so effortlessly. Did you lie because you didn't trust me?" And imagine the idiot I felt like when his father was the one to tell me in that condescending voice why I shouldn't play with fire.

We were starting to make a scene with raised voices and his crossed arms and my flailing ones. "Let's just forget about this for tonight. I don't want to upset my grandparents. Things don't have to be awkward, you know?"

I pinched my brows together. "Do you even remember me?"

He smirked, a bit cocky, a bit sad. "I remember everything."

He lifted a hand toward the backyard, allowing me to walk ahead before he appeared at my side. He stuffed his hands into his pockets while I tried my best to focus on the doors. Awkward was an understatement. All I wanted was to get away from him—and at the same time, all I wanted was to be glued to his side.

I rubbed my arm, trying to press away the goose bumps skittering across my skin in relentless waves. Why was he walking so close? Why did he smell so good? Like rain and cinnamon.

Daniel cleared his throat, his chest going in and out with heavy breaths. He raised his hand to his neck, maybe to scratch? He used to do that when he was nervous.

Brandy appeared just beyond the sliding double doors, all smiles and looking cute in a dark green knee-length dress. Her dimples were as deep as Daniel's, her skin shimmering in the evening light.

"You made it!" she said.

"Yeah. Thanks for telling me this was at your parents' house. And also...a welcome-home party?"

She sucked her teeth. "Yeah, about that...my grandparents made me."

"Mm-hmm."

"Well, Grandma has a bag of food for you to take home afterward, I kid you not. Complete with an entire pie."

"Wait a minute." Daniel's chest was now a torturous few inches from my back. His warmth seeped through my silk blouse and tingled against my flesh. My brain told me to step away while my body screamed, *Merge into him and become a coalesced fusion of sexy flesh.*

"Does that mean I'm not getting a pie?" he asked, appalled, while I walked alongside Brandy across the lawn.

She clucked her tongue. "You're such a grandma's boy, of course you're getting your own pie. Let's go! I'm hungry."

My tongue tied itself into knots wanting to object to staying and eating, and Daniel didn't make things any easier.

"Are all these people family?" I asked Brandy.

She waved off the others behind us in the house. "Every event is an opportunity for business, so says Dad. Don't mind them."

Brandy helped Grandma Thompson set one of the long tables, saying, "Look who's here, Grandma!"

"Preeti!" Grandma Thompson said, waving me over and then hugging me even harder than Grandpa Thompson had. "Sit right here! Oh, don't you look lovely in that shade of pink. What a classy fit."

"Thank you."

Jackson jogged over from the house and kissed Brandy's cheek. "Hey, sweetie."

"Right here, baby girl. Have some Kentucky porch tea." Grandma Thompson handed me a glass filled halfway with the sweet drink with a bourbon kick.

"Oh, I should get going," I protested.

"Nonsense."

There was no denying her. Before I knew it, amid the fuss of making plates and creating a corner for the few of us, I bumped into Daniel as his grandparents orchestrated seating assignments.

"Sorry," I muttered, our arms brushing. A tingle started at the base of my neck and trickled down my back. Goose bumps. We hadn't touched in years and one simple accidental brush threw my entire body back in time. Memories floundered around my head, and my skin was on fire.

Basically, I hadn't been ready for that graze and barely kept my body in check.

He cleared his throat, his chest expanding and then deflating in quick succession, like maybe he hadn't been ready for that minimalistic touch, either. I wondered if he felt something nice and memorable, or if he was just annoyed.

"Grandma, we can sit right here," he said instead with a nervous laugh, his focus entirely on her now. Those. *Dimples.*

After what amounted to a warped game of musical chairs, I ended up settled into a seat between the grandparents and Daniel with Brandy and Jackson across from us. Brandy shrugged, not quite apologetically, as she had just sat there watching our entire awkward interaction, amused. My cheeks flared hot, but when I was cushioned against the grandparents, I couldn't help but feel their never-ending comfort.

All right. I could eat quickly and get out.

The first bite of warm, crispy, baked tortilla-chip-crusted catfish and savory grits with a smear of spicy, robust creole remoulade speckled with crawfish was a heavenly thing. I ate slowly, against the tendencies that I'd picked up over the years of cramming my face in two minutes flat between classes and cases. My eyelids fluttered and I might've let out a soft moan. Wow. There was no mistaking Grandpa Thompson's cooking.

"Right?" Daniel said as he took a bite.

Ah! Had he heard that? Oh my lord.

"For you, my dear," Grandma Thompson said as she handed Daniel an icy glass of Kentucky porch tea.

"I've been waiting for this all year." He looked at the floating ice cubes melting beneath a setting sun and drank the entire thing in one go.

"Calm down!" Brandy said. "This stuff is strong."

He coughed. "Oh, man. It sure is."

"I'll get you another, baby," Grandma Thompson said and kissed his cheek before pouring another glass. "I've been waiting for you to come home for six years, young man. You were supposed to come back after grad school, not run off to New York. Don't you leave again."

Being away must've killed him. He might not have been close to his parents growing up and in college, but he had the most amazing relationship with his grandparents.

"Why'd you stay in New York for so long?" I asked, making small talk, if for no other reason than to appear unaffected by him.

"Why do you think?" he mumbled, giving me a look so cross that it gutted me, and went back to eating.

As I watched him, wondering if I was truly the only reason, he squared his shoulders. His face hardened and his entire body went rigid.

"You stayed away from those appetizers?" Grandpa Thompson asked. "I brought some real food. Right here." He added another fillet to Daniel's plate beside a serving of cranberry and almond salad, and I swore Daniel had heart-eye emojis pop out of his head.

He took another sip, leaned toward me, and said quietly, "Listen. You don't have to stay."

I gulped down a bite of salad. Was he trying to tell me to leave? "Okay." I spoke up and announced, "I should really get going."

"But you haven't had pie," Grandma Thompson said as she plopped down a giant piece of...oh my word, was that buttermilk pie? Now who had heart-eye emojis popping out of their face?

"You made buttermilk pie?" I swooned.

"Isn't this your favorite?" Daniel asked.

I nodded. But why was she making *my* favorite pie for Daniel's homecoming dinner?

There were other pies on the table, too, and Daniel was going in for the kill, uncuffing his shirtsleeves and folding them up partway.

It was impossible not to stare at those wide, brawny forearms—like forearm porn. Why was he doing this to me? I had the mighty need to fan myself. Must've been the bourbon. Had to be the bourbon.

Grandma Thompson pushed a plate toward me. "Don't worry, baby girl. You have your own pie to take home."

"Really?" I squeaked.

Daniel muttered, "Thought I was the favorite one?"

Grandma Thompson gave that heartfelt, musical laugh of hers. "Next time, I expect you to make *me* a pie, Daniel. I know I've taught you how to cook."

"That's the truth," Daniel countered. "I would love to make you all the pies from now on."

"And cobbler," she added.

"And cobbler, Grandma."

I savored another bite of buttermilk pie and recalled how every time I'd seen Daniel with his grandparents, he was cooking with them. Baking, marinating, grilling, smoking, sautéing. No wonder he cooked like a chef. He'd learned from the best.

"Going to make some young woman very happy," Grandpa Thompson added.

Daniel stiffened, glancing at me with his head lowered, and poked at his slice of pie. "Let's not go there, please."

My stomach sank. Yeah, some woman would enjoy the food that Daniel made with his own hands, and then enjoy those hands all over her body.

I tried to focus on the soft, delicate sweetness of the pie, but it turned a bit sour in my stomach at the thought of Daniel's future wife.

"You know who doesn't love pies, though?" Brandy cocked her head toward the house. "Can you trust a woman who doesn't like pies?"

Grandma Thompson clucked her tongue. "Bless her heart."

"*Grandma!*" Brandy snickered.

Grandma Thompson swatted the air. "Hush, now."

To the left, Alisha emerged from the house in fluid motion between businessmen, chatting, laughing, drawing a small crowd, which didn't go unnoticed by Grandpa Thompson. "She's quite the woman, that one. No fear. Look at how she wraps those vultures around her finger," he said with a hint of admiration.

Grandma Thompson, on the other hand, responded, "I thought this party was for Daniel, not another reason to talk about work. What she *should* be doing is sitting over here and eating. Or at least sitting near the man of the hour."

"I don't mind," Daniel mumbled, casting a glance at me from the corner of his eye.

"Now, why can't y'all get back together?" Grandpa Thompson asked, looking from me to Daniel.

I froze midbite.

Daniel had gone motionless, too.

Brandy smirked from across the table and Jackson just watched the entire exchange with that goofy grin. "Awkward" was an understatement. So was "setup."

"Let's not go there," Daniel said in an even tone.

"Whatever made you two split, anyway? Can't y'all work it out?" Grandma Thompson prodded.

I stuffed the rest of the bite into my mouth and almost choked, much like Daniel, who had a coughing fit before he downed half a glass of tea, blushing as hard as I probably was.

"You sitting here, welcoming Daniel home, enjoying our company, appreciating my food? And where is Alisha, huh? Talking business over there. You know priorities," she said to me.

Daniel interjected, "Now's not really the time or the place, Grandma."

She plopped some more salad onto his plate as he protested, "I can't eat much more. But I can't stop, either!"

She laughed. "I already set aside enough leftovers for a week. Where are you staying, by the way?"

"Don't worry, Grandma," Brandy promised. "I found him a nice temporary place closer to north Houston." Oh? So Brandy had set him up with Liya's apartment. That made more sense than Daniel directly asking Liya for a place, seeing as Liya and Brandy were still friends and kept in touch.

"That's so far. Why not stay here? Or at our place? Or at Brandy's? Honey, did you offer your extra room to your brother?"

"Of course! He wants some privacy, I guess," she said, but shot a subtle glance at me.

"You mean *you* need some privacy," Daniel retorted, contorting his face.

I finished my pie before Grandpa Thompson could circle back to why Daniel and I hadn't worked out, and insisted, "I should really get going. I have a busy day tomorrow, starting early."

"Okay," Grandma Thompson relinquished, and then asked Brandy to grab my bag of food.

When Brandy returned a few minutes later, handing me a generous amount of goodies secured in a cloth bag, she gave me a sly smile. I wasn't sure if that look was aimed at the food that would last for days or at my predicament with Daniel. I gave all the thanks and praise and was almost home free when Grandpa Thompson nudged Daniel. He pushed his seat back and stood, watching me with those intense, soulful brown eyes.

"I'll walk you out," he said.

Before I could decline, his hand landed softly on my lower back. He pulled away and apologized.

I bit the inside of my cheek, annoyed by how his touch still incited flutters in my stomach. I could be irritated, angry, tense, awkward, anything in the world, but his touch never disappointed. Which wasn't a good sign. Not when I was on a path to get engaged to someone else. I could count on my fingers everyone in the world whose touch I didn't mind, and Daniel was still one of them.

We went around the side of the house. Without running into his parents. There was that, at least.

"So, you've moved back? Permanently?" I inquired on the walk down the driveway.

"Current plan. Have to join my family business sooner or later. Your residency almost over?"

"Yes. A couple more months."

"Congrats."

"Thank you. How did you know?"

He leaned his head back and whistled. "Think my grandparents don't give me an update on you during every phone call?"

Eek. Did they tell him about me hanging out with them once in a while, too?

I unlocked my car from afar and Daniel opened the door for me, gripping the top so that I couldn't just jump in and drive off.

"I'd better get going," I said and slipped into the car.

He smirked. "See you at home."

Oh, crap. What had I gotten myself into?

Chapter Five

Saturday mornings were not for sleeping in. It was a scientifi-
cally proven fact that kids, from in utero onward, would throw
a wrench into any schedule. Also, cut-and-go was an actual game
plan when it came to emergency C-sections.

This residency with *this* practice of family physicians had labor
and delivery privileges, as well as surgical first assist privileges.
It wasn't common, and I might never find a job that allowed me
to deliver babies ever again. So I pretty much lived at the hospital
trying to deliver as many bundles of joy as possible.

While I loved the rush and celebrating the momentous arrival
of life, I didn't love having to wake up at three in the morning,
hurry to the hospital, throw on a surgical gown, and dive red-
eyed into a delivery. And then rounds at seven and finishing up
side projects and scheduling by end of day.

My feet hurt. They were actually throbbing. Standing in the
OR was not conducive to happy feet and ankles. I should really
look into orthopedic shoes. My legs ached. I could just imagine
a little blood clot with a devious ability to expand forming and
traveling its deadly way to my brain.

Late Saturday afternoon hit in the blink of a weary eye, and I was scurrying to finish packing before Liya arrived from Dallas.

Sana came over to the apartment to help after my shift. She always spoke softly but had much to say, which was a fantastic but gentle shot of energy. We'd almost finished packing before Liya's grand arrival, which led to chatter and updates. She talked about everything from her new job to Dallas air pollution to Jay, but she had yet to mention her scandal. I wasn't going to push. She needed time.

"I'm going to India to meet the guy my parents want me to consider," Sana said nervously, avoiding Liya's gaze.

"Oh, terrific!" I replied, holding the edges of a box while Sana taped it closed.

"It's wise to spend time with him before agreeing to marriage," Liya added.

We gave her a long blink.

"What?" she said.

"Usually you have some strong opinion," I reminded her.

"I already voiced my opinion. But if you must entertain the notion of allowing your parents to set up your marriage, then spend as much time with him in person as possible. He should come here, too."

"He is!" Sana said, her face lighting up. "In six months."

"So, this isn't a quick wedding?" Liya asked as she placed the last of my study supplies into a box and folded over the cardboard flaps.

"No! You assumed it was."

"My fault."

"Yes, your fault," she said with a hint of unexpected sass.

Liya smirked. "Make sure to interview everyone he's ever come into contact with so you get all views and not just what he's selling."

"My list is ready. Covert interviewing to commence ASAP."

"That's my girl."

"What about you, Preeti?" Sana asked, taping another box. "How's it going with Yuvan?"

"Okay…" I winced, my gaze flitting around the room to find something else to busy myself with.

She scowled. "That doesn't sound good."

"I dunno. When we first met, he seemed great. That perfect Indian guy, so to speak, who has an established career, takes charge at mandir, is respected by everyone and adored by my parents. He didn't seem to care about my past or what people said, which is always a relief. But there's no connection. No sparks. Maybe I was hoping for a whirlwind romance, or some butterflies in anticipation of seeing him again. I just expected to be more excited."

"It doesn't always happen that way," Sana said. "How many people do we know who weren't in love with their spouses before marriage, or were more nervous than excited? All of our parents were matched and didn't know the other person. All of my cousins. Some of Preeti's cousins. Lots of your cousins, Liya."

"Yeah, I just think there's something wrong if the man you think you're supposed to marry doesn't incite some enthusiasm when we all know it's possible for a man to do that for you," Liya said, looking pointedly at me. Subtlety was *not* her forte.

Sana got quiet, knowing full well that Liya was referring to Daniel. Sana had been there for all the love and drama and breakup tears.

"By the way," Liya continued, "I told Daniel that you come with the apartment and he said, and I quote, 'Perfect.' Guess you two will be living together for three weeks."

Sana swerved her head toward me. "Um, *what*?"

I groaned. "Can we not discuss that?"

"Wait a minute. We most certainly need to discuss you living with your ex. What's happening?"

"It's nothing. Just a weird, temporary living arrangement. Can you please not tell anyone?"

"Of course I won't tell! But I need to know every detail."

Liya grinned. "Methinks that even the most traditional of us is Team Daniel?"

"Yes!" Sana squeaked. "As if there was ever a doubt. Listen, I might be traditional in many ways, but love is love, woman. You make things work with him."

"But Yuvan—" I protested.

She waved him off. "I don't even know Yuvan."

"Oh, boy." I glanced at Liya, who was trying not to laugh. I checked my watch dramatically and said, "Oh, no. Look at the time. Sana, you're going to be late for mandir."

Her excitement fell flat as she announced, "I'll help get these boxes into the car, but don't think I'll forget this whole thing."

I gave her a quick hug on her way to the car, grateful for the out. "Thanks for helping."

With the strength of womanpower, we loaded my car and Liya's, made one trip to my new place, and lugged everything inside. Who needed men?

About three hours later, we had everything in my temporary place and had unpacked quite a bit.

"Here are the rest of your things," Liya said as she brought the last box inside. I was hanging my clothes, all while ignoring the suits and men's shoes on the left side of the closet. Just knowing that my clothes were going to be alone with Daniel's felt naughty.

I stepped back and bit my nail. Daniel had several suits and slacks and a few shirts in here, but probably not all of his clothes. He must've left some in storage for now.

My items didn't take up much space in the walk-in closet. There was plenty of room to spare. Lots of shelves helped organize folded clothes and shoes. I only had four pairs of shoes, but Daniel? Why did he need so many shades of brown and gray?

There was even more room in the tall five-drawer dresser and the longer but shorter dresser with a mirror. His watch and cuffs were on the tall dresser. Seemed as if he'd moved in already. Maybe he was with his family right now.

"Thanks so much for letting me stay here," I said to Liya.

"I should be thanking you. I won't have to worry about someone breaking in and stealing my stuff."

Both of our phones went off, and Liya checked hers. "Oh, shoot. Reema's flight is delayed. They won't get in until one a.m. and her parents will pick them up from the airport." She pouted. "I was really hoping to see her and Rohan."

"Oh, no. That sucks. I can't stay up that late. Guess I won't see them today, either."

"But you have tomorrow. I have to get back to Dallas and prepare for a meeting."

"On a Sunday?"

"Welcome to international affairs. The client is fourteen hours ahead and wants the meeting first thing their Monday morning."

I didn't have much time on my hands between work and studying and family and mandir, but I absolutely loved hanging with my girls. At the end of our too-short visit, I sent Liya off with a little bit of Grandma Thompson's leftovers and a slice of pie and set out to organize my things in my new place.

I walked through the roomy apartment and glanced around.

All alone.

For the first time in my life, I wasn't living with family or friends.

The place was quiet. And so big. All I really needed was a corner to study in, a decent bed, a bathroom, a small fridge, and most importantly, a microwave to reheat leftovers.

I checked every room and closet and triple-checked the locks to the door and the balcony. Everything was secure. Then why was my skin itching and my nerves on edge? What was I so afraid of? Of being alone? In the dark? Of facing Daniel? Or all of the above?

To calm myself, I finalized the resident holiday schedule, realizing I'd have to pick up extra shifts here and there. But that was fine, seeing that I was able to accommodate everyone. I sent it off in an email to my colleagues and boss.

After a quick shower, I slipped into pajamas and wiggled. I *loved* comfy clothes, and this was the best part of the day. Another lock check and I turned off the lights. One by one. The darkness grew.

I shook my head and muttered, "You're a grown woman. You can't be afraid of sleeping alone."

Then I crawled into bed, pulled the covers to my chest, and glared at the door.

Just waiting for Daniel to walk in and wreck my world.

Chapter Six

My arm went over my head to hit snooze when my alarm went off at five in the morning. Wow. Praise the stars! A full night's sleep during residency was better than sex.

I swung my arm back, excited to wiggle deeper into the mattress for another five minutes, but the back of my hand hit something hard.

I shot up, dazed and clutching the bedspread to my chest. I turned on the bedside lamp and yelped at the sight of Daniel in bed with me.

He groaned, his face buried in a pillow, his hands beneath said pillow, and the bedspread tangled at his waist. The man was shirtless, displaying solid back muscles with perfected ridges and dips. "Can you not make so much noise?"

"Daniel!"

"That's the opposite of what I just asked you to do," he grumbled, his voice guttural and sleepy.

"Why are you in bed?"

"I mean, I was trying to sleep. Where am I supposed to sleep?"

"On the couch."

"Nah."

"I can't share a bed with you for three weeks."

"First of all," he started, showing more of his face in the dim light and squinting, "I was here first. You can sleep on the couch if you don't like it. Secondly, you won't combust from sharing a bed with me."

My face heated up like a blazing sun. I might combust, actually, in some weird, restrained mixture of embarrassment and arousal.

"Can you turn the light off and get on with your day?" He smashed his face into the pillow and went back to sleep.

I guffawed. Seriously? I jerked the bedspread off me, climbed out, and went into the kitchen, as far away as I could get from the man in my bed short of leaving the apartment.

With my jaw still hanging open, I decided to catch up on my infection project by starting a presentation slideshow. I hunched over the kitchen counter, but my eyes kept wandering toward the bedroom. Having to share a bed with the finest man this side of Texas, in addition to the fact that after years of school I still couldn't put together a decent slide deck, had me crawling out of my skin.

Slamming my textbooks closed after an hour, I went for an early-morning run. Life didn't always allow time for a workout, but I had a lot of tension building between work, interviews, living arrangements, engagement, and Daniel. Instead of revving it up by blasting a playlist through my earbuds, I put on a calming app—an anxiety reducer Daniel had suggested back in college.

I faced off with the treadmill in the spacious, quiet gym on the first floor of Liya's apartment building. The ache in my feet and legs felt good, for once, invigorating and much needed.

Instead of fretting over things, I took in calming sounds: gentle songs, crashing waves, singing birds, and gusting wind. Afterward, I wiped the sweat from my brow and from the machine and sat on a bench to angry-text Liya.

She was most likely asleep, all cuddled up in Jay's arms living her best life. But I hoped that she'd forgotten to put her phone on sleep mode and startled awake with every notification chime.

She might've expected this. Me freaking out. But as I considered my reaction, I realized how immature I sounded. So, instead of dragging myself down a rabbit hole of negativity, I decided to have fun. What better stress reliever?

Me: *So, um…do you think I should call off this whole thing with Yuvan if I sort of accidentally slept with you know who?*

Ha! That would get her attention. In a matter of seconds, the bubble indicator popped up. Guess she wasn't asleep after all.

Liya: You're lying!

Me: *You knew leaving me alone in an apartment with him would lead to this!! I hope you're happy! What am I supposed to do now?*

Liya: Shut up!

Me: *What did you think would happen? I mean…there's only ONE bed.*

Liya: AHHH!!! Get it, girl! ONE bed? You should interest him in the ONE shower while you're at it!

Me: *This is NOT funny. You set me up to fail!*

Liya: This is all circumstantial; Brandy said he needed a place for a few weeks and I was leaving town anyway. Then you needed a place. Was I supposed to say no to you, or go back on my word with him?

Me: *I guess there are worse things in life than waking up to a fantasy in my bed.*

Liya: I don't really believe you, but nice try. Y'all need to work out your issues before you decide to marry someone else. So. Talk. And maybe get some. Just to make sure you're over him.

Her text was immediately followed by a bunch of emojis. Heart eyes, water squirts, devil horns, eggplant, and a fire. How could one get so raunchy with cartoons? Leave it to Liya.

The time on my cell phone flashed six thirty. I hurried back upstairs.

When I ducked inside, Daniel was still asleep in bed, lightly snoring as I stood over him with arms crossed, wondering if I could drag all two hundred pounds of muscle out of bed for the next three weeks or erect a barricade between us at night. The sound of him sleeping thrust me back to college. The best morning had been any morning waking up beside him.

I shook my head, shaking loose any images of what we often did in the morning after waking up.

I took a quick, frigid shower to cool off and changed into a pair of gray slacks and a lavender blouse.

In the living room, I shoved everything I needed for a day of work into my backpack and was grabbing Grandma Thompson's leftovers when Daniel emerged from the bedroom. His sweatpants hung low, exposing the V-cut of his hips. And shirtless! The shame! The flagrant display of side muscles had me gawking so hard that I might as well have given him a thumbs-up when he caught me staring.

Daniel scratched his head and casually said, "Your jaw's about to unhinge."

I clamped my mouth shut, then sputtered, "You slept topless next to me."

He turned toward me and smirked, running a hand down his rather well-maintained abs, then disappeared into the bathroom.

I swerved around and chugged from my water bottle, then promptly refilled it before heading to work. The thirst was real…in more ways than one.

※

The best thing about going to the hospital was that no one ever told me to leave. It was my day off, but I needed to study and catch up on this presentation and make a slide deck so amazing that attendings would use it to teach residents how it was done. The lord knew I wouldn't be able to concentrate at the apartment, waiting for Daniel just so I could avoid him.

The hospital was eerily quiet, like the days-leading-up-to-a-full-moon sort of quiet.

The physician lounge was barren and boring, especially when all the pastries had been picked over, leaving the least favored: bran muffins, plain Danish, and half-torn bagels. Heathens.

Instead of working, I found myself wistfully replaying the morning in my head—because bless the gym that had catered to Daniel for the past six years—when Reema texted.

I leaped for joy! Mama Duck was home from her honeymoon and finally awake! I headed over right away. With Rohan out, it was just me and Reema at my old place. She was on the couch in her sweats, her hair damp, and eating treats she'd brought home from her honeymoon.

She ate another Parisian chocolate and groaned. "Ugh. I'm about to start my period. I feel the cramps coming."

"Crampus is upon us. My app notified me that I have another week."

She giggled at my menstrual take on the demon Krampus. If men had battled him once a year and thought it a victory, then we women who slayed the monthly version should be revered as heroes.

"We're still synched? At least I'm not pregnant," she said. "What kind of mess would that be? All the aunties would be wagging their tongues, busting out calculators and calendars and pregnancy date wheels to see if there's even the slightest chance we did it before the wedding."

"But if you were!"

She grunted. "Yes. For sure you would have your hands all up in me. I wouldn't want any other woman probing my lady parts."

"I'd be the best auntie." I paused. "Oh. Ugh. I'd be an *auntie.* I'm too young for that."

"No, you're not. None of us are. You just refuse to mingle with people who have kids, aside from a few. Once their kids start to speak, you're going to be Preeti Auntie. All day, every day. Face it, we're becoming the next generation."

I'd like to think age was nothing but a number, but in my world, each day was a ticking clock, a countdown to an engagement, a wedding, kids of my own. The mention of things to come pushed Yuvan to the forefront of my thoughts. I wondered if I could be as happy with him as Reema was with Rohan.

"Well, for now, hooray for menstruation to remind you that you've successfully evaded the purpose of your uterus for another month," I said. "I'm not ready for my period. Stop putting me off schedule."

She rolled her eyes. "No one is forcing you to menstruate. I didn't have a private talk with your uterus to purge."

"You don't have to. It's science."

She laughed. "*Okay*. I'll try to hold off as long as possible."

"That's all I ask. Just grip that membrane tight."

"Oh, boy..." She pushed the box of chocolates toward me. "You have to try some of these treats I brought back."

In one indulgent bite, I saw why people made such a fuss about Paris. "You must be so tired from getting in late last night. You're absolutely glowing, though! Did you enjoy your honeymoon?" I asked longingly.

"Yes! It was magical. Maybe it was the whole newlywed thing, or getting a wedding done and over without a hitch, or getting a vacation, or all the wine and food...it was probably the wine and food."

"I bet it was delicious." I could almost taste the decadent cheeses and world-renowned bread. This chocolate was amazing, but it wasn't enough to satiate my desire to try Parisian food in actual Paris one day.

"We couldn't stop eating!"

"I would love to eat all day on vacation." I slouched and patted my belly. I'd been gorging on leftover wedding food for too long.

"You deserve one after residency is over. I recommend Paris. Hey! Maybe we can do a girls' trip. After your residency but before Sana gets married."

"Yes! I'll need the time to just veg and not think about work or studying. It's going to be weird not to be in that mind-set."

"Until then, I didn't forget about my girls!" Reema ran behind the counter and returned with a bag. "For you!"

I squealed with joy. "You didn't have to!"

"You'd be mopey if I didn't," she jested.

"What is this?" I pulled out the largest item, which was heavier than I expected. "A bag of...flour? I know the bread is to die for, so it must be the flour, right?"

"It's a dummy-proof crepe mix from one of the top cafes that makes these mouthwatering crepes. We were eating crepes all day long. This is it! For the, um, culinarily challenged, an easy step-by-step package."

"I mean, how hard is it to make crepes?"

She scowled. "Coming from you? Who cannot make a decent pancake without wrecking the first three attempts?"

"Thank you. I love it." I pulled out a smaller bag within the larger one. It was stuffed with fancy shimmering paper.

Reema snatched the bag and said sheepishly, "Oh. This is something that you should open when you get home. It's a surprise."

"It's not something dirty, is it? You didn't buy me a Parisian vibrator?" I quirked a brow. "Because I don't know what I've said that leads you to believe that I use one or need one."

"No! A woman should buy her own vibrator. We're best friends, but we're not *that* close."

I peeked into the bag. What could possibly fit into a square the size of my hand? "I might end up leaving sooner just to see what's in here."

"Keep looking."

"There's more? Oh, my goodness, Reema." I pulled out two containers of jam.

"For your crepes, of course."

Then my fingers caressed something cool and smooth. I held up a silk scarf. "Oh, wow. This is *gorgeous*." I hugged Reema and then studied the scarf with romantic watercolor-style flowers in various shades of blue, hints of green leaves, strokes of lavender stems, all set against a backdrop of cream and a golden stitched hem. I wrapped it around my neck and clutched the front to my nose.

"It smells like Paris!"

She clapped. "I knew you'd love it! Do I know my girls or what?"

Reema flipped back her hair and ran her hands through it
before leaning against the couch arm. "I got this new shampoo
over there and my hair feels nice and nourished. But so glad to
get a shower and nap in after that long flight. I talked to Liya
this morning. She…unloaded. A lot of stuff happened while I was
gone. I still need to process her situation. Holy hell."

"I know," I said sadly. "But there's an overwhelming auntie
squad rising to support Liya, including our moms."

She gnawed on her lip, her brows creasing with worry and
anger over Liya's ordeal. But she needed time to get her thoughts
straight, which I absolutely understood, and I knew now wasn't
the time to talk about Liya. As if Reema had to make the point
clear, she added, "She said you're staying at her old apartment
until her lease is up?"

"Yes. Did she tell you who else is staying there?"

"Yes. Spill the cha," she demanded with a snap of her fingers.

"Eh?"

"You know: spill the tea. But desi. 'Cause cha is tea." She
swatted the air like she was fighting off a horde of gnats. "Never
mind! Anyway, woman, spill it."

"I think Liya is trying to set me up with Daniel." I made a face.

"Are we saying his name now? Is that allowed?" Reema asked.

"Yes."

"Liya knows you're ready to get engaged. But honestly, girl,
not all of us think you are."

"Oh." Talk about blunt. And a little hurtful. Here I was
trying to go full force into commitment and the only people who
believed in us were Yuvan and our parents.

She patted my hands in that motherly way she sometimes did.
"It's coming from a loving place, Preeti. We know you want to
move on and make your parents happy, and that you thought
maybe this thing with Yuvan would help. But should you really

be pushing yourself into this? It shouldn't be this hard. And we all know you still love Daniel. We don't want to see you keep hurting. I don't always agree with Liya's tactics, but she didn't do this on purpose. Since you're with Daniel for a few weeks, you should take advantage of it. You need closure to move on. And maybe the right thing is to try again?"

I sank into the couch. Leave it to best friends to tell you the truth. Not exactly what I wanted to hear, but probably what needed to be said. "You're not worried?"

"Why should I be?"

"Oh, I dunno..." I gestured wildly and added, "What if my parents found out? My aunts, Yuvan, his parents?"

"No one will find out. It's just a few weeks, right? And besides, I'd be more worried that you'd fall—" She caught herself, the room suddenly silent save for the rhythmic churning of the washer and dryer in the background.

Worried, huh? *Yeah, you and me both.*

"Maybe you need this," she said softly.

"This torture?"

"Are you still in love with him?"

A denial planted itself on my tongue, ready to spring from my lips, but there was no point in trying to deny it. I wasn't a great liar to begin with, and Reema caught my lies like a net catching fish. Maybe tiny white lies might get past her, but not this ginormous whale of one.

She went on, "Maybe you need this closure, a final goodbye to him. You have to give up any feelings that you have for him if you're going to marry Yuvan. It's not fair to either of you. You wouldn't want to marry a man who's in love with someone else."

"I know. I know. I should suck it up and interact with Daniel and prove that I'm over him."

She considered my words for a few seconds, but Reema knew

me well. "You haven't even had a real conversation with him, have you? Let me guess. Are you avoiding him? Avoiding eye contact? Avoiding all interaction?"

I groaned and threw my head back. "Yes."

"You can't dodge him much longer if you're living together."

"Sure I can. He's only going to be there for three weeks. I work late, I can sleep in the on-call room. It's easy to avoid him."

"If you cannot be normal around Daniel, lock eyes, exchange a few words, have coffee together, be in the same room and not want to be with him, then there's some serious self-evaluation that you need to do."

"Anyone ever tell you that you're great at lecturing?" I asked sarcastically.

She shrugged. "Are you in love with him? Is he still in love with you?"

"Why does it matter if he's in love with me? I'm sure he's not."

"Because if he is, maybe y'all can make it work."

I guffawed. "You're forgetting that he's—"

"Black?" she asked dryly. "I know things were hard when word got out about you two, people were cruel and your parents got the brunt of it, but it's time to woman up if you want to be with him. It's not like you cowered away or were trying to save face. You were young and scared and made mistakes. You were being human, but this hiding and keeping the truth to yourself is not the you that you are today. You can't escape being judged in this world. Everything is hard. You have to choose your hard. Someone is going to shove out their unsolicited, hurtful opinion no matter what you do. You can't live for others."

I nodded, knowing she was right. I was forever grateful for friends who were honest but patient. Tears pooled in my eyes and I gripped the pillow to keep from crying because, despite Reema's understanding, she would never be in my shoes.

"Maybe that's easy to say when you're in love with the man your family and community and society want you to be with," I found myself saying before I could think it through. "Same race and culture and religion. Do you think that you'd as easily have married Rohan if he were different? If it hurt your parents so much that your mom had a heart attack because of the community lashing out at her? That the gossip surrounding everything put her in the hospital? Love isn't just love with us. It affects the entire family.

"How can it be as simple as love, Reema? When it's really deciding between him and my parents' health? I can't make that choice! It *kills* me to be away from him, like my heart has holes and is deteriorating. But it kills me to turn my back on my parents, too. I had to choose. And my heart would've broken either way. Look at what happened to my mom last time. How would she survive that again? I can't do that to her."

"That wasn't your fault. It was the gossiping, your aunts."

I turned toward her, my back rigid, and hit the pillow in my lap with balled fists, white knuckles, tears brimming, my skin flaring hot. "Of course it was my fault! *I* did that to her. I'm supposed to protect my parents, and instead I put her in the hospital."

"It wasn't you."

I was shaking out of control when I replied, my voice cracking, "It was the stress and ostracizing and cruelty she received because of *my* actions. When she collapsed, it didn't matter if their attacks were racist or uncalled-for or wrong. It didn't matter if I was young and didn't know how to stand up for them. The only thing that mattered was that it got to her, it hurt her, it damaged her. That was the scariest time of my life and it would've never happened had I not dated Daniel. So yes, it is *my* fault."

Suddenly, my face was wet with hot tears, my entire body quivering with sobs.

"Shh. Shh," Reema whispered and crawled toward me on the couch, pulling me into her.

I rushed to wipe the tears from my face. But there were so many, falling and vanishing into Reema's collar, that I couldn't keep up.

I shuddered, trying to compose myself. "None of this matters because the fact is that I did what was best for my parents. And I would do it again if I had to."

Chapter Seven

That evening, I'd managed to pull myself together long enough to get to mandir in time for the weekly Sunday program. I wasn't so into religion that I conducted classes or dances or performed in plays or anything of that nature. Heck, I didn't even care to set up for things, and cooking? My reputation as the only woman around who couldn't cook rice preceded me. That, along with my history of having dated Daniel, clung to me wherever I went, so the judgmental looks continued.

It was daunting. Draining. But leaving the community wasn't a simple thing to do. It meant cutting ties with a lot of people, family even. It meant not being invited to gatherings and feeling more awkward than usual at festivities. There was no separation of religion and culture here. Community was either all in or not at all.

I couldn't break my mom's heart that way. My parents loved this place. They felt this was their entire connection to being Indian. When my fois had seen me and Daniel six years ago, holding hands and kissing in a park, they had swerved into vicious-beast mode. Not to "protect my name," but to tear my parents down. They were, in the nicest words possible, the most heinous aunts imaginable. Papa's sisters were nothing short of witches, if not, well, a much stronger word that rhymed with "witch."

My fois would be here tonight, since they were as devout as they were hypocritical. No wonder they were so close with Liya's assaulter. Frankly, I hoped they all got what was due to them.

I slipped off my shoes at the main entrance and walked across cold marble floors.

There were plenty of things I enjoyed here. Seeing friends, detaching from everything going on outside of these doors, meditation, seeing my parents and their friends, the rise of my mom's auntie squad, appreciating shimmering décor, festivities, and food. Mandir was like life, a mix of joy and hardships.

As I searched the room for Mummie, I spotted one of my aunts.

My body turned rigid and fraught at the sight of Kanti Foi in the distance, merrily greeting people and chatting with the younger girls. She taught Gujarati class and dance class and led the girls in plays. She also worked seven days a week. Where did she find the time to gossip?

Part of me wanted to be polite, to show that she had no effect on me. A larger part wanted to drag her onto a stage and play a PowerPoint presentation of all the horrendous things she'd done. There were so many. The presentation could take hours.

It would begin with how she tried to turn Mummie into a servant in India when my parents had first married. Papa was still in college then and away for most of the day while Mummie had succumbed to a life of servitude, of cleaning and cooking for the rest of the family, taking her meal last if there were leftovers, and starving if it meant making sure that I'd eaten when I was a small child.

The presentation would chronicle how bitter Kanti Foi was toward my dad, dragging his name through the mud when he was nothing but sweet and kind and wanted to be a positive aspect in the community. In fact, his favorite saying was "Don't focus on negativity, but instead be a positive force."

Then we'd move on to how terribly the fois treated my mother, inciting eruption-worthy levels of anger in my dad. They always spoke badly of Mummie behind her back, twisting her words and actions. In order to be friends with Mummie, an auntie had to have a strong backbone to take the lashing. Which was why my mom had a small but mighty squad, whom I was eternally thankful for.

Of course, the presentation wouldn't end there. Because when Kanti Foi had seen me with Daniel, she didn't take me aside and lecture me on how improper it was for a girl to date an American, or to date at all, as was the custom in my family. She didn't talk to my parents to intervene in order to "save my reputation." Nah. That wasn't how Foi played her game. She went straight to the gossip mill. Whatever naive admiration I'd had for my aunt had been shredded the day I walked into mandir and was hit by an agonizing, blaring abundance of hate, racism, and gossip.

I'd never felt more helpless because I'd made things worse by standing up to my fois in a culture where respect for elders was prime. I went from being a "slut" to being a disobedient disgrace.

Liya had been my rock. Reema was my buffer. Sana was my calm. And somehow Brandy hadn't forsaken me and her grandparents hadn't abandoned me. They didn't know the entire truth, and I didn't deserve them.

My cousin twirled in her new outfit, the princess of the mandir. She had it all: beauty, brains, friends, respect, and an unsullied reputation. She was being pursued by a nice guy, a dentist at that. He walked up beside her and smiled, his hand brushing her lower back in an imperceptible yet forbidden touch, considering where we were. She flirted and tapped his chest.

If having had physical intimacy with Daniel made me a "slut," then well, I supposed we had two sluts in our family. But she was Kanti Foi's daughter. She was untouchable. I wouldn't wish upon anyone what Foi had put us through, but well, I was also sort of petty. It took everything in me not to lash out at Foi and expose her daughter. Eye for an eye.

Yeah. Pettiness wasn't becoming. Anger wasn't kind. But accountability *was* needed.

Ahead, Mummie chatted away with an auntie. Mummie stood out in a vibrant red-and-green salwar kameez that brought out the amber hues in her eyes. She was one of the few older women who rarely wore a sari. Everyone in the auntie legion around us wore nice silks and chiffons in the wraparound style, while my mom was decked out in loose trousers and a long top. Like mother, like daughter. Pants to the end.

Upon closer look, the auntie who giggled and chatted with Mummie was Yuvan's mom. I didn't know how to address her. "Auntie" seemed too informal and "future Mummie" seemed too personal.

All I felt around her was confusion about proper etiquette. I should feel some sort of excitement seeing her. A desire to know her better, to appease her, to figure out living arrangements and her expectations of me as a daughter-in-law, to discuss engagement details. After all, she would become a permanent and influential fixture in my life.

"Preeti," someone called.

I swung around and almost knocked over Yuvan. "Oh my gosh! I'm so sorry."

He held his hands up and laughed. "It's okay. No harm done."

A few people watched our exchange. So nosy. There was no such thing as dating privately in this community, it seemed. Which was why I had to be fully, one hundred percent sure about Yuvan before we went public. Until then, we kept a casual distance.

He crossed his arms, stretching the fabric of a shimmering dark green kurta. The color enhanced the rich hues of dark brown skin and eyes, a nice contrast to the jet black of his newly cut hair.

Yuvan was several inches taller than me at just under six feet. He was handsome and all that, but there weren't any tingles. No funny, delightful sensations. No hitching of breath or wobbling of knees. However, he was a logical choice. A doctor, adored by my parents, respected by the community, patient, kind, energetic, well-spoken. He was basically a walking accumulation of attractive biodata.

"Where are you in a hurry to? We haven't talked since Reema's reception," he said.

"Has it been a week already? So much work. I was actually trying to get to my mom. I missed last week's family dinner, so I haven't seen her since the reception, either."

He checked over my shoulder. "My mom's talking with her. I'll go with you."

"Sure," I said as he walked with me.

"Beta," Mummie said when she saw me. She hugged me from the side and pressed her cheek against mine. Never had I felt so squishy.

"Preeti, beta, how are you?" Yuvan's mother asked.

I touched her feet, or rather let my fingers hover at the tops of her feet as a gesture. I rose before she had a chance to touch me.

"You don't have to do that," she insisted. But we both knew that I did. Mummie hadn't raised a rude child.

"Hello," Yuvan said, touching Mummie's feet in respect as she raised him by the shoulders and smiled at him.

Mummie looked up at him with adoring eyes, like a proud mom. "You look so nice."

"Thank you," he said with a grin. "You two look lovely, as always."

His mom playfully hit his arm. "Oh, stop that."

"What? I'm being honest." He laughed as Mummie teased his mother about being too hard on him.

"Did you come straight from work?" his mother asked me, a tinge of disapproval in her eyes.

"Studying. Lost track of time," I replied.

"Oh, no matter. What's important is that you're here."

What she meant to say was that what was important was how she observed my worship habits. Heaven forbid her son marry a woman who had no clue about anything without a prayer calendar and a how-to book for Hindu dummies.

"I've something for you," she said excitedly and handed me a bag.

I looked to Yuvan for a clue. He shrugged, seemingly as surprised as I was by her gift.

"So nice of you," I told her.

Within it was a box. A...prayer box, engraved and decorated with silver carvings of elephants and peacocks. Complete with beaded necklace, pictures of idols, a mat, and everything else one needed to be today's virtuous and devout girl even on the go.

"It's beautiful," I said.

She touched the top. "You can take this anywhere so you can observe prayers no matter where you are. It's important to have a regular prayer schedule."

"Thank you?" I replied. I didn't know how to take this. Seriously? Because it was a fancy box with exquisite contents. Offended? Because she hadn't gotten the clue by now that I wasn't very religious. Pressured? Because she expected me to get my religious act together.

"How generous," Mummie commented.

"We must keep up proper worship, hah?" she told Mummie. "Otherwise, what are we living for? But I have no doubt that you trained her well."

Mummie smiled that tight-lipped smile. Oh, boy. If Yuvan's mother only knew. Mummie had taught me well. I brushed off her comment, and hopefully Mummie did as well. I didn't need a mother-in-law coming at my mom every time I did something that was subpar. My observance level wasn't a reflection on how well Mummie had raised me.

Yuvan's mother lowered her voice and *tsk*ed. "Can you believe the rumors about Mukeshbhai?"

"I can," I replied firmly, annoyed to hear the name of the elder who had sexually assaulted Liya and berated me for having dated Daniel.

She startled and stared at me. "You're friends with Liya, hah?"

"I'm best friends with Liya, actually."

"Such bad company, no?" She frowned.

"You don't even know her."

She waved a hand. "So much gossip about her from so many. She has a deplorable reputation, beta. I don't think my son should be around her company."

Then maybe he should marry someone else.

Yuvan sighed. "We discussed this. You can't say things like that, Ma."

"Oh? Am I supposed to keep my mouth shut about everything?" she rebuked in an eerily calm manner.

"Liya has gone through something terrible. We can't judge her and dislike her without ever having met her. We talked about this." He turned to me and apologized.

"You know that I'm never leaving Liya, don't you?" I asked him, but I looked at his mother. There was no wiggle room or gray area when it came to anyone's stance on Liya's assailant. Liya was my ride-or-die chick, and I would raze cultural etiquette to the ground over her.

Yuvan touched my elbow and I froze. It lasted all of two

seconds but sent shivers down my back. I clenched my teeth and counted to ten to fight off the overwhelming anger triggered by nonconsensual touch.

"I know. Sorry," he said, looking to my arm.

"I'm working on it," I muttered.

He frowned despite knowing, despite my profuse apologies over something I couldn't always control. He didn't understand touch aversion. He didn't understand why I had such a harsh reaction when it didn't stem from trauma. It was just my brain.

It sounded illogical. That a simple touch or brush or hand-shake made me want to scream and punch someone in the throat. Absolutely abnormal.

He cocked his head to the side and led me away from our mothers.

"Is your mom serious?" I asked quietly once we were far enough from others.

"She's trying to understand the entire situation."

"Is she, though? Because to me it sounds like she heard a bunch of gossip and defamed Liya's character right along with the rest of them."

He clenched his jaw. No guy liked having his mother called out, but this was something we had to get straight. "Ma's not perfect."

"It's harmful and hurtful. We need to side with Liya and protect her and hold her attacker accountable. He can't walk around like nothing's wrong while she's banished."

His mouth twitched with a smile. "I love how you defend your friends."

"If I didn't, then I'd be no friend, would I? But it's more about doing the right thing. You don't have to be friends with Liya, but you shouldn't let destructive comments slide."

"No. I get you. I'll keep talking to Ma. She really doesn't mean to be that critical." He leaned back and looked me over. "You look very nice in this color."

"Oh. Thanks. Are you flirting with me?" I quirked a brow. Flirting wasn't strange, but lacking the tingles associated with it was.

"That's allowed, right?" He came closer and muttered, "It's not *that* soon?"

"You'd better stop. We're at mandir and people are already looking at us." There were several inquisitive looks being thrown our way, some plain nosy but some very hopeful. I guessed more people than I'd thought considered us a good match.

"People know we're dating."

"What?" I gasped.

"Don't worry. Let them talk."

I looked around pointedly. "Gossip incubators."

"I don't let it bother me."

"You must've never been the center of a scandal, then."

His smile faltered as someone rang the bells. He knew exactly what I meant. "It's almost time to start. I have a meeting afterward and then I'm helping the younger guys in the group I'm leading. Filling in for...Mukesh Uncle's absence."

"*Don't* call him Uncle. He doesn't deserve that respect."

"Can we talk afterward? I'll be done maybe around ten?"

The thing was, I wasn't interested in talking it over. There was nothing to say on the matter of gossip or Mukesh. Why should there be? The elder had hurt me, too. And once I was home, there was a certain ex who waited for answers. My brain couldn't handle it all. The carefully built compartments of my life were beginning to crack.

Chapter Eight

I sat in the parking lot of my new apartment building, glaring up at the bedroom window. The lights were on, the shades closed.

The lights flickered off and I dragged myself out of the car. I'd been out all day, from studying to Reema's place to mandir to the taco truck. I'd had one too many horchata refills and needed to pee. So up I went, all the while silently praying that Daniel was asleep. Somewhere. I would take whichever room he didn't want.

I studied the front door for several long minutes before quietly opening it. The lights were off but the gentle green and red glow of plugged-in electronics in the living room showed that the bedroom door was ajar. A corner of the throw blanket sat on top of the couch. An arm dangled off one end. Daniel must've decided to take the couch. Oh, thank the lord.

I hopped on one foot, then the other, trying to get my shoes off in the near dark so as not to disturb him, and also to avoid him. My shoes thudded against the wood floor of the foyer and I bit my lip, freezing like a statue. Maybe if I didn't move, he wouldn't notice me?

Daniel didn't stir.

I walked in the dark and stubbed my big toe against that idiotic corner beneath the kitchen bar counter.

"Ah!" I muffled my cry and cursed the pain throbbing up my foot.

My backpack knocked over something near the edge of the bar. "Oops!" I gasped.

Ugh. This wasn't working and every second weighed down on my bladder like a boulder. I was ready to pee in my pants. I was literally waddling with my knees glued together.

Daniel sat up, his head and shoulders popping up from over the couch.

"You okay?" he asked, his voice gravelly and doing all sorts of weird, glorious things to my belly. You could hear the sleep deprivation in it, though. Poor thing.

"Oh! Yeah!" I called back and ran to the bathroom before my bladder burst. I was not going to get a UTI today!

Oh, but what sweet, sweet relief. I sat in that blissful state of having emptied out a bladder so full it had become painful.

I took my time, washed my hands and face, brushed my teeth. I scraped my tongue and flossed and put on night cream. Then I studied my reflection and plucked all the stray hairs. Then I sat on the edge of the bathtub and cut my toenails.

Let's see. What else can I do in here?

Twenty minutes must've elapsed. Daniel had to be asleep by now.

I turned off the bathroom lights and closed my eyes, regulating my breathing and getting used to the dark again so I could make a quick move to the bedroom.

But when I opened the door, the living room lamp was on and the apartment was aglow. Daniel had his butt against the back of the couch and his arms crossed, waiting for me. He'd been staring at the carpet and dragged his gaze up to meet mine.

I gulped. He had that look in his eyes, the one that said we needed to talk.

Seconds crept by. He waited. Quietly. I stood immobile like a child about to get scolded.

"Sorry to wake you," I muttered and went to the bedroom.

"Are you avoiding me that hard?" he asked in a level tone. "Come on, Pree. Let's not do this, not for three weeks."

"Okay. I think we should stay out of each other's way, though," I said in a small voice, still facing the door and glaring into the darkness of the bedroom. Because that was a lie. I didn't want to avoid him. I didn't want to throw away my last few days of being around him. But seeing him made me want to be near him. Being near him made me want to touch him. Touching him made me want to be with him forever. And that simply wasn't possible.

"You really can't stand me? Not even long enough to tell me the truth?" he asked with an unexpected sharpness to his tone.

A deafening silence clenched around us. The sounds of soft footfalls and a light breeze hitting my back let me know that Daniel stood behind me. I could smell his cinnamon-and-rain scent and feel the heat of his body.

"You really don't want anything to do with me? *Damn*," he said harshly.

I clamped my eyes tight, anxiety building and bubbling in my head, ripping apart my chest. "It's not that at all."

He scoffed. "Whatever. Go to sleep. I'll be happy with us staying out of each other's way. You're pretty much a pro at evading me anyway."

"Daniel…" I turned to him, and suddenly our faces were inches apart. He towered over me, inciting a confusing mix of feeling protected by his closeness and the fear of talking to him. I wanted to reach out and run my hand down his arm, take his hand, sit with him, and spill all the guilt I'd been trapping inside me for six years.

The words choked themselves out at the back of my throat.

"I don't want excuses," he said, his voice a bit softer but his brows furrowed, serious, unyielding. "We're going to talk before three weeks are up."

He went to the couch, dropped onto the cushions, switched off the lamp, and covered himself with the blanket. His unbelieving grunt echoed in the room.

My stomach dropped, followed by nausea. All that horchata was about to come back up. I didn't know what I'd expected. Of course he was going to be upset. Of course he was going to get answers. It was the entire reason he'd agreed to stay here.

My body trembled. My lips quivered. My heart splintered. I wanted to lock myself in my room and cry. Instead, I closed the bedroom door behind me and turned on my calming app, filling the room with sounds Daniel himself had recommended to soothe me.

Anxiety inched closer and closer. I closed my eyes tight, gripped the sheets in my fists, and tried to find a calm that never came.

✳

Morning approached. Having a top-floor apartment with a bedroom window allowed lots of warm sunlight to filter through partially opened blinds. The light, and sleeping on edge, awoke me before my alarm had a chance to go off.

I should go to the apartment gym. A treadmill run would relieve some stress and wake me up after a dreadful night of half sleep. Maybe even some weights? But then my stomach grumbled, loudly. Really? After all those chicken tinga gorditas last night? There was a small amount of leftovers and a lot of dessert from Grandma Thompson in the fridge. Pie sounded like the breakfast of champions anyway.

But when I opened the bedroom door, the deep aroma of coffee percolated through the air and woke me all the way up. Daniel was not only awake this early in the morning, but he was in the kitchen cooking. He had his back turned to me as he quietly worked around the stove, surrounded by the sounds of coffee dripping and butter sizzling on a skillet. A snug T-shirt stretched over the expanse of his back, leaving little to the imagination as muscles contracted and released with every move. Not to mention the, um, *very* well-fitting sweatpants.

I whipped my head toward the bathroom and went through my morning routine before my brain started mentally undressing him. I couldn't even brush my teeth without stabbing myself in the gums.

Cleaned and minty fresh, I contemplated how I could evade Daniel. Perhaps slip out the front door while he fished for something in the fridge and wasn't looking?

Daniel glanced up from the kitchen sink when I emerged. His gaze penetrated right through to my bones with the type of stoicism his father possessed. There was no reading him until his gaze slipped down the length of my body in a blink. My pajama pants were old and faded, and the thin top wrinkled from all the tossing last night.

I wriggled my toes into the carpet and offered a slight smile. Anything bigger would be fake. Anything less was harsh. "Hi."

He pulled up a piece of toast and buttered it. "Morning."

I made it to the bedroom door, eager to get dressed and hurry out, when he said, "Listen. I'm sorry about—"

"Don't be," I interjected, facing him. "I really didn't mean to upset you last night. It's just…awkward being around you after all this time."

"So you don't know how to act?" He slid a rubber spatula between eggs and the skillet and gently folded them. There was a real technique to fluffy scrambled eggs.

"No," I said bluntly and shrugged. "I *don't* know how to act around you. But I'll try to be normal and considerate and stay out of your way so you can work and relax when you get home. No apologies necessary. It's really on me."

He quirked a brow as he plated the eggs. "I was actually apologizing for taking up the bathroom when I know that you have to get to work."

"Oh." Right. Right. I nervously tugged on the hem of my shirt. "Well, no apologies needed for that, either. You were out before I got up anyway. I should get ready for work."

I changed into slacks and a blouse, dabbed on a layer of tinted SPF cream on my face, tied my hair back into a low ponytail, lugged my backpack full of necessary daily items, and carried my trusty pair of comfy loafers to the foyer.

When I set my tumbler on the counter, Daniel said, "Wait."

I sighed, my shoulders slumping, my words coming out rushed. "Listen. I know you want to talk. And I *will* tell you the ugly truth about why I left. But not right now. Okay? Please. I have to get to work and focus."

His lips twisted, his eyes squinted. "*Okay.* I was just going to offer you a breakfast sandwich to go."

"Oh," I mumbled, heat rising up my neck. "Thanks."

Without a word, he laid down a buttered-to-death piece of toast on a sheet of foil; added a slice of smoked Gouda cheese; topped it with fluffy and lightly seasoned eggs, a dollop of salsa, a sprinkling of cilantro, and a layer of baby spinach and arugula; and finished off with another slice of toast. Because of the many times he'd cooked for me in the past, I knew that the cheese at the bottom and the greens at the top acted as barriers to prevent sogginess, and a nice, firm wrap in the foil would keep it from getting cold or spilling over when I took a bite.

He slid a plastic container toward me as well. "Leftovers from Grandpa for your lunch."

"Thank you," I said, dumbfounded. "Why are you being so nice to me?"

"As opposed to...?"

"Being angry."

He scoffed. "Oh, I'm angry as hell, Pree. I thought I was fine seeing you, since it's been six years, but no. Leaving the way you did when I loved—" He paused and swallowed, letting out a rough breath. "But I'm also not an ass. If you're stuck in this apartment with me for a few weeks, then you don't have a lot of places to run off to. Just like this bread, I'm going to butter you up and get answers." He leaned his forearms on the counter and glared at me. Then he glanced at the tumbler in my hands, took it, and filled it with a precise mix of coffee and heavy cream, no sugar. "Still like your coffee this way?"

"Y-yes."

I quickly slipped into my loafers, pulled my backpack over both shoulders, and balanced my keys, the tumbler, and a bag with my breakfast and lunch. "I have to go to my parents' house after work. Feel free to do whatever you want around here."

"Running, huh?"

We looked at each other and lingered. I inhaled a deep breath like I might say something long-winded and defensive. Instead, I pivoted on my heels, opened the door, and called back dryly, "Have a good day, then."

"Yep."

※

I swiped across my work tablet at the counter of the nurses' station, shifting from one foot to another. A little more charting and I could head to the clinic to see patients.

"Who is *that?*" Olivia, another resident, asked on her way toward me.

I looked down the hall and did a double take, almost dropping my tablet. The CEO of the hospital strolled down the hallway with none other than Daniel freaking Thompson.

"Fine as *hell*," she added.

Well, that definitely got everyone's attention. I hadn't realized there were two other residents and a scrub tech around the door to the second, more private, computer station behind the wall. In a matter of ten seconds, every staffer in the vicinity was peering around the counter to take a gander.

The CEO waved a hand here and there as he spoke. Daniel took notes, keeping up with a purposeful pace. Both men wore the heck out of tailored blue slacks and button-down shirts. The CEO had a jacket, while Daniel had only a dress shirt and tie. A light brown belt and matching shoes added the right amount of pop.

How did he do that? Take something as everyday as dress clothes and wear it like a model, all color-coordinated and on point? Daniel knew how to turn heads, but he probably didn't realize he was even doing so.

He happened to glance up as they walked past, adding, "Ladies," with a nod and a smile. His gaze faltered when it landed on me, but only for the briefest of seconds, and then he moved on.

I stared at him, shocked, my stylus frozen over my tablet. All my eloquently phrased, detailed notes suddenly vanished from my mind. I loved my workplace, and one second ago, it had been my reprieve where personal drama didn't follow. Having Daniel living in the same apartment was bad enough; the last place I expected to see him was at the hospital.

The CEO was talking about structure and budget, which led me to believe that Daniel, or his father's company, was spearheading a new development.

I didn't snap out of my stupor until they had passed.

Olivia, who happened to be pursuing the same in-clinic position as myself, leaned back to check out the men.

Olivia commented, "That ass, though."

Yep. The truth was that Daniel could ruin entire civilizations.

"And big feet..." another resident added. "You know what they say about men with big feet."

Flushed, I whipped my head back to my tablet, trying to recall my notes from the procedure I'd just emerged from.

"Oh, Doctor. Never seen you flustered," the nurse said.

I spoke in my stern, authoritative physician's voice. "It's inappropriate to speak about someone that way. You know better." I looked at my colleagues. "You guys, too. We can get into so much trouble."

"Would love to see more of him." Olivia waggled her brows. One couldn't blame her, and yet the fact that she was ogling my ex tripped a nerve. Jealousy, was that you?

When the men reached the end of the hall, they turned to walk back past us. This time, Daniel looked directly at me as he approached. "Preeti."

"Hi," I said, fully aware of the women around me blinking with a hundred silent questions.

"Ah," the CEO said to the unit secretary and then spoke to all of us, probably because he obviously didn't know who was in charge. "I believe the department manager informed you that we would be by to look at the OR. Could we get the necessary items to go back there?"

The unit secretary jumped up. "Everything is in the locker room. You can use the disposable yellow gowns if you don't want to change into scrubs. Booties and bonnets are in a bin beside the scrubs rack. I can show you to the locker room."

As soon as they disappeared through the hall behind the

nurses' station, the residents and nurse let out a collective sigh and bombarded me with questions.

"How do you know him?"

"Are you two dating?"

"Have you hooked up?"

"Who is that?"

"How did you meet?"

"Does he have a brother?"

"Can you introduce me?"

I rolled my eyes. *No, Olivia, I'm not going to introduce you to my ex so you can pounce on him.* Although Olivia, with her gorgeous frizz-free hair, amazing posture, and extroverted charm, didn't need any help from me.

"*No,*" I said firmly. I tucked my tablet to my chest and marched off.

But I had to go in the direction of the locker rooms to get my stuff. If I hurried, I could get in and out before Daniel emerged. Unfortunately, I wasn't that fast, or maybe he was too fast.

I halted with my backpack over one shoulder just outside the women's locker room, directly across the hall from the men's, with the surgical area several feet to the left. He waited by the double doors to the OR. He'd opted for the disposable gown that went over his clothes.

"You look like a yellow bunny," I said, snickering.

"I was going for the doctor look, so yeah, don't start." He looked down at all the yellow.

"Oh, you have to cover the sideburns, too." Having had it drilled into me that all hair must be covered when going past the red lines of surgical areas, I approached Daniel and covered his ears and short sideburns, brushing my fingers against his warm skin in the process. My fingertips tingled, yearning to press against his cheek, to wander across his sharp jaw to those lips. Instead, I stepped back and resisted the urge.

Touching people was a complicated thing for me, sometimes okay, sometimes not my preference. But touching Daniel was as natural as breathing. I didn't have to think about doing it, only about refraining from it.

Worse than that was the fact that he leaned into my touch. His features softened, as if, maybe, he wasn't as pissed as he seemed to be.

"Thanks."

"And your gown has to cover every inch of clothing," I muttered and adjusted here and there while he watched me.

"Are we talking now?" he asked softly, almost whimsically.

"I can't let you walk past the red tape like this. What are you doing here?" I asked instead.

"My dad's firm was contracted to design the new wing of the hospital, so he put me on grunt work duty."

"Why? Aren't you high-level there?"

He hesitated before replying, "We've been arguing a bit, so this is his way of getting me out of his hair for a while."

"What are you arguing about?"

"You really want to know?" he asked.

"Yeah. You two still fight a lot, huh?"

He scratched the back of his head. "Yep." He used to always tell me about his fights. I found myself missing being there for him when, at least back then, he didn't have anyone else to talk to.

Chapter Nine

The gold-and-red foliage that had created such a gorgeous canopy of colors over my parents' suburban street had withered down to a few brown leaves clinging for dear life. I knew how they felt. Vulnerable, depleted, desperate, and susceptible to even the barest breeze. But the last leaves were the most resilient, and one had to step back and look at the organism as a whole. The tree might seem frail in its worst time, but spring was just around the corner. It only had to withstand winter to flourish later. Much like myself.

I parked in the driveway, beside Mummie's old green Camry, and hauled my backpack out from the passenger seat. I rang the doorbell to announce myself, and then shuffled through my keys to find their house key. It was also green, Mummie's favorite color. I'd just turned it in the lock when Mummie opened the door and grinned ear-to-ear.

"Mummie!" I squealed and hugged her tight.

"My beta!" she replied, like she hadn't seen me just yesterday at mandir. "Come in! There's a cold front coming."

And by "cold front," she meant anything below sixty degrees. She was already bundled up in a burnt-orange sweater, a pair of cream-colored wide-leg trousers, and socks. Her hair was back in her usual braid that reached her waist with a coconut oil sheen, the gray tinted burgundy from mehndi. She smelled like the gardenia soap I had shipped in for her from Hawaii, very subtle but soft and fresh.

I took off my shoes in the foyer and walked through the hall, passing the door to my old bedroom on the left and following Mummie into the kitchen, where the house opened up to its epicenter. Our lives revolved around the kitchen. When I was growing up, Mummie made sure that we cooked together, ate together, and cleaned up together, all while discussing life.

I took a second to stand by the fridge, close my eyes, and inhale the rich aromas of family cooking. Spices from curried veggies and ghee on hot buns sizzling on the griddle hit my nostrils.

"What can I help with?" I asked as I washed my hands.

Papa walked by and patted my shoulder. "Nothing, beta. We're done."

"Really?"

"You worked all day." He set the dining table.

"So have you."

"Well…"

"What your papa is trying to say," Mummie interjected as she filled a pitcher with water, "is that we didn't want you to cook."

"What!" I objected. "I can cook."

Mummie arched an eyebrow while Papa tamped down a laugh. "It's not a bad thing. No one expects you to do it all."

I frowned. "You'd think I'd have better cooking skills after spending every day in the kitchen with you."

"To be honest, you were always preoccupied with studying."

"Probably should've paid more attention to cooking, huh?"

"Studying was a good choice," she reminded me as she brought over a large bowl filled with pav bhaji filling—a mixture of curried mashed potatoes, cauliflower, and peas.

Papa grabbed the platter of stacked, warm, and grilled-to-toasty-perfection hamburger-style buns nearly saturated with ghee. That scandalous amount wasn't the best for our cholesterol, but no one in this house could resist butter. And cheese. In fact, a rather large bowl of grated cheddar was already on the table, beside small portions of chopped onion, diced tomatoes, cilantro, crispy sev noodles, and lime wedges.

I pulled down six glasses from a cabinet, my thoughts drifting toward Daniel at work. He'd looked so adorable as a yellow bunny.

"Why are you smiling?" Papa asked.

"Oh, isn't it obvious?" Mummie answered. "She must be so happy to see Yuvan tonight."

My smile faltered, even as I nodded.

Yuvan and his parents arrived as we finished setting up. I opened the door for them on the first ring. I immediately, albeit barely, touched his parents' feet and clasped my hands at my chest in respect for my future in-laws.

Yuvan's parents were full of smiles and laughter and warmth but maintained their physical distance. His dad hardly ever touched females outside of their family and kept his hands clasped behind his back in a nonverbal announcement that he wouldn't be offering a handshake. I wished everyone could be that way. His mom patted my head the way elders often did.

My parents greeted them behind me and lured them away while Yuvan walked up the driveway with a small bouquet of Stargazer lilies.

"For you," he said and handed them to me.

I smiled as I took them. "Thank you. They're beautiful. I don't think I'll ever get used to this."

"To me getting you gifts?"

"Yeah. Is that weird?" I asked, stepping aside to let him in.

"We're still new. Honeymoon phase, right?" He took off his shoes on the porch and came in, his hand landing on my lower back. I froze.

The very slight, very fleeting touch had me clenching my teeth and fists.

My parents greeted Yuvan with praise and hugs. When had he become so much a part of my family? Had I been *that* busy that I never noticed? We'd been dating for six months and it was all a blur. And by dating, I meant texting, phone calls, and family dinners. Maybe a movie? It was all so sterile and unmemorable.

I hadn't dated anyone other than Daniel before Yuvan. I'd never been interested in dating, was too busy, too focused. Then I'd met Daniel and after a few innocent run-ins, things avalanched into a furious need. A need to talk, to be close to him, to touch him and be touched by him. While marriages didn't always start with whirlwind love, I'd really expected mine to.

All this with Yuvan was simplistic, ideal given how our families, culture, religion, and backgrounds coincided. But he wasn't the love of my life, and I was beginning to wonder if he ever would be.

Mummie shooed him away when he offered to help in the kitchen, not that there was anything left to do. She had impeccable timing when cooking for guests. We all sat down to eat in the dining room. When I scooted my chair closer to the table, I also, hopefully imperceptibly, scooted away from Yuvan. I couldn't stand that his shirt grazed my arm.

We fell into chatter about life and work. Papa and Yuvan took up the majority of the conversation while I plated for everyone. Three buns to the side, heaping dollops of filling, and all the garnishes and toppings, minus the cheese, in imaginary compartments. We served guests first, and I always made sure my parents had their food before I started eating.

I laid my buns open-faced on my plate and topped them with a good heaping of filling, a super helping of cheese, a fair amount of onion and tomato, a sprinkle of sev and cilantro, and a squeeze of lime. Before I dug in, my mouth watering, I caught Yuvan watching me.

"What?" I asked around a bite, savoring the crunch of sev and onion and the burst of lime on my tongue. I wiggled in my chair, it was so divine! Mummie grinned at me, knowing my favorites.

"Is that how you eat pav bhaji?" Yuvan teased.

"I know, you're supposed to tear off the bread and eat it like roti, but whatever."

"I meant with...cheese."

"In this house we eat cheese with everything."

"Try it. It's very good," Mummie insisted, but Yuvan looked skeptical. In the end, he decided not to be the least bit adventurous. Oh well, he was missing out; more cheese for me.

"This is amazing," he said around a bite. "Did you make this?" he asked me.

"No. I don't really cook," I said quietly, bracing for his reaction.

"What do you mean you don't cook?" his mom asked, peering around him. "Beta, you must learn quickly."

I tried to control my RBF for the sake of respecting my elders and not shaming my parents...but wow, was it hard!

Yuvan asked, "Not even this? You can cheat and use a spice packet."

"Do you know how to cook? Even with spice packets?" I asked, because we'd been through this before. We'd had lots of meals together and not one of them had I cooked. Yet he always seemed determined to remind me in this sort of passive-aggressive way that I should know how to cook. I didn't look at any of the parents but felt their silence thicken around us.

"Not much, honestly. I was too busy studying and hanging

with friends. My sisters were the ones who cooked. My parents are really proud of that, girls who can cook."

I gritted out, "My parents are proud of a daughter who's a doctor."

"My sisters are doctors, too," he reminded me as he bit into his bun, absolutely unaware of how tense I'd become.

"So...are you expecting me to cook after we're married?"

He laughed. "Of course. I don't know how to cook."

"What if neither of us knows how to cook?"

His right brow hiked up, as if I'd thrown some lengthy physics equation at him.

"We should both plan on cooking after the wedding," I clarified.

"We can get into the kitchen with our moms, maybe take some cooking classes? Sounds fun."

"I don't mean once in a while cooking together. I mean cooking together every day."

His eyebrows knitted together, as if the concept confused him. "I don't think every day is viable long term."

"But it is for me to cook every day? Long term?"

"I mean, you're...the...wife. Every wife I know is the cook."

His parents nodded, chattering about how young his mother had been when she began cooking and how they'd taught his sisters to cook from an early age, too.

I stuffed another bite into my mouth to keep from snapping. Thank god for Papa, who swooped in and defused the tension. "You know, I've cooked with my wife since we married. I strived every day to help her. And trust me, it's a great way to spend time together. You're working with your hands and talking about your day, about any discussions to be had. You're enjoying your time and not wasting it in front of a TV or apart, reading or studying or with other people. And as for Preeti, who doesn't always like to talk a lot, she's a great listener. I really miss having you here."

My heart melted. "Aw, Papa! I miss being here, too."

"You could always move back in," Mummie suggested. "Save some money."

I smiled. "Nice try. The house is too far from work."

I ate dinner faster than anyone else and leaned back into my seat, satiated.

"You eat much too fast," Yuvan commented.

"By-product of working at the hospital."

"You can slow down and savor at home, though."

Not when I wanted to get out of here and get back to…Daniel? No. No. I just wanted to breathe and get away from Yuvan and take a shower and sleep. It was only six thirty. It'd been half an hour since he'd arrived.

"Speaking of home, where are you living now?" Mummie asked. "Did you ever find a new place? You hadn't mentioned moving. Or are you still with Reema? Beta, that's not good. Reema is married now. You can't live there if a man is there, too."

"No, Mummie. I left before she returned from her honeymoon."

Papa added, "Your rooms are just the way you left them if you want to move back home."

"Rooms?" Yuvan asked.

Papa laughed. "Yes. Plural. This daughter of mine had too many things to fit into one room. The guest room became the overflow area. Make sure you have lots of space in your house for her to move into."

Yuvan grinned. "That much stuff, huh?"

"In my defense, Indian clothes take up a lot of space. I needed a bigger closet. Plus, it was nice to use the guest room as a study. I needed a place for my books." I shrugged, hoping that my mom didn't volley the conversation back to my current living arrangements. Not that the subject of my postwedding living arrangements was any better.

"We'll have plenty of space for Preeti," Yuvan assured us and placed an arm over the back of my chair, forcing me to sit up and away from his touch. I sipped water as he continued, "We'll look at two-bedroom apartments after our engagement. We can convert one into a study and all that space will be for Preeti."

"An apartment?" his mother guffawed.

"Don't be ridiculous," his father added with a wave of his hand. "You're going to live with us. As is the Indian way."

No. No. *No.* I couldn't. I didn't want to live with a bunch of other people. I needed privacy and quiet and not to be expected to clean up after everyone or be looked down on because my cooking was subpar. I needed the ability to come home, shower, and pass out without any other responsibilities for people who could take care of themselves.

His mother added, "Right. What will people say if you live on your own when you're so close to us? We don't want others to think we don't get along or have diverted from tradition."

I looked to Yuvan to speak up, because if I said anything in this moment, it was sure to come out scathing and tactless.

He nodded once to me and told them, "Newlyweds need their own space. Time to adjust to each other."

His mother opened her mouth to argue, but Mummie intervened. "Oh, it's fine. They need to learn to take care of responsibilities and become comfortable with each other. I think an apartment is a fine idea."

"Why don't you start looking at a house? Investment," Papa recommended.

"Well, I don't have a job secured yet," I reminded him, then said to Yuvan's parents, "Which is why we can't decide on where to live just yet."

Papa asked around a bite, "Why wouldn't the practice give you a position? I thought they liked you and you were doing a good job."

I shrugged. "It seems like they will, but they have lots of residents and external applicants and only one position."

"Don't worry. You'll get something soon," Yuvan assured me. "Have you been applying to other places?"

"Of course," I replied. "I've had several interviews."

"Where are you living now?" Mummie asked, as if she'd been waiting patiently to broach the subject again.

"I took over Liya's place for a couple of months, since she's in Dallas," I replied.

"Oh! That worked out perfectly, gives you time to find a permanent place."

"Hopefully."

"You are living by yourself?" Yuvan's mother asked, concerned.

"They have security on premises at all times, and it's an upscale area. It's a perfectly safe apartment," I reassured her.

Mummie said, "You're always saying that her place is very nice. Send us the new address and maybe we can stop by."

"Of course." Only if she insisted that I write it down right then and there as she stood beside me and watched every stroke of the pen.

The conversation quickly moved on to more pressing matters.

"Are you two any closer to setting an engagement date?" Papa asked, looking first to me and then to Yuvan.

He replied, "We're working on it. Actually, letting Preeti take the wheel on that. Gor dhana and wedding dates will revolve around her work demands. But I think as soon as she gets her new position, we can move forward."

"Great!" Mummie beamed and clapped her hands. "Ah! I'm so excited to send out invitations and get all the emblems ready."

"Ready?" Papa asked. "You already have them."

She blushed. "Oh, well, maybe I got ahead of myself."

"I must see!" Yuvan's mother said, and, of course, Mummie was ready to show them the entire display.

"We'll be ready to go at any given time, right?" Yuvan looked to me.

I nodded. Yeah. Sure. Watching how lovingly my parents reacted to Yuvan, talking to him at all hours of the day like he was their son, I knew this was the right thing to do. I wanted to make my parents happy and proud, and marrying Yuvan would do that. I couldn't stay planted in one spot my entire life. I had to move forward. While seeing my mom giddy made my heart burst, the anxiety started creeping back into my brain.

I breathed in and out, concentrated on my plate, and managed to keep my fists from balling up.

"Good. I had your foi bring some items from India," Mummie said.

I almost choked on my water. "Didn't she go to India six months ago?"

"Yes."

"So, you've been planning ceremonial things since last summer?"

"Yes. As soon as you and Yuvan started talking."

"Mummie. You really did jump ahead of yourself." I almost laughed. Saying that Mummie was prepared was an understatement.

She waved off my remark. "I knew Yuvan was the one the moment you told me you began texting."

Yuvan's mother giddily added, "No need to waste time! You two are a perfect match."

Oh, boy. Eight months ago, Yuvan's mom and my mom had suggested us as potential marriage partners. Seven and a half months ago, Yuvan and I agreed to text. Seven months ago, we agreed to meet. Six months ago, we had our first date, and despite social rules not to unleash all your baggage on the first date, I had to be up front with him. I'd told him about Daniel.

He knew that we'd dated and that I'd loved him. He knew that

I'd been intimate with Daniel and that it still circulated within the gossip mill in the community. And he didn't care, as long as I was over Daniel.

I told him that I was. I thought I was.

"Your sister had beautiful engagement pictures that she sent out with the invitations," Yuvan's mother said to him. "You should do pictures."

"We can go together," Mummie suggested. "Or make a girls' trip with Reema? She must be up to date with all of the latest trends. We'll need a nice salwar kameez. Or gown? For the pictures. What about the engagement: lengha or sari?"

"Oh, lord no. I can't handle a sari," I reminded her.

"And bangles to match. Some new jewelry?"

"No, no. We don't need to get so extravagant."

"Nonsense," Yuvan's mother said. "This is a very special occasion. Please, let me gift you both with engagement attire. I insist."

"You only get engaged once," Yuvan said. "We should look extra nice. We can shop together, match?"

"That's a wonderful idea!" Papa agreed. "Why don't the six of us go shopping together?"

"Shopping!" our moms said in unison, all splendidly with a clap of their hands.

"And you can pick out engagement photo outfits. At least three to mix up the photos. You should really do engagement photos, beta." Yuvan's mother clucked her tongue. "All the young people are doing that these days. And it looks very professional, huh?"

Papa added, "Reema and others used their engagement photos as decorations and slideshows during their reception. It would be very nice for you to do that."

"I think so, too," Yuvan agreed and turned to me. "What do you think? As soon as you establish a permanent position, and I'm sure you're going to land the job at your current practice, we can start scheduling all these things. We can start a list tonight."

I stuttered over my thoughts before my parents jumped back in.

"Ha! Great idea!" Papa grabbed the notebook and pen he kept by the phone and brought it over, while the moms began a side discussion about all the ornate details with great enthusiasm.

Papa wrote as Yuvan spoke. "Things to do. Let's see: engagement photo session, gor dhana date and invitations and menu, shopping for three engagement photo outfits, shopping for all six of us for gor dhana outfits. Then we need to pick a date for the wedding and a venue. Look at mehndi party details, pithi, garba if we decide to do that, have to find a horse for the baraat, reception theme. Colors for each event…"

My heart skipped a beat, and not in a romantic, warm, lovey-dovey, be-still-my-heart way, but in premature ventricular contractions. I'd only had PVCs before episodic panic attacks. My heart skipped a beat and then pounded so fiercely with a premature contraction that it literally knocked the air from my lungs. I wheezed to catch my breath, but Yuvan simply rubbed my back and I stilled, tightening my fists. He didn't stop to ask what was wrong, but instead checked his phone as it pinged with a message.

Goose bumps puckered up and down my arms. My head was getting too crowded with a growing cacophony of whispers and questions and reminders. Was this too soon? Could I be happy with him? Was this the right thing to do?

Yuvan snapped his fingers. "Ah! I just received an email that there might be an opening for the group engagement at mandir at the end of the month."

The moms were immediately enthralled with the idea, ignited by chatter and excitement.

I sucked in a shuddering breath. "End. Of. The. Month? *This* month?"

"Yes! Isn't that perfect?" he asked.

"Ah! What a blessing!" his mother exclaimed, while Mummie added, "A group engagement means being blessed personally by His Holiness. You'll be the first in the family to receive such blessings, beta."

"We have to act fast, though," Yuvan said. "Before the spots fill up."

"Oh! Wouldn't it be wonderful if you partook in a group wedding, too? Maybe next year they do the wedding portion, and your wedding will be personally blessed again by His Holiness," Yuvan's mother added.

"Actually, in Chicago, the mandir is performing group weddings next month," he said.

My PVCs went into overdrive. I gripped the edge of my seat, focused on catching my breath. "Oh, no. I'm not…not ready for a wedding."

"Yeah, of course. I'm just throwing that out there. I mean, all we would need are airline tickets, a hotel room, and nice clothes. But think about it, we wouldn't have to pay for anything, just a donation to mandir. We wouldn't worry about the procession and all that wedding stuff. They have all the emblems needed, everything is taken care of. And it's quick."

"If you were married by the end of the year…" Mummie said dreamily. And off she went chattering with Yuvan's parents over pros and cons.

But Papa caught the panic that I felt was so abundantly twitching across my face. How could no one else see it?

"Well, let's just relax on the wedding portion," Papa said, his hands moving outward in a calming motion. "Even a group wedding has to be planned a few months out."

Yuvan took in a large breath, his chest expanding and then deflating with disappointment. He cleared his throat and turned to me. "I'm getting ahead of myself. I'm just so excited to start married life with you."

He placed his hand over mine, but I flinched and retracted my hand to my lap. The look of rejection on his face pained me, but I still couldn't force myself to hold his hand.

"Sorry," I muttered.

"Don't worry about it," he replied in a flat tone.

I blew out a breath and Mummie nodded. "You're right. It's too soon, too rushed. What if people talk?"

Although my mom didn't mean it in any sort of foreboding way, a hush washed over everyone. Every person at this table was unwillingly thinking of my past relationship and how people gossiped. That was all it took: harbingers with torches lighting rumor fires all over the community. A quick wedding meant only one thing, right? That I *must've* been pregnant. Why else would we rush?

"Let me think about the group engagement," I told Yuvan after dinner as he walked me to my car.

"The sooner, the better," he insisted. "The seats fill up fast."

I nodded. It was a very big deal to get blessings, which was why people didn't mind group engagements and group weddings. But once we were engaged, it was almost as final as being married—without the benefits. Engagements were rarely broken in our community and in my family.

"Can't believe it's been six months already," he commented.

Six months of dating, of barely realizing I was finally in some sort of relationship geared toward engagement and everyone was waiting on me to announce a date. And as of tonight, everyone was waiting on me to agree to the group engagement at the end of the month.

This was happening too fast.

"I would really love to be blessed," he started.

"I know. I just…need to think about it. It's so soon."

"It's logical, right?"

Logical? Yes. Idyllic? No. Feeling right and absolute down to my bones? Not at all.

He continued, "Everything is set, ready to go. We show up in our best threads. We don't even have to go shopping if you don't have time. We have plenty of heavy outfits. I mean, if we're getting engaged anyway, might as well get blessed, right? Jumping to the wedding, sure, I get that it's too much, too fast, although I'm not concerned about gossip. But the engagement is doable."

"Mm…" I pressed my lips together with a grunt.

"How far is the drive home?"

"Almost an hour."

He checked his watch. "It's getting late. Text me your new address. I'd love to drop by."

"Sure."

He came in for a hug, albeit slowly and cautiously.

I tried. I really tried. I managed to stay in place but stiffened with fists at my side.

He hugged me gently and pulled away, frowning. "You really have to learn to let me touch you."

I really have to do nothing. "You say that like it's my fault, or like it's anything personal against you. It's not. It'll become more natural over time," I said, trying to convince myself more than him. Six months of getting to know each other for the purpose of determining if we would make a match and not being able to touch? Maybe even Yuvan could see through it. "I'm perfectly fine hugging my parents and my close friends. You've seen that."

He reached out for my hand, but his slight touch felt like burning coals branding my flesh. I jerked back.

"See?" he said, his voice edging toward irritated. "That's not normal. You should be okay with a hug or a touch. I don't understand why you can't stand to be touched to this extreme."

"You don't have to understand it. But you should respect it and be patient," I replied, sifting through my own irritation and matching his tone.

"How patient can I be? We've been dating for six months and I can't even hold your hand. How did you get so far with him?"

And by "him," he meant… "I was comfortable with him. I'd been in love with him. You know that."

"So. You're not comfortable with me? You're not in love with me? Yet we're about to get engaged?"

I swallowed as his gaze bored into mine. A disturbing silence engulfed us because we both knew the answers.

Yuvan was *not* Daniel Thompson.

Chapter Ten

When I got home around eight that night, mildly prepared to deal with the ex who'd been on my mind since the hospital, Daniel had just slipped into the bathroom, leaving the lamp on at his desk in the corner. I'd always been fascinated by the way his mind worked, how he brought together design, math, and physics in his projects. My brain couldn't fully grasp it.

I took my things to my room and then walked over to the desk. Lines and numbers and symbols in a complex labyrinth. Complicated and beautiful.

I leaned over the desk and was trying to figure out what Daniel was creating when he was suddenly behind me, his arm brushing my back, his breath crashing against my hair. I jumped.

"Like what you see?" he asked, coming to stand beside me. Close enough that his body heat curled over me like a blanket. I wanted to snuggle into him. I pushed the thought out. No. This was how I was supposed to feel about Yuvan, and not about my ex.

Yet I didn't move away. I loved the smell of him, and right now he smelled like body wash with a hint of musk. "You're so quiet, like a yellow bunny," I teased.

He half smiled, like he wanted to crack a grin all the way but fought it. "Funny. It's this plush carpet."

"I didn't mean to be nosy, but I was always amazed by your designs. I don't understand it, though."

"It's part of the new hospital wing, actually." He swiped across the large tablet, zooming out until it resembled an actual building. The 3-D effects were incredibly realistic, like I could reach inside and be in the building. Technology blew my mind sometimes.

"When did you stop using paper?"

"I design electronically for the most part. Paper design is for passion projects and calming down. Like the house." He looked at me then, his eyes searching mine as I recalled how we used to spend much of our alone time designing a dream house. It was fun and relaxing but never came to fruition. We'd had our entire futures wrapped around each other, blooming in a dream home where we imagined celebrating, living, growing.

I saw his thoughts materialize on his face. The reminiscing about good times, the power duo we'd been as I sat against him on the floor while he drew my rooms, the sense of us having a future, the joy in our plans. And now, the irritation and hurt because I had thrown it all away.

I straightened while he sat down. He tapped the earbuds left on the desk, his expression pensive, his brows furrowed until he finally grunted. "You wanna talk?"

"Oh. No. I'll leave you to your work. I didn't mean to interrupt."

"You gotta talk to me sooner or later."

I studied him as he leaned back, his knees apart, one hand on the chair arm, the other rubbing his chin. I bit my lip. The last time we were like this, he'd invited me to sit on his lap and explained the complexities of his latest design for his thesis. Right now, he looked drained. Exhausted. His lips pressed into a tight line, the cut of his jaw even more defined, and his eyes narrowed.

"Are you that mad at me, or is there something else?" I asked.

He rolled his eyes. "I'm also fighting with my dad."

"About me?"

"What? No. About work."

"Oh." My hands clenched and unclenched at my sides. I knew as well as most that talking it out made a lot of things feel less compact. I wanted to be there for him, but surely, by now, he had someone else to lean on? I also knew that talking to him would alleviate some of my own issues, and that...seemed selfish.

I asked, "The delegating you to grunt work? Do you want to talk about it?"

He watched me for a long minute, as if he was contemplating the implications and consequences of letting down his walls. "Sure."

I pulled over the round cushioned footrest and sat down beside him. And waited.

"Things were never great," he finally started. "You know that. Don't get me wrong, I owe a lot of things to my dad. He pushed me to be my best, but anything less isn't worth it for him. Things haven't been the same since he found out about us dating."

I chewed on the inside of my cheek as I wondered if Daniel knew about his dad running me off, and if so, how Daniel had reacted, whether he thought his father had a point.

"He's groomed me to take over the business but won't listen to a single idea, won't let me make a single decision. Like I'm a child. Like I didn't graduate with honors or don't know what I'm talking about or didn't make my own way in New York. He makes me want to leave again. It's always his way or no way."

"Oh, Daniel. I'm so sorry. Is there any other way to reach him?"

He shrugged. "I'm out of ideas. He has to listen in order to communicate. All we do is fight."

"Are you going to stay?"

His expression fell flat, as if Houston had one too many pains for him to endure. We talked a bit longer about the stunts his dad kept pulling, his mom's absence from the equation, and how his grandparents didn't need to be stressed out by an already strained relationship. Essentially, he had no one to vent to.

He half chuckled. "Sorry. I'm unloading a lot of crap on you. Not many people to talk to down here. Jackson was the guy, but there are no secrets between him and Brandy, and she doesn't need to get involved again. My other friends seem to be too busy with their own stuff."

"Don't worry. I'm happy to listen. Wish I had something more to offer." I gave a soft smile, feeling less and less wound up.

"It's not an easy fix. What about you? How you doing? Seem to be working nonstop."

"Work is intense" was all I said.

He lifted his chin and looked down at me through drowsy, weary eyes. "Nah. Something's going on."

I scoffed and jumped to my feet but ended up wobbling.

"You okay?"

"My feet are killing me. Thrombosis is a real fear. My brain might explode from a traveling clot one day."

"Damn, you're morbid sometimes. Here." He shot to his feet, whirled me around, and eased me onto the chair while he took a seat on the footrest.

"What are you doing!" I squealed when he took my foot onto his lap. A bout of uncontrolled laughter burst from my lips. "Stop!"

He laughed at me. "Calm down."

"I'm ticklish!"

"I know!" His soft touch turned firmer as he kneaded the crap out of my arches and oh my lord...

I gasped with the most unexpected, intense explosion of pleasure and relief.

"You should try massages on the regular," he said as my head floated back.

"Yep," I mumbled.

"Is this helping? Too hard?"

"Perfect," I moaned, then stilled, realizing how that sounded.

"So I see that I still got you making those noises."

"Shut up." I pushed my foot against his stomach.

"This isn't free, you know."

"Yeah? How much do I owe you?"

He pulled my ankles toward him so that he dragged the rolling chair and suddenly he was sitting in between my knees, his hands gripping the chair arms, his biceps and forearms strained as he leaned into me. "You know what you owe me."

"Um…" Wow, it was suddenly hot in here.

"Um?"

"What exactly…"

"An explanation, Pree."

My stomach dropped. I should've pushed back, gotten up, anything, but Daniel was a force field and I'd gotten sucked into it. "I-I can't right now."

"Why not?"

"I'm going through a lot."

"So am I," he replied, his tone sharp.

"Not right now, Daniel."

"You gonna run again?"

"Kind of hard to run when you have me trapped."

"I've got a lot of problems being back in Houston. Can you alleviate just one?"

"I've got a lot of stress, too!" I shot back. "You being in my face doesn't help. And why do you care so much about what happened six years ago?"

"Because one doesn't just get over the love of his life walking away! What the hell, Pree? Why can't you just give me a damn answer?"

I blinked, a nauseating sensation rumbling through my insides. How hard was it to tell him that I never stopped loving him, and worse than that, that I left him for the wrong reasons? The words were simple and few, but they knotted on my tongue and refused to come out.

Daniel grunted and tilted his head back, biting his lip to keep from cursing.

I stood then, still straddling his thighs, and looked down at all the pain and turmoil I'd caused, plain as day on his face. I touched his cheek as tears welled in my eyes, my thumb grazing his lips.

His hands touched the backs of my knees but quickly fell away when all I could muster was "I'm so sorry that I hurt you." I walked away as tears blurred my vision.

I closed the bedroom door and wiped away the tears and tried not to succumb to the growing, overwhelming panic. I wanted to ease his pain and anger. I wanted to be better. I wanted to not be that person who ruined things. I wanted to be stronger than this.

But I wasn't.

I didn't have anyone to talk to. My parents would be concerned about Daniel being back in my life and worry about my anxiety. Yuvan seemed to see only black and white when I was full of gray. Liya had her own problems. Reema was on a honeymoon high. Sana was too busy.

After several minutes of lying in bed in silence, I heard the front door open and close. Daniel must've left while all my attempts to fall asleep failed. I plugged in my earbuds and listened to the calming app, contemplating why I hadn't gone to my doctor to get diagnosed for this throbbing, engulfing anxiety that prowled toward the verge of depression.

I closed my eyes tight. There was a huge stigma around doctors having mental illness. No one wanted to be treated by them. No one wanted to work with them. The same stigma existed in the community, in society in general, and in my family. It was taboo, shameful. I didn't agree with any of it, but it had prevented me from seeking help.

I needed help. With gnawing anticipation and trembling fingers, I booked an online appointment with a shaky breath. Why was I, a physician, so scared to face my issues? Guess even doctors weren't perfect or logical all the time.

I couldn't sleep and there was no time to feel pity or overwhelming confusion. I had things to get done, projects to finish, and a job to nail down. I grabbed chips and salsa, opened my laptop and pulled up my slide deck. Now to transfer essays' worth of information into a presentation worthy enough to wow my boss into giving me the job. Olivia was my closest competition for the position, and her case studies were typically brilliant, so I needed to bring my A game and had only another week to prepare.

When Daniel returned, it was midnight and I almost walked right into him when I came out of the bathroom.

"Oh!" I jumped, placing a hand to my chest. "Sorry."

"It's fine," he said, a little startled to find me awake.

"Where were you so late?" I asked out of curiosity, realizing only after the fact that it prodded into an area I had no right asking about.

He tilted his chin up. "Drinks with Alisha. You might've met her at my parents' house."

My heart sank into my stomach, my head dizzy. I didn't understand why. Of course Daniel would've moved on. He didn't love me anymore. He probably didn't feel half the things I still felt for him.

I hardened my emotions. "You make a nice couple."

"Thanks," he gritted out.

"Good to know things worked out for both of us."

There was a flicker of anguish in his expression, a flash in his eyes. "You're dating someone?"

"Yes," I said boldly, proudly, my chin up.

His gaze swept down my body, leaving a white-hot trail. "You have sauce on your socks," he said dryly and went to the bedroom.

I scoffed, letting out a tattered breath, and exchanged my salsa-stained socks for a new pair.

Daniel stripped off his shirt and undid his pants at the edge of the bed.

"What are you doing?" I demanded, begging my eyes not to glance down. *Don't do it, eyes, don't you dare peek or I will end you.*

"Going to bed."

"I thought you were sleeping on the couch."

He stepped out of his pants, letting them drop to the floor, and slipped underneath the covers and closed his eyes. "Nope. But you can."

I could. Reason told me it was best. But the bed was more comfortable and warmer. I wasn't going to relinquish a good night's sleep for the sake of being stubborn.

I huffed and climbed underneath the blankets. Daniel was sprawled across his side of the bed as if he'd fall asleep any moment in restful bliss, whereas I lay as stiff as a log staring at the ceiling. Another night of sleeping together in silent war.

Chapter Eleven

There were a few exciting things to look forward to at mandir the next night: family, food, and friends. I lost one of the latter before even setting foot inside the magnificent marble building.

> **Reema:** Bad news, babe! I literally just started my period. Won't be there tonight!

> **Me:** *I really don't understand or agree with the archaic belief that menstruating women are unclean and have to stay away from worship.*

> **Reema:** Same. But I can't, in good conscience, go and touch anything. Sorry! We'll catch up soon! When I don't feel like I'm dying . . .

> **Me:** *Godspeed in your battle with Crampus.*

Ugh. Why was the *literal* blood of new life considered unclean? I searched for my parents but instead spotted my aunts near the tables and went to them. It was rude not to greet them once in a while.

I approached while their backs were turned to me, swallowed by the crowd in the usual frenzy just before the program started. They spoke with two other aunties.

Kanti Foi said to them, "My bhai told me that Preeti's marriage has been nakkee to someone."

The aunties nodded with interest. Really, Papa? I hadn't even told my friends about an impending engagement with Yuvan, and here he'd let it slip to his sisters. I expected happiness from them, but their next words had my smile slipping off my face like melting ice cream.

Jiya Foi added, "Smart young man. Yuvan. He's here today. Does he even know?"

Kanti Foi clucked her tongue. "Surely he must not know about her past, otherwise why would he want to marry her? He seems like a good boy, religious, good family. Poor thing, getting someone so defiled as a wife."

"No surprise to her behavior. Just look at her parents. I tell you, I don't know what went wrong with my bhai, but there's the proof. Kids reflect their parents, no?"

"She doesn't observe anything at mandir, she eats meat and drinks, and she dated an American boy. I just wouldn't be able to show my face in public if my child behaved that way. Sharam nathi?"

The aunties agreed with a *tsk*. I had no shame, huh?

Let's not forget Kanti Foi's daughter, who had been sleeping with her soon-to-be fiancé since high school, if my fois really wanted to judge a woman based on her virginity.

Sometimes my aunts made me feel like a little kid, all giddy to see them and nostalgic over memories of them feeding me and letting me sleep over with my cousins. But then there were moments like this that reminded me of why we had distanced ourselves so far from my dad's side of the family. Papa was a giant bear of a sweetheart, so kind and warm, and it was a mystery how these vipers were related to him.

It was easy to believe one could simply speak up. Speaking out was a basic right, but one stifled by traditional etiquette. When they did this right in front of me, my anger sparked and suddenly I wasn't the "well-behaved Indian woman" I had been taught to be. Which probably shouldn't matter because, according to my aunts, I wasn't well behaved in the first place.

The thing about standing up to your elders in a culture where such a thing was considered a sin was that it caused rifts and feuds and dissonance. All while villainizing the youth who spoke up and protecting the elders, no matter what they said or did. Respect was valued, but it could be lost.

I marched the last several feet toward them. My aunts startled when they saw me and tried to play their comments off with forced smiles. I felt my RBF weighing down my expression as the aunties around us faltered and turned quiet, dismissing their own fake smiles. This passivity would turn into biting words behind my back later.

I'd already confronted my aunts many times over, despite my parents' disapproval, as my parents believed the "grown-ups" should deal with one another and leave the kids out of messes. But I had stopped being a kid when my aunts had dragged me into a war over my relationship with Daniel and had put my mother in the hospital. I had battle scars and armor now.

They had once spat venom to my face. But the thing about them going up against a woman who'd learned to be stronger was that my aunts sure hadn't said anything to me since.

"Were you saying something?" I asked curtly.

"Oh! Preeti! No, nothing," Kanti Foi replied.

"Oh, good. Because we wouldn't want the Sunday school teacher to be hypocritical," I said in a cheery voice. Then my voice dropped to a level, heated tone that Liya had once said intimidated even her. It came from the pit of my being, curling like flames at the back of my throat. It arose from the early months of my departure from Daniel and what my aunts had done, sprouting as anger and evolving into righteous indignation. "*Don't* mention Daniel again. Period. Don't talk about me like I'm worthless, coming from you of all people. And don't *ever* speak about my parents like that."

Turning to the aunties, I added, "I can't care if you think I'm being rude, because this is a circle of toxicity. Shame on you, too, for adding to the cycle. I hope you're aware that my fois say similar things about your daughters, so stay in this hot mess if you want, but keep me and my family out of it."

"Preeti!" Kanti Foi objected, but I wasn't here for this.

"Have a blessed session," I told her. "We'll be discussing the importance of truth and kindness, and how those who act pious but behave against the basic teachings are much loathed in His eyes for causing undue distress among His followers."

At this, she blinked repeatedly at me, baffled and thwarted.

I huffed and pivoted on my heels, marching away from them. I just couldn't wrap my head around malicious people. They *lied* all the time. And everyone knew they were lying! They preached sermons from such high and mighty pedestals and then spoke so unkindly of others. Everyone could see their hypocrisy! Yet they wielded a huge platform. Maybe some people were inherently bad and wanted drama.

"Preeti!" Yuvan called from the doorway, waving me over.

I met him where the crowds parted; females on one side and males on the other.

"What's wrong?" he asked.

"Huh?" I asked, distracted with thinking that everyone in the near vicinity had been swept up in my aunts' tales.

"You look upset."

I shook my head. "It's nothing."

"Don't do that. Tell me if something's wrong, even if you think you're overreacting."

"Why would you assume I'm overreacting about something?"

"What's wrong, then?" He leaned against the wall and crossed his arms, the fabric of his baby-blue kurta stretched across his biceps.

I blinked a few times and looked over my shoulder to where my fois rattled on and on about whatever nonsense with a captive audience. "My aunts are talking crap is all."

"What're they saying?"

I made sure no one was close enough to hear when I replied, "They're gossiping about my past relationship and how you must not know about it if you're considering marrying me."

"Do you want me to talk to them?"

"No!"

"Because I will if this is bothering you. I don't care what any-one says because I already know the story. My family and I are over that. It's not ideal, but it happened and it's in the past," he said a little too casually, even lackadaisically.

"I hate how they twist everything to make my parents look like horrible people."

"You have to get over it. You can't get defensive over every little thing."

I glared at him and enunciated my words when I replied, "Little? You think them saying I'm a slut and ruined for any man and then calling my parents a disgrace to the community and unworthy of basic respect is a *little thing*?"

"I didn't mean that."

"You did."

"Don't get defensive, and don't take it out on me. You knew this type of thing happens around here when you decided to be in a relationship with some Black guy."

I stuttered over my thoughts. My lips had parted, but words couldn't form on the tip of my tongue, at least nothing that wasn't ragey.

"Wait—" He reached out for me but I stepped back.

"Don't say you didn't mean it that way, because we both know you say what you mean."

He sighed and then rubbed the bridge of his nose.

"Am I exasperating you?" I scowled.

"Don't turn this into a fight."

"Does it bother you that I was with someone else?"

"A little, but not enough that I don't want to marry you."

"Does it bother you that I won't let you touch me?"

"Yes. I don't understand why you shrug off my arm when we're posing for a picture or step back from a hug or holding hands. I can't even sit close to you without you getting up. Those are *basic* things *normal* people do. But what bothers me the most is that I know you don't mind being touched by the right person. Your parents hug you all the time. You hug your friends. You've obviously been intimate with someone. What is it about me that you can't stand being touched?"

I bit my lip. That was the golden question. I'd started dating Yuvan because he'd been okay about my past, seemed like a good person for me, and my parents liked him. But six months of trying to accept his touch hadn't led to much progress. I thought it was my touch aversion being random, that I just needed to get comfortable. But a few accidental touches from Daniel, and I wanted more. This was all wrong. Nothing aligned.

He shook his head, dismissing his own question. "Come on. Let's talk about this later? The program is about to start."

Every muscle in my body turned so rigid, my joints ached. My breathing escalated into pants as the tendrils of anxiety prodded for a way into my brain. The physical tension that came with keeping things bottled inside was like a spring coiling tighter and tighter, until it was too taut. Sometimes everything came rushing out in an angry, annoyed, garbled mess. Sometimes only a few things slipped.

I didn't even think about the words, but they were honest and came out in the bluntest way, and saying them relieved so much of the tension, the wrongness of it all. "Yuvan. You're right. Something *is* wrong if I can't stand your touch. I need time and space to reevaluate."

He creased his brows. "Wait. What are you saying?" He took a step toward me, closing the space between us, his eyes scanning others around us. "Are you breaking things off because we had a fight?"

Anxiety wasn't going to take me down today. Instead of hemming and hawing and forcing myself to move forward with the pressure of what felt like the entire world on me, I hit the brakes on thinking and let my heart push out the words. A gush of terror, relief, honesty. "I need time for me, and a break from us, or the potential of us, or whatever the crap we are."

Someone called Yuvan over into the room behind him.

"Looks like they need you."

He looked back, pleading with the guy for another minute. In the end, he said to me, "I'll talk to you later about this, okay?"

I guffawed. Seriously? Well, I knew where I stood on the ladder of his priorities, and apparently the rung of mandir duties was higher than his potential future fiancée slamming the brakes.

"You just need time to calm down," he insisted.

"Calm down?" I fumed. Maybe it was the residual anger over my aunts. Perhaps it was his casual and dismissive reaction to all of this, or the buildup of everything that was glaringly wrong with our lack of connection. Whatever it was, if not all of it, had just toppled over with being told to simply *calm down.* "All right. This isn't going to work between us. You don't understand me, or aren't trying to, and I feel like you're trying to fit me into a neat little box of expectations when I'll never fit. I'm trying to make this feel right when it doesn't. You'd better go. The uncles are calling for you now."

He looked over his shoulder and huffed as if he wanted to stay and talk it through, but in the end, he scratched his head in disbelief and went into the adjacent room with the other men, while I found my place beside Mummie and her friends.

I trembled, realizing what I'd just done. And that now I'd have to break my parents' hearts all over again. My own heart shattered at the imminent conversation, and the tendrils of anxiety reared themselves again.

"Beta, so good to see you," Mummie said and beamed up at me as I sat beside her.

I closed my eyes and tried to relax, focused on my breathing, and concentrated on Mummie's delicate rose oil scent.

She stroked my hair in a very maternal, loving gesture. I hugged her from the side and rested my head on her shoulder. How to tell her?

"My sweet girl," she whispered and kissed my head.

From our spot four rows behind Kanti Foi, I saw her twist in her seat to adjust her sari. The auntie behind her had tapped her shoulder and they laughed over the displaced fold of fabric. She caught my eye and her smile stretched, phony, as she waved and mouthed, *Hi, Preeti!*

My face turned heavy, weighed down by the stoicism that I knew was evident in my expression. If there were a medal for how fast and furious RBF came on, I'd be platinum champion every time. I'd even have a medal for holding the most medals in the RBF Games.

My aunt would not get a smile out of me.

*

The past couple of days had brought climbing anxiety levels, but at least today started with some much-needed cheer.

It was a big day for Laura, a patient who had tried for years to get pregnant with various interventions. She was full of joy and had that radiant pregnancy glow. She'd been in a few days prior for routine fetal heart rate monitoring and all had been exceptionally well. Today, she was going to have her baby.

My boss and head of the practice, Dr. Wright, had left it up to me to get to the hospital by seven and induce Laura. So even though I was sleep-deprived and anxiety-ridden, it would be a good day because we'd all been waiting so long for this delivery.

I washed my hands and greeted Laura with as big of a smile as possible while the nurse got her situated in bed. Our giddiness was palpable. I loved seeing good things happen for my patients, and such times were priceless. I felt incredibly honored being here.

"Today's the day!" I said to her as she adjusted her green gown while her husband placed a small suitcase in the corner. He had a pillow for her and a giant tote full of other belongings.

"So close!" he said and kissed Laura's temple.

"It'll be nice not to have to come in every few days for monitoring and checkups," she said with a sigh as she lay back on the inclined bed.

I put on sterile gloves to check her cervix. I dared to hope that she was fully dilated and one hundred percent effaced. But as I sat on the rolling stool and listened to her excitedly talk and laugh and show pictures of the nursery, I watched the fetal heart monitor. The nurse struggled to adjust the straps and monitor, checking all over for the baby.

"Try the lower right side," I suggested. "Baby was loving it there a few days ago."

She tried there. And everywhere. I rose to my feet and tried myself, asking her, "Can you get another pair? Maybe these are faulty."

Please be faulty.

She hurried off and returned with a new set. Still no fetal heart rate. I remained as calm and convincing as possible, but Laura had read everything on pregnancy and knew when to worry. The hospitalist came in and examined her as I nervously stood on the sidelines, helpless.

Bubbling thoughts of a worst-case scenario had calcified, turning soft, annoying edges of anxiety into jagged ones.

My PVCs surged back to life, but I fought through them, struggling to stay focused even as my patient quickly went downhill.

Everything happened in a flash. Laura's heart rate skyrocketed and baby's fetal heartbeat was...gone. The hospitalist had his hand inside Laura, checking for the baby's position and trying to get an internal Doppler attached. But when he removed his hand, it was covered in dark, clotted blood.

Crap.

It was a surreal moment. An agonizing one. Intrauterine fetal demise rarely happened this late in a healthy pregnancy, and to a woman who had done *everything* in her power to give this baby its best chance. But here we were. I had my hands clenched into fists trying to hold myself together as Laura's wails filled the room.

I couldn't comfort her. I didn't know how, didn't know what to say. There wasn't anything a person *could* say. The first thing in my head was that we still had to induce her; she still had to go through labor and deliver her child and make awful decisions regarding next steps.

The hospitalist excused me with a nod of his head because he saw it on my face. I couldn't hold it together, and this wasn't even about me. I went straight to the restroom and bawled. This wasn't right. I had to pull myself together and be there for Laura, because my patient mattered more than my emotions.

I hardened myself, although there was still a crack in my mental armor where the tentacles of anxiety pierced through. I wouldn't show it, though, the chaos battering my head. I returned to Laura, determined, helping the hospitalist where I could and helping Laura where she allowed me.

The chaos and all the things that could go wrong didn't stop there. Because I was part of a large family practice and we had patients all over the hospital whom I needed to check on, I couldn't go home early. I saw an elderly patient taking her last breaths in the ICU with respiratory illness. Following that, I dealt with another patient receiving the always heartbreaking news about positive cancer test results. Then I tried to reason with a pissed parent about why vaccines for their child were safe. Right after that case, I had yet another patient whose symptoms were across the board and who could have a number of diagnoses but in the meantime endured incredible pain and frustration.

Many of these patients took their stress out on me. If not the patients, then frustrated family members with sharp accusations of what *I* was doing wrong and why my best wasn't enough to fix the issue.

Some days, doing everything that I could felt like only a drop in a deep bucket. It wasn't that I'd helped save a baby and mom's life just the other day, but that I hadn't caught this demise in time. It wasn't that I sat with a dying patient when their family was out, but that I couldn't stop them from dying. It wasn't that

I caught cancer in time to treat it, but that I didn't have a cure. It wasn't that I patiently educated someone about vaccines, but that I was shoving my agenda down their throat.

There were no pats on the back or thanks for working long shifts with little sleep. There was no gratitude for having to skip meals and suffering leg aches because I couldn't afford to sit down for more than a minute.

And when the time came to deliver Laura's stillborn child, there wasn't a dry eye in the room.

Dr. Wright had asked me in the hallway half an hour prior if I was all right.

"No," I'd said. "But whatever I'm feeling is nothing compared to her. I have to be here for Laura."

She nodded. "These things never get easier. Excuse yourself if you need to, but you have to keep it together in there."

I was terrified, powerless. There was nothing to do but watch as Laura, in complete agony and pain, cried and pushed. Her husband sobbed beside her but made every attempt to hold her leg and wipe her forehead and support her neck.

Teary-eyed, I watched as Dr. Wright placed the baby on Laura's stomach, as she had wanted to see her daughter and her husband had wanted to cut the umbilical cord. But as soon as Laura saw the baby, her wails ignited and engulfed the entire ward.

The nurse took the baby away to clean her and take measurements and record all findings. I pushed through my touch aversion and sat on the bed beside Laura, took her hand in mine as she gripped it to death, and consoled her.

There just weren't enough words.

Chapter Twelve

Some days, giving my all wasn't enough.

I sat in my car in the parking lot after the hideous nightmare-incarnate day. The light in the apartment was on. Daniel was home.

My phone pinged with a text.

Yuvan: Still mad at me?

Was that really all he had to say after I essentially broke things off with him? Or did he think I was simply upset and would go running back to him because who else in the community would marry me?

I couldn't deal with him right now. I didn't respond, nor did I answer his call ten minutes later.

My eyes fluttered closed as my thoughts drowned in wave after thrashing wave of anxiety. My head throbbed. My legs and back ached.

I finally dragged myself out of the car and lugged my backpack after me. The strap snagged on the seat belt buckle. I tugged harder and harder, but the thing about loops was that they didn't just unsnag themselves. I crawled back into the car and undid the loop, but the backpack was so heavy and forcing it to squeeze between the console, and then against the wheel, turned into a battle.

I wanted to scream. Why couldn't the freaking bag just come out! Why the crap did I always try to lug the stupid thing through my side? Why didn't I just walk around to the passenger door and open it? Wouldn't that make sense?

When I succeeded in the most basic thing I had to do today, I took the elevator to the top floor and opened the front door to my apartment. My shoulders drooped beneath the weight of the backpack as I took off my shoes and nearly stumbled over them. For goodness' sake. Could I just do something right today?

"Ready to talk?" Daniel said from his desk. He wasn't slumped over his work. He had the TV on and was eating out of a bowl.

I really hoped he'd at least cleaned the stupid kitchen. Fortunately, when I glanced at the countertops through the corner of an eye, I saw only a spotless kitchen. Even the dishes that had been left on the drying rack this morning had been put away.

"Are you okay?" he asked.

I could've said a number of things: My patient lost her baby today. I was having an anxiety attack. I was on the verge of depression. I was on the cusp of hating myself for not being good enough.

"Yep," I said instead, avoiding eye contact and lugging my crap into the bedroom. I dumped it all in the corner by the window, grabbed my sweats, undies, and towel, and went to the bathroom.

My shower was neither as hot nor as long as I would've liked.

Once dressed, I fished through the medicine cabinet and checked out my options. NyQuil always knocked me out fast and hard, but it left me feeling groggy in the morning. Maybe Motrin

PM? Yeah. I was a lightweight and didn't need two tablets. One would suffice, although two or three seemed tempting.

I downed one pill and anticipated the druggy sleepiness that would hit soon.

"Do you want something to eat?" Daniel asked cautiously when I emerged. He washed his bowl and fork in the sink.

"No, thanks."

"Are you sure you're okay?"

"Yep." I pressed my lips together and turned toward the bedroom.

"Pree?" He walked around the counter. "What's going on?"

I wanted to tell him, because I just needed to unload on someone. Anyone. Part of me knew without a doubt that he'd understand, because he had been there for me in times like this before. But part of me knew better than to lean on him in any way.

Even a conversation.

Even when I needed him.

Even when I knew that his response would alleviate the tension burning in my veins, a wildfire scorching my insides to ashes.

I'd come home looking a haggard mess with dark circles beneath red-streaked eyes, furrowed brows, slumped shoulders, and a quiver that came with every breath.

No one had ever seen me get this bad, except once when I had too many classes and too many projects and too many labs and studying for the MCAT on top of worrying about my entire future and letting my parents down.

I'd crashed that day. Literally. Into a tree while riding my bike across campus in the evening. Liya had taken one look at me and demanded to know what was wrong. I told her, but there was nothing she could do. So she'd called Daniel, despite me warning her not to.

"Great distress leads to desperate measures. Or else I call your parents," she'd said.

I hadn't wanted anyone to see me that way, out of control and agitated beyond belief. That had been a dark, scary time.

I'd pushed Daniel away, even snapped at him. He'd gotten frustrated, upset, but always came back to try again. He never left me.

He'd sat with me through many nights and checked in on me throughout the days. He'd asked what had happened, listened to me rant about feelings, sat with me when I didn't want to talk. I'd leaned on him for my life. That was how Daniel found out about my anxiety, how it sometimes led to depression.

It wasn't easy in times like this to simply look to God or prayer, to talk to friends, to remember how all the blessings outweighed the bad. There was no way to take a minute and calm down, or view things in black-and-white, to give it an easy fix.

Daniel had seen me then, and he saw me now.

His eyes went wide. "You're having an episode."

He took three long strides across the expanse between the kitchen and the bedroom. For a second, my shivering stopped and I closed my eyes, relaxing.

He maintained a short distance, didn't speak, didn't touch me, didn't probe. He knew me better than anyone. He knew that I was hard to read at times, that a gentle touch could either soothe or trigger. He waited. I leaned toward him, almost as if I'd fallen asleep.

I jerked back. The calm vaporized.

"I can't. I just can't," I snapped before hurrying into the bedroom.

Daniel came after me but the door went flying shut in his face. Oh, no. I didn't mean to throw my anger at him.

I heaved and backed away from the door as if it were about to explode.

A knock. A gentle, calm-evoking knock.

"Please go away. I just want to sleep," I said from the darkness of the bedroom, my lips quivering, trying to keep it together. Even now, I spiraled into depression, that vortex of negativity, losing the chemical and mental fight.

Anxiety attacks were like being on the failing side in the battle to keep the *Alien* facehugger from attaching to my head. When it did latch on, it not only suffocated the airways, but the tentacles clawed into the brain and squeezed. If it squeezed even one second too long, a full-on mental breakdown ensued.

Daniel's shadow faded beneath the door.

I was alone, which meant my hands and my mind needed busywork.

I was in my favorite sweats and concentrated on positive things. I had a happy playlist on my phone for such episodes. There was a compilation of comedic shows and movies that fluttered through my thoughts because pairing auditory and visual was best in order to use up as many senses as possible, reducing the chance for my brain to start thinking and dreading again. I needed something for my mouth to do. Singing was an option, no matter the level of tone-deafness. Eating or drinking was better, though. Hot tea. Cinnamon and orange pekoe black tea with a sprinkle of sugar.

I had a tea bag somewhere in my backpack, but just looking at the bag slumped in the corner had me seeing red. It was illogical to get this upset at an inanimate object.

Even as I rummaged around the bedroom, my thoughts fought an imbalance. I had to try harder to keep negativity out, but pessimism was a wildly strong beast that grappled to the death. And mental health decline was surreal. I'd experienced it one too many times, and I didn't want to get near that again.

I swallowed hard as words formed in my head, all triggers that created holes in my poorly barricaded mental fortification.

Bad doctor.

Worthless.

Incompetent.

Pointless.

Each word created splintered images of my poor patients and their sobbing families.

Tears stung my eyes and my lips quivered. Then a new section broke open at the sight of Yuvan's name flashing across my phone.

Bad wife.

Can't cook.

Can't be touched.

Can't commit.

Has a history.

Why did he want to marry me, anyway? Didn't he see that I was worthless? He was already getting agitated with me.

No. I am not *worthless. I* have *to fight it.*

Even as I thought the words, they disintegrated. The darkness rose like colossal waves and crashed down with the weight of a million suns. The mental assault was becoming less and less bearable and more and more critical. My breathing escalated, turning harsh and ragged. My pulse raced.

Maybe wine instead of tea? Or maybe more sleeping pills? The fogginess and sleep wouldn't erase it all, but it would blur the sharpness of misery.

I scratched down my arms to alleviate some of the tension building inside my bones and grunted out a muffled scream. Just as tears rolled down my cheeks, music floated through the room.

I glanced around for an entire minute trying to figure out where the sound came from. The TV was off and my phone wasn't playing music. My confusion ebbed away when I realized that the music hummed from the living room.

It took another moment to pinpoint the song. That melodious, humbling, comforting song that dove straight to my soul. It was a soothing balm, placating the fires and torrents that tried to destroy me from within.

The heaviness in my chest receded. The gnarling thoughts gnashing around in my head subsided. My skin cooled.

"Oh," I breathed, staring at the closed door that separated me from these healing sounds.

Thrumming music.

Daniel still played the guitar?

The music got a little louder, a little closer. The ideal medicine that had helped me years ago came back in that heartbreaking way. It was a magical remedy to these acrid mental wounds.

The music started low, quiet. He played right outside.

I rested my forehead against the door as tears streamed down my face. On one hand, Daniel's gesture quieted the storm raging through my mind. On the other hand, he reminded me of just how much I'd loved him.

Daniel was…as easy as Sunday morning. Maybe that sounded cliché, but it was the truth. Remembering every song he'd ever played for me and how much it meant was as natural as waking up to a lazy Sunday morning. A morning spent wrapped in blankets and sipping on hot coffee with the right amount of robust flavor and a dollop of homemade whipped cream. The smell of country ham and bacon mixed with sweet maple syrup drizzled over pecan waffles on those amazing, unexpected long mornings when he had time to cook masterful meals. Buttery sweet grits and honey-glazed buttermilk biscuits. A pitcher of fresh-squeezed orange juice. The spread on white lace tablecloths around a bouquet of purple and yellow wildflowers when I'd stayed over at his place. Clanking fine china and silverware muted by haunting laughter and conversations those times when we ate with his grandparents and Brandy.

Sunday morning was about comfort and grace and gratitude and all the feel-goods life had.

Sunday morning was about blessings and taking a step back from hectic life.

Sunday morning was... any morning waking up beside Daniel.

As his fingers strummed against the strings, the tune vibrated through the walls and straight into my chest.

His shadow crested beneath the door, moved to the left, and stayed there. Music softly, delicately filled the space between us.

Please be enough. Please let this music floating beneath the door be enough.

He remembered this after so long? This music that had been my safety line, the only thing to grab on to when there was nothing else. In a world where tangible things weren't enough, when I felt like I was mentally and emotionally drowning, these intangible notes had become the only thing I could latch on to.

Back then, it had been just enough to keep me from reeling away and tripping over the edge.

Please be enough again.

Chapter Thirteen

Coming from Daniel, music took on a whole other meaning. It became an entity that sifted through the air and hummed into my skin. It wove a blanket around my soul and cushioned me from the darkness. When I couldn't barricade myself from myself, his music managed to do the job.

My vision blurred behind tears.

He remembered. And more than that, he knew. He knew me well enough to know what I was fighting without my even having to say it. And he knew exactly what to do. His music was stronger than any drug.

Sometimes Daniel was the only thing I needed. And right now, that simple truth couldn't be any clearer, any more apparent.

I slid down to the floor and brought my knees to my chest. My head touched the wall. My eyes drifted closed. And the music swam through me. It battled the darkness on my behalf, just enough for me to continue on, even if I had to crawl.

My breathing eased and so did my pulse.

Daniel must've played for some time, moving through several songs. Happy songs. Songs that held so many memories. Songs that we'd danced to, eaten dinner over, heard on the radio when we studied together. Songs that filled the silence around us when we cuddled up together on the couch or on a blanket beneath the stars. Songs that were everything to me.

He remembered them all.

I sighed, long and draining, as if my breath carried half of my burdens with it, and wiped my tears. They'd been flooding down my cheeks and dampening my shirt.

The music stopped. I opened my eyes and glanced at Daniel's shadow beneath the door. He was still there.

Despite knowing better, my body knew what it needed. I reached up and grasped the doorknob. Part of me warned against this. One thing always led to another when it came to us. We weren't snowflakes of innocent moments. We were snowstorms of powerful emotions.

I breathed faster, telling my hand to stop, but everything faded into white noise as I tamped down my thoughts.

And opened the door.

Daniel was sitting on the other side of the doorframe, his guitar off to his left, his knees to his chest, a hand on the carpet between us. He gave a soft, defeated smile, the kind that could calm a blizzard and melt snow. The kind that could calm me. He'd always done that. His mere presence had staved off so many anxiety attacks in the past.

I glanced at his fingertips, twitching as if they yearned to reach for me. "Your fingers are going to bleed."

He moved into the room, sat with his back against the wall. "Come here."

I crawled toward him and sat in between his legs, facing the window, my back to the apartment, my shoulder to his chest.

"Is this okay?" he asked, his voice gravelly, his arms wrapping around me. Such a warm, protective touch that warded off negative feelings. Sometimes I needed Daniel more than I needed air, and it had never been so devastatingly clear as it was right now.

I nodded.

He held me against him, my cheek against his chest. "Nothing in the world would have made me stop, if it helps you."

"Thank you. But why would you care after the mess I created?"

"Are you joking right now?" he asked, his voice soft.

I shook my head.

He sighed and hit his head gently against the wall. "Because caring for you is as natural as it's always been."

"Oh." My heart twisted in my chest, full of hope and regret.

"Do you want to talk about it?"

"No."

"Okay. I'm here when you do."

As my emotions simmered down, the adrenaline wore off, the meds kicked in, and my eyelids grew heavy. Sleep was a no-nonsense stalker at my gates.

As soon as I yawned, Daniel shifted and I pulled away.

"Let's get some rest?" he asked.

He stood. I took his hand as he pulled me up. He let go as soon as we realized how long our hold had lingered. He rubbed the back of his neck as his gaze flitted to his feet. What was better than his music to calm me? His embrace, undoubtedly.

"I should get some sleep," I whispered.

"Yeah," he replied but didn't move, his focus on the small space between our bodies. "I should probably take the couch tonight and let you rest."

I frowned, not wanting that at all.

"Pree?"

"Yeah?" I asked, hopeful that he'd sleep in the bed again.

"Are you...getting help for this? I know in the past it was new and scary, and you'd told me about the stigma among doctors and in your community and family, but I'm really worried."

"I have an appointment for it coming up tomorrow, actually." I offered a small smile. "Thank you for caring."

"We might not be in the best place with each other, but for things like this...I'm right here if you need me," he said, his gaze intent on me. His fingers twitched. So did mine. I wondered if he wanted to hug me as much as I needed him to.

I took a step back and slowly closed the door after he walked out. Behind me, the bed was cold and empty, much like how my mind would be any given minute. I went to bed and lay down. Yep. The sheets were like ice, but my body raged hot. I tossed and turned and tried every position, then groaned. Loudly. I just wanted to scream. I even clenched my eyes and gritted my teeth, clutched a pillow over my face and almost... *almost* let it all go.

Daniel knocked on the door. "Are you sure that you're all right?"

I shoved the pillow aside and gasped for air. Had he heard any of that? Had I actually screamed? "Yep."

No.

I shot out of bed and reached for the door just as he pushed it open.

"I know you're not okay," he said. "Why are you lying to me?"

My lips quivered and I tried to blink back tears. I might've won the fight against my emotions if he hadn't taken me into his arms. He pulled me against the warmth of his chest. His broad arms wrapped snugly, perfectly around me. Not too tight, not too loose.

I clutched the back of his shirt as soon as the shock of his touch wore off. I held on to him like I might die otherwise. Then the sobs came, muffled against him. My tears would ruin his shirt.

Daniel didn't care. He held me quietly and caressed my back. Sometimes all a person needed was for another person to just be there. No words. No explanations. Just silence. And tears. And hugs.

I inhaled a deep breath filled with Daniel's scent as the sobbing eased. I rubbed my tears against his shirt as I pulled away and wiped the rest of my face. I must've looked a complete mess.

His hands were still around me, one on my hip and one low

on my back, when I asked, "Um. Do you mind...I mean...is it awkward if...?"

"Do you want me to sleep in here tonight?" he asked.

I nodded.

"Of course."

"Thanks," I mumbled as he closed the door and got into bed.

The bed wasn't eerily chilly anymore. It was warm and glowing and full of hope. But also awkward. We both lay flat on our backs on opposite sides. There was enough space in between us for another person. I was so close to the edge that I would fall off with any minor movement.

I scooted closer to him.

He inched closer to me.

Until finally, I surrendered to the awkwardness and rolled toward him.

Sometimes Daniel read my mind. He stretched his arm over my head. "Come here."

I lifted my head as his arm slid down my neck and wrapped around my shoulders. I nestled against him, curled into his side as he held me.

I tried not to enjoy this.

I tried to remember that, until a couple of days ago, I was getting engaged to another man and that I could not still be in love with Daniel Thompson.

I tried not to relax and melt against him.

But the moment I snuggled into Daniel, I was done. Because instead of abhorring his touch, I craved more of it. Daniel instantly eradicated so many anxieties swarming in my head. There was no such thing as feeling scared when he held me.

As much as the better part of my brain told me to not even think it, I already knew.

I really missed this. I really missed *him*.

Chapter Fourteen

I hadn't slept most of the night, but I must've passed out pretty hard at some point because my own snoring jolted me awake. That only ever happened when I was dead tired. I kept my eyes closed for as long as possible.

Until I felt a warm hand brushing hair from my face. I tucked my chin down and burrowed against him, the bedspread to my nose.

Yum. Someone smelled like soap, clean with a hint of vanilla.

I pried open my eyes, stuck together by tear-dried lashes, as realization dawned on me. I was not alone. My face turned hot as I blinked up at Daniel. He watched me with concerned eyes and an imploring smile.

"Oh..." I pulled back, embarrassed.

Daniel lay on his back, his head turned toward me, partway covered by the bedspread while I was turned into his side. He had one hand beneath his neck and the other on his stomach. The last time we'd lain like this, so comfy and at peace, had been days before the breakup.

My blaring alarm pierced the tranquility from the nightstand behind me, that sober tune I most despised hearing. I turned off the alarm and sat up in bed, way, way on the other side, far from Daniel and his perfect, welcoming body.

He followed suit and sat up, stretching his back and neck, and leaned back on his hands. "Morning," he said, his voice gritty and rough. He sounded like sex.

No. Stop it. That was just my out-of-control emotions talking.

"Oh, no. You didn't sleep, did you?" I asked, my voice small and a little hoarse. "Why are you smiling?"

"Am I? Oh, it's just…you instinctively knew I didn't get much sleep. Or do I look that awful?"

"I can tell from your voice."

"Still know me so well, huh?"

My skin flushed. Knowing Daniel this well was easy. "I could say the same for you. For the music last night."

He licked the corner of his lips, his expression soft, relaxed. "Some things are impossible to forget."

My breath hitched. "Thank you for the music. I *really* needed it."

"I'm just glad that it helped. And my offer stands if you want to talk about it."

I offered an appreciative smile, trying to hold my tears at bay, struggling to cage the horrors of all the bad things and at the same time diving headfirst into the normality of waking up to Daniel. The anger he'd had since we moved in together had taken a back seat as his natural concern and warmth permeated the space between us. No one had to ask him to help. He just simply knew. He just did it.

"Is there anything…I can do?" he asked, watching me, his body tense.

Yeah. There was. He could hold me, kiss my forehead. But I couldn't admit that.

"No, thank you," I replied. "I really shouldn't."

"Shouldn't let it out? If not with me, then with someone else. Your friends?"

"They're all going through something right now. Reema is on a honeymoon high and I don't want to fracture that. And Liya, well, she's dealing with something awful and I can't add another burden."

"You are not a burden to any of your friends. Don't even think that. In fact, if they knew you were suffering this bad and you didn't tell them, they'd be pretty upset. They were there for you years ago when they called me. Your friends would do anything for you, and none of them would see this as a burden. I can promise you that. Just like I don't see it as a burden."

I stared at the bedspread scrunched in my lap and ran a fingernail over the abstract design. "Part of me knows that."

"Yet the other part prevents you from leaning on them. Doesn't have to be them. Maybe your parents?"

"They'd worry way too much and they have so many things going on. The next thing I know, they'll be pressuring me to move back home so they can baby me."

He smirked. "You were always a daddy's girl."

I coughed out a laugh. "I'm an only child. My parents dote on me, and there's nothing wrong with that or with being close to them."

"Nah. I'm glad that you are." He cleared his throat, his expression a little bitter, probing as he asked, "Maybe you can talk to your boyfriend."

My eyes went wide. "He doesn't get it. At least, not the way you do."

He sucked in a big breath, his chest expanding and slowly deflating. Our eyes locked in an intense, unbreakable moment. My chest tingled, in a good, calming way. Our fingers twitched, my hand pressed against the mattress beside his. Without moving his hand, he swept a fingertip over mine. My insides sank like quicksand. His touch was feathery, energizing, and shot a lightning bolt of desire straight to my core.

The alarm shrilled and I startled, my thoughts reeling back into order, to reality.

Saved by the buzzer! I turned it off again. Holding the phone in my hand, my pulse racing, I groaned. "Another day."

"It'll be better than yesterday," he said.

"Probably not," I replied and slid out of bed. Because death didn't just disappear after one day.

He outstretched his hand. "Can I add my number to your phone?"

Perplexed at the request, I signed in with my thumb and handed my phone over.

Daniel entered his name, then looked surprised. Oh. Yikes! I still had his old number *and* a photo of us programmed in.

"You still have this old picture?" he asked, a cocky smile on his face.

I flushed. "Guess so."

"I remember that day."

"Me too. There you were, pouting about having to walk because you were so done with school."

He chuckled. "And their ugly gowns. Is that bad for me to admit?"

"Sort of. I was really proud of you. I mean…we all were."

My words ended quietly. That was a time when he hadn't wanted to walk the stage, but earning a master's degree was *his* accomplishment. His parents and grandparents had worked hard to make sure that he earned one. I'd convinced him to walk for them. They were so happy. And then things changed. When his father told me in clear-as-day, sharp-as-a-razor words that I was not good enough for Daniel. When around the same time, everyone in the community caught wind of our relationship and it hit my parents like a speeding bus out of nowhere.

He handed me my phone after updating his number and

clarified, "Today is better than yesterday because no matter what happens today, you know that I'm here. Doesn't matter if you call me or text me or see me when you get home."

Warmth filled me from his kindness. "Thanks, Daniel. I should get ready for work."

"Yeah. What do you want for breakfast?" he asked, yanking the covers off and swinging his legs over the side of the bed.

"You don't have to make me anything. You should try to get a couple of hours of sleep."

But he was already at the door. "Do you want buttermilk pancakes? I feel like some pancakes. They always help the mood."

"Um…" I watched his backside as he strolled into the kitchen.

"With that butter-crisped edge?" He glanced up from the kitchen as the lights flickered on.

I couldn't hide my tiny smile at the thought of his pancakes.

He cocked his chin toward the bathroom. "I got this."

I nodded and disappeared into the bathroom for my morning routine, then came to the kitchen still in my pajamas but with hair combed, face washed, teeth brushed. "What can I help with?"

"Can you not burn the coffee?" he joked, setting out the butter beside a bowl of batter and a cup of freshly whipped cream.

"Hey!" I said, feigning insult.

"I mean, you *did* burn coffee once."

"That was my very first time even seeing a coffeemaker." I poured water into the coffee machine and adjusted the settings. This one was super fancy, seeing that it was Liya's, but I'd used it before.

"Be right back," he said and hurried to the bathroom.

Hmph! Like burning coffee was a repeat offense. I heated the skillet and proceeded to make a pancake instead of standing idly by and leaving room for the panic attack to creep back in.

"What are you doing?" Daniel asked.

I jumped. "God, were you trained by ninjas in how to sneak up on people?"

He was at my side, towering and crunching the space between us. "Seriously. What are you doing, though?"

"If I can simultaneously handle L&D and the ER on-call during a full moon, I can handle a pancake," I argued, armed with a spatula.

He slipped behind me and watched over my shoulder as a dozen bubbles erupted in the pancake. I jammed the spatula underneath it. Daniel hissed.

"*What?*" I asked tersely.

"Not enough bubbles yet. And gently. The pancake isn't one of your L&D patients."

I paused and glanced at him over my shoulder. "You think I ram my hand up my patients?"

He shrugged. "I don't know how you shove anything up anyone, but that pancake needs a softer touch than this. Let me," he insisted and went to take the spatula.

I twisted away and muttered, "I don't understand why everyone acts like I should know how to cook. It's condescending."

"I'm not trying to be condescending. Cooking isn't your thing and nothing's wrong with that, just like medicine isn't my thing. How about you let me help you?"

I felt him flinch behind me when I flipped the pancake over, splattering the uncooked side all over the pan. The top was barely golden. It looked so... sickly and pale.

"First one is always bad," I explained.

"True..."

I shoved the spatula underneath the sickly pancake and dropped it into the trash. Poor thing didn't stand a chance.

Daniel greased the pan with a nice helping of butter. I took a measuring cup filled halfway with batter and dumped it into the pan.

"Slowly," he said, lifting my hand to ease the flow of batter. He helped me lower the cup and spread out the batter more evenly by using the bottom of the cup.

I armed myself with the spatula again. I kept trying to check the underside and every time, Daniel tugged my elbow back.

"Wait for the bubbles," he reminded me, now standing with his chest to my back and his hand on my wrist.

I swallowed hard and stiffened, resisting the urge to melt against him. The last time Daniel taught me how to cook something, this exact same scenario led to his pressing against my backside. Which led to me arching against him. Which led to him kissing my neck. Which led to me gripping his hip. Which led to him running his hands underneath my shirt and...burning pancakes.

He explained, "There's a good amount of butter in the batter, but adding it to the pan creates nice aromatic, browned, crisped edges and ridges. See?"

I carefully scooped up the pancake and flipped. It was perfect.

"The best pancake flipper in Houston," he teased.

I transferred the finished pancake onto a plate, my body gliding to the left and then to the right against his chest with barely-there grazes. My skin burned as his chin tickled the back of my head. I inhaled him like he was the breath of life.

What was I doing? What in the world was wrong with me?

When I got the hang of it on the third and fourth pancakes, he stepped away and made a cup of coffee. I had an amazing stack of four pancakes piled perilously high for myself. While I made three more for Daniel, he garnished my stack with powdered sugar, freshly cut strawberries, whipped cream, and, of course, more butter. I liked my pancakes without syrup. He liked his with a bit of everything.

"I'm going to have a sugar crash," I said as I stuffed a giant bite into my mouth and took a seat on a barstool at the counter.

The toaster oven dinged and Daniel held up a finger. He brought over a plate of breakfast sausage. "Protein. Extra to take with you for when you have a sugar crash."

"Thanks. I knew I smelled something other than pancakes and coffee." I stabbed a sausage with my fork and gnawed on it through the heat. My gaze fell to his shirt. "You have some flour there."

"Where?" he joked, as if he didn't notice that he was about half covered in flour. "Ah. I accidentally dropped the measuring cup into the bowl and up went flour flying all over."

"And your hair..." I reached up to scuff off some particles from his twists, my fingers lingering, savoring the touch. "It's really in there. How... *what*?"

He leaned down at the same time I jumped up from the barstool. We knocked heads. Hard.

"*Ow!*" I groaned and grabbed my temple, fully aware of how close he stood to me, our chests only inches apart.

"Sorry!" He cupped my face and kissed my forehead, as if it were simple instinct. The touch was quick, innocent, but his lips were sensual, intoxicating. I shuddered.

I loosely held on to his wrists and a soft breath escaped from my parted lips. His gaze dropped to my mouth, mine fell to his. His lips probably tasted like buttermilk pancakes and whipped cream and strawberries and syrup. I could practically taste him on my tongue.

I winced, pulling away instead of giving in to test my hypothesis. "That really hurt. You're so hardheaded."

He chuckled. "You're one to talk. You might need ibuprofen for that."

"Sugar high and head injury... are you trying to make me pass out?" I rubbed my forehead and walked to the bedroom before I let out a tremulous sigh.

A forehead kiss was nothing. It was innocent. Right?

I returned dressed in black slacks and a wintergreen blouse, my hair pulled back in a low ponytail. I took the foil-wrapped sausage with thanks, filled my water bottle and coffee tumbler, and left.

My heart rammed in my chest. We couldn't do that again.

I was determined to face the day, to push aside all the negativity thrown at me and focus on my patients. They weren't just cases or bad days. They were people and they needed me.

The first thing this morning was rounding. Laura was my second patient.

I sat beside her bed, held her hand, and let her cry.

Chapter Fifteen

Yesterday had been miserable, and today wasn't much better. There were still patients and families receiving bad news. People continued to blame me.

Today, for lack of a better word, sucked. But it *felt* a hundred times better. And I knew exactly why every time I peeked at my phone and saw Daniel's occasional check-ins. And there was, of course, Liya reeling the conversation back to my so-called hookup with Daniel. She actually had me cracking up, which made me feel weird and guilty. Maybe I didn't deserve to be happy when Laura and so many other patients were suffering.

By now, Reema and Sana had jumped into the conversation.

Reema: Seriously! Liya just told me what's going on in that...apartment of ill repute.

I laughed so hard that water almost spurted out of my nose. The text sex joke was just the distraction my day needed. So silly and lighthearted and anything except serious.

Reema: Don't you think about using my gift toward this madness.

I hadn't thought about that. But maybe I could repay Daniel's kindness by cooking him dinner. Maybe having that relaxed type of evening would make it easier for me to tell him why I'd left the way that I had. I didn't have to use Reema's gift to show my gratitude. Although, how impressed would Daniel be if I came through with Parisian crepes? More importantly, why was I even thinking about impressing him?

Vegetable stir-fry and noodles seemed easy enough. Cook veggies, add sauce. Boil noodles for three minutes, drain, add to veggies. Easy-peasy. Yet I found myself standing in the international grocery aisle after work wondering which sauce and which type of noodles to get. There was a better selection at the actual Asian supermarket down the street, but that store had an entire aisle dedicated to noodles alone and another for sauces, and I wasn't ready for that.

I texted the girls for advice, since everyone was already on the sex text thread.

Me: *Making dinner for my man. Quick! How do you make stir-fry noodles? Which veggies and sauce should I buy? Also, which noodles?*

Liya: Mm! Food is definitely the way to a man's heart.

Sana: So NOT funny (if this is a joke)!

Reema: You lie. You're not getting along with him, much less doing it.

Liya: We're adults. We can say screw. And she's screwing him hard. I mean...LOOK at him! He's like Trevor Noah and Michael B. Jordan smashed into one fine-ass man. Rawr.

Sana: Okay, yes, I do agree with Liya about the level of fineness.

Reema: No one is questioning Daniel's attractiveness, but I demand proof or stop playing this dumb game. Why are you doing this?

Me: Guys. I'm standing in front of the noodles. I need help.

Liya: Chow mein noodles are easy, quick, tasty, and won't get soggy. Don't do cruciferous veggies...ya know, the gas...

Reema: OMG. Just sauté red bell peppers, mushrooms, baby corn (in a can), and add spinach at the very end. Keep it simple if you're actually cooking. And use a splash of soy sauce and some chili paste or get a stir-fry sauce in a bottle. Be basic.

All right. I could do that.

With everything I needed in hand, I arrived home without a trace of Daniel in sight.

That gave me time to shower and change. With Reema's text still fresh in mind, I couldn't believe that I'd forgotten all about her wrapped gift that I wasn't supposed to open until I got home. It was still in the bag with the crepe ingredients, which sat on top of the long dresser. As my hair air-dried, I unwrapped the delicate lavender tissue paper and unraveled lacy fabric.

*Oh...*Maybe when she'd said not to use her gift with Daniel, she wasn't talking about crepes at all. Maybe she meant this very sexy, very lacy Parisian underwear and bra set. The fabric was soft and textured in a gorgeous shade of pinkish-purple. The panties were, um, a thong. How daring! And the bra wasn't padded at all. My nipples didn't stand a chance in the air-conditioned world without padding.

Might as well wash these. I tossed them into the hamper

and went to the kitchen, washed my hands, then scrubbed the vegetables. I took my time. I found a wok in the cabinet and started heating some sesame oil instead of olive oil.

The door opened as soon as I'd finished cutting up veggies with Liya's expensive and super-sharp knives. Good thing I had a physician's bag with an emergency kit just in case.

"Hey," Daniel said from the foyer as he locked the door and stepped into the kitchen with his *shoes on*. I glared at them and almost jumped out of my skin. Seeing someone walk into the home with shoes on made me want to claw my face off.

"Shoes, please."

"Oh yeah. Sorry about that." He slipped out of his shoes, leaving them against the wall in the foyer.

"What's going on?" he asked, peeking over my shoulder, his body heat meeting mine and making me want to arch into him.

"I thought I would make dinner to pay you back for breakfast."

"Uh-huh," he mumbled skeptically.

I glanced at him from over my shoulder. His eyes narrowed with curiosity, and his lips parted as if he couldn't figure out what in the world I was doing. His face was so close to mine that I could see his pupils dilate, pushing against a ring of dark brown irises.

"What?" I scowled.

"Need help?"

"Nope. I have it under control."

He removed his messenger bag and tossed it onto the couch. "Cool. Are you feeling better?"

I smiled as the veggies hit the sizzling pan. Boy, sesame oil sure heated up fast in a wok. "Yes, thanks."

"Just going to wash up and change, then." He winked, seeming thoroughly entertained, and disappeared into the bedroom to grab his clothes and then to the bathroom.

Reema: Please tell him hello for me…if you're actually getting hot and heavy…

I was in the middle of texting her back with the next level of this joke when I smelled something pungent.

"Oh!" I rushed to turn off the stove and remove the wok from the heat, waving off smoke. The veggies would be okay. Who in Texas didn't like barbeque-style food, anyway?

Daniel emerged from the bathroom and snickered. "Are you sure you don't want help?"

I guffawed. "I can make stir-fry veggies. Thanks."

"Yep." He tossed his clothes into the hamper and sort of did a double take. He pushed his clothes aside and raised a sharp eyebrow. "Nice…"

"Hey!"

"What?" He laughed. "Since when do you wear lacy underwear?"

"Not polite to look at those, and anyway, I didn't buy them."

"Did your boyfriend buy them?" he asked, his tone sharper than it had been a second ago. Was he jealous? No, that couldn't be. Why would he be jealous of anyone in my life?

"No. Actually, Reema did, as a gift from her honeymoon in Paris."

"Ah. Are you going to wear them?" He waggled his brows.

I tamped down the fire in my veins. "You shouldn't flirt with me."

He chuckled from the other side of the counter. "If you think that's flirting, then your boyfriend is doing it all wrong. I mean, flirting is pressing my chest against your back and watching you cook."

I swallowed. Crap. It was.

"Or taking my shirt off in front of you." He lifted the hem of his blue T-shirt like he was about to strip, flashing those infamous abs, only to wipe his face with it. He grinned at me as he lowered his shirt back into place.

I bit my lip. Double crap.

"Brushing the hair from your face and telling you that you look beautiful first thing in the morning. Or does he not do any of the things I used to?"

I gripped the handle of the wok even tighter and changed the subject before it wandered too far down the wrong road. "Anyway. How's the hospital project going?"

"Fine. Dull. Rudimentary." He crossed his arms on the counter, his biceps straining against his shirt, and leaned down just as my phone pinged. He glanced at my lit screen a couple of seconds longer than he should've. His eyebrows went up. Way up.

He laughed. "So, uh, we *did it*, huh?" He looked at me, his head cocked to the side and amusement flourishing across his face.

I panicked in a flood of mortification. Exes should never know that you told your friends y'all were getting busy, even as a joke. "You can't just go around reading people's text messages."

"I didn't mean to, but you left it open to the message and the notification sound had me automatically looking. Hold up. We have to backtrack," he went on and took the phone, although he didn't scroll through the rest of the message. "You told your friends you're getting some from me?"

Heat sprang to my cheeks as I hurried around the counter and tried to get the phone back from him. "I'm pranking Liya for setting us up like this. She can't just shove us into an apartment expecting something to happen. I don't know what that woman was thinking."

He chuckled, holding the phone high and forcing me to claw at him to get anywhere near it. But he was so tall! "It's kind of amusing. The sex is better than it was before, huh? I mean, damn, Pree. We had some amazing sex before, so how am I topping that now?"

The heat at my cheeks? All-out flames scorching my flesh off as I clambered up his body to no avail.

"According to your last response, which Liya just quoted and added an eggplant and an emoji with an open mouth, it says something about how I can get you wet with just one look."

"Daniel! Oh my god!" Even on my tiptoes I couldn't reach.

His hand landed softly on my waist as he held the screen down to read. "Liya wants to know if we…um…have tried other things? Because in the past you made sex sound kind of boring, unless you weren't telling her everything, in which case she wants all the deets now. The dirtier, the better, because she's here for it." He laughed, his body rumbling against mine. "What kind of freaky things does she think we're doing?"

I tumbled against him, tangled in arms and laughter. I poked him in the armpit, a ticklish spot that I hadn't forgotten about.

"Can I play along, too?" he asked, laughing and turning from my poking. "Can I add to this entertainment?" He typed.

I gripped his side, clutching his shirt in my hands, fully immersed in his scent and touch and warmth. I wouldn't mind being glued to him forever. "I give up. Oh my goodness. This thing is spiraling out of control."

"Might as well have fun, right?" He handed me the phone. "After all, she did put us in this situation."

I huffed and stepped back to read his message. I didn't want to smile, but the mortification slipped away as I smiled anyway. "I'm going to delete this entire, absurd thing."

"Ah, don't be petty. You know it's good."

"Ugh, you're right," I admitted.

"Can we hit send, or what?" He leaned against the counter so that he could peer over my shoulder.

"You're kind of full of yourself, aren't you?"

"You think so? That sounds pretty believable to me…"

"You walked in on me taking a bath and things kinda escalated from there? You do understand that I think baths are like simmering in your own body oils and dirt. Very gross."

"But I drew you a bath."

"With candles and rose petals?"

"And lots of suds." He winked. Yeah. When he said it like that, the idea did not totally suck. It took everything in me not to let the visual image intensify from there.

"And then you stripped down and I was done for?"

He grinned, so proud of himself and his little erogenous tale. "Yep. See? Sounds very believable to me. Bathtub sex is the most erotic way to get it on. All that slippery skin and easy gliding."

I swallowed hard and wished away the mental images of being butt-naked with soapy, wet skin slipping and sliding. Two people could easily accidentally have sex. Was it getting hot in here? Or was it the burnt veggies? I blinked a good few times and read more of his reply.

"Your...kisses are like drugs that have me hooked and pining for more? And your touch has my body on fire; I can't stop think-ing about you and can't wait to get home? Forget about the extra on-call. Okay. *That* part? Sets off an alarm. I would never cut back on on-call shifts right now," I said and deleted the last section.

We faced each other as my smile slipped. He blinked down at me and lifted a hand to brush the hair from my face, his fingertip lingering and gliding from my cheek to my jaw, sending shivers down my spine.

His voice lowered. "But if I'm that good and I keep you coming back for more...doesn't it make sense?"

"Umm..." Talk about a man who stole my breath and my words.

He cleared his throat and backed away, rubbing the back of his neck and letting his hand hang there for a few seconds as if maybe his tale of eroticism was partly wishful thinking.

I took a much-needed deep breath and regained my senses, but sent the text and nudged him away from me. "Go eat your veggies."

"The burnt ones?"

"The...pan-seared ones."

"Pan-searing is for meat and fish. Not veggies."

I stuck a fork into a piece of perfectly browned baby corn and winced. "Yum. So tender."

Daniel opened the fridge, pulling out all sorts of ingredients. "I can't with you, sometimes. You may be a rock-star physician, but you can't eat burnt vegetables for dinner."

I leaned a hip against the counter as he posed with a smile and a wink. He stayed that way for a good ten seconds. "What's that for? Did you just freeze?"

"Photo ops. For the, uh, prank texting sex joke or whatever you're calling it."

"Oh! Yes. Perfect." I took a picture, admiring how photogenic Daniel was. The way the light and shadow created perfect contours and highlights, accentuating the sharp cuts of his jaw, his framed cheekbones, the defined edges of his haircut, the formation of his muscles beneath the taut fabric of his shirt. Even his eyes glimmered. He might as well have been a model.

I studied the picture on my phone a little longer, zooming in on his face, on his smooth skin, on those eyelashes that I couldn't get on my best eyelash curler days, on that amazing smile. Daniel had a mandibular structure that belonged in a textbook, dimples that should be considered lethal, and perfect teeth with oddly mesmerizing pointed canines that just did it for me. Like Henry Cavill canines. He hadn't grinned at me like this in ages.

My heart fluttered and my belly did flips. Even though I knew perfectly well that the guts did no such thing, my body had me challenging basic medical facts.

I sent the picture to the group text and could practically hear the squeals of unadulterated joy through the screen.

"I take it they're loving it?" Daniel asked while he deftly

prepared vegetables and then moved on to cutting chicken breast into near-paper-thin strips.

"At this point, I think they're just playing along to be rowdy. They can't possibly believe this."

"Why not? Is it so far-fetched? Even with a picture as proof?"

"That picture is proof that you're cooking in this apartment and we're actually having a good time."

"Ah. So what you're saying is that we need a more convincing picture?"

I shook my head. "No. This joke isn't going to escalate any further. Besides, as soon as I see my friends, they're going to know. I don't lie well. Even with pranks. I'm the worst person to tell a secret to, much less invite in on a joke."

"That's too bad," he said with a shrug as he glided back and forth across the kitchen to cook the chicken first and then added veggies. The succulent smell of butter, garlic, and parsley filled the room. "We could've had some real fun with pictures," he added playfully.

"Like what? The only way they'd truly believe is if...we were kissing or in some indecent pose or in bed together—" I stopped myself.

His face was turned from me, but I could still see a sliver. He was grinning. He thought this was funny! "I was going to say something like having my shirt off while cooking...but the bed, huh? Okay. I could do a few boudoir pictures."

"Stop enjoying this."

"It's kind of hard not to."

"Aren't you in the least bit upset with Liya about this situation? Or at least annoyed? I'm sure you didn't expect me to be living here when you took the keys."

"It's not that bad. It's not like we hate each other, right?" He looked at me, as if waiting for an answer.

"No. At least, I hope not?"

He shook his head and replied distantly, "I could never hate you."

Hearing that confession lifted a small weight off my shoulders. "Is there anything I can help with?" I asked, pulling out dishes and forks.

"Nah, I got it." His shoulders relaxed as he cooked. He was so at ease, almost fluid in the kitchen, that it was mesmerizing to watch. The play of muscles in his arms, how he timed every portion of the meal from cutting to cooking.

As he sautéed and the savory aroma of a well-cooked, unburnt meal made my stomach rumble, I greedily looked around for something to busy my hands with, for something to do.

I went to work on my failed dinner and poked a piece of bell pepper with a fork. Then I brought it to my mouth. Surely it was still edible.

"Don't eat that," Daniel said and took the fork from me.

"But we can't waste it."

"It's done." He scraped the plate into the trash.

"But...all the hungry kids in the world..."

He raised an eyebrow. "We'll find a way to donate to a reliable organization that feeds the needy. But this ain't it."

He took a different fork, pierced a piece of asparagus with a cut of chicken and a sliver of almond, blew against it, and brought it to my mouth.

"Did you just blow on my food?" I cringed.

He gave a real RBF. "Like we've never swapped spit?"

"That was a long time ago. I don't know who you've been exchanging germs with."

"No one, Preeti. My germs have not been getting freaky with other germs. Try this."

Before I processed his words, I took the fork and savored the perfect combination of herbs, meat, vegetable, and a nutty crunch from the almond.

My mouth watered even more. All right. Forget my burnt veggies. I needed an entire plate of this. "Um, are you going to eat all of that?"

"Good, right?" he asked, pointing the tongs in my direction. "Need to give you a cooking lesson while we're in this living arrangement."

"Hey! I can cook."

"Can you, though?" he asked as he drained pasta.

"Hush up. Just plate me." I held out my dish.

Daniel mixed the pasta in the skillet with the veggies, chicken, and buttery garlic sauce. He used the tongs to scoop up a little of everything and then twisted as he pulled them away from my plate, creating a cute little spiraled ball of food.

"Uh-uh. Wait," he said when I took the plate back. He drizzled extra sauce around the edges and then sprinkled vibrant green chopped parsley over the top.

I smiled and walked around the counter to a barstool, holding the plate almost reverently, and inhaled. By then, Daniel had already grabbed his plate, dished up, and met me on the other side of the counter. His shoulder almost touched mine. There were four stools to sit on, yet we occupied the middle two.

"This is heaven," I said around a bite.

"You haven't seen me get fancy." He slurped a noodle, and a drop of butter sauce splashed against his cheek. Maybe he didn't notice it, because he didn't bother wiping it away. It just sat there on his otherwise deliciously perfect face. It was making my eye twitch.

"Will I see you get fancy?" I asked.

"Do you want to?"

I took a napkin and dabbed his cheek, realizing too late what I was doing, being so casual. "You had sauce on your face."

He held my hand to his face for a second before letting go.

"Thanks. How are you feeling? You had a rough day yesterday. I'm here if you want to talk about it."

I regarded him for a moment before checking the time on my phone. "Is that a genuine offer, or are you offering to be polite?"

"Now, you know me better than that. I want to listen. I want you to be well. I know from the past that this is a current that can take you under, and neither of us wants that."

We ate quietly while I mulled over his words. Very few knew this side of me, and Daniel was the only one who'd gone above and beyond for me during these episodes. Not because no one else cared, but because no one else knew. I never had to tell him. He saw it on my face, in my movements, in my behavior.

I took a deep, meditative breath and turned to him. "Can I ask a favor?"

"Sure."

"I have an appointment with a therapist tonight, perks of being virtual. Um. It's my first time and, you know…it's…" I exhaled, annoyed with myself. How could I put together an eloquent and detailed presentation on infectious diseases and not say these few simple words? "Can you sit with me during my appointment?"

He set his fork down and twisted toward me, his left shoulder hunched over the counter. For a moment, I thought he'd decline or ask why I couldn't ask my boyfriend. Instead, he gave a soft, encouraging smile. "Of course."

"Okay." I smiled nervously.

We finished our meal. Daniel soaked dishes while I sat on the couch with the laptop prepped for a virtual appointment. My first therapy session. My first time letting some things out, but not everything. There wasn't enough time in our allotted hour.

After I checked in but before the doctor joined, Daniel sat down about a pillow's distance away. Close enough that he reached out and gave my hand a gentle squeeze, but far enough that he wasn't on-screen.

I practiced my breathing, my palms clammy as I rubbed them against my pants. "I know better, and still it took me this long."

"I'm proud of you," he said with a warm smile.

Chapter Sixteen

After the call, we sat on opposite ends of the couch, my legs tucked beneath me as I sipped on warm sakura tea reserve imported from Japan. Daniel's treat. I delighted in the light pink blooms blossoming in my cup.

"Well, that was pretty much what happened with my anxiety attack."

"That sounds like an extremely difficult time with work," he said sympathetically. We would never truly understand the stresses of each other's jobs, but both had their sharp edges.

"Sometimes I wonder if I'm meant to be a doctor."

"If I recall, your brain is wired for medicine. You've always seen the human body and microbiology components as machines. You wanted to dissect and heal since you were in middle school. You're the person who rallied for a zero-hour Anatomy & Physiology class and graduated high school at sixteen with a definite plan. Don't let a few bad days and a few idiots unravel the determination that you've had since you were a kid. You'll make mistakes, Pree. You're not perfect, no one is, and although you hold yourself to incredibly high standards because you take your responsibility and privilege seriously, you can't beat yourself up for every mistake. But the fact that you do shows how much you care. Mistakes are just that. They don't always reflect your skill or intelligence.

"Sometimes you can't control emergencies any more than you can control illnesses. They'll happen, but you're equipped and prepared to handle them. No one could ask for a better doctor. And you can't control how patients and families react to bad news. You can't stop or repair every bad thing that happens. You did your best and sometimes, unfortunately, you're the one who bears the brunt of patients' frustrations and anger. Some of them will never get that, but that shows that you're strong and humble and considerate. You're an amazing doctor, and from where I'm standing, you're doing it right."

I blinked away tears, mumbling, "Thanks, I truly appreciate your words, but it doesn't diminish the fact that a patient lost her baby."

"I'm sorry. I don't know why things like this happen." He rubbed my knee, and I relished his comforting touch.

Research showed that humans were meant to be touched, craved it from infancy, lost part of themselves when touch was absent for too long. I never related, couldn't comprehend it until now. I'd gone most of my life with limited touch before Daniel, but with him, I'd found myself hungering for more and more. When he was gone, I was deprived. Over the past week, that hunger had returned.

His touch was both pleasure and calm, both exciting and comforting.

I wiped away more tears, the product of my anxiety, Laura's loss, and Daniel's tenderness. "People think it's easy, that being a doctor is all about prestige and I'm the one who needs to get over bad times. As if I mean things to be a big deal, adding drama. Like maybe I can control my thoughts more? Like they're a faucet that can be turned off at any point. But it's not easy. It's like a million arrows hitting me and some of them penetrate my armor. Some things will haunt me forever."

"Do you agree with the therapist that talking it out with your parents will help? Letting them know how some of the things they might say, or allow others to say, affects you?"

I nodded. It was more about me getting to the point of telling them that these seemingly tiny, abstract comments hurt me when I'd done much worse to hurt them.

He added, agreeing again with the therapist, "Removing yourself from stressful situations when possible is helpful."

"I can't do that at work. I have to face it. Maybe at mandir I can just avoid or walk away if I can't make a difference."

"And this... Yuvan guy? Sounds like an ass," he said bluntly and took a sip of tea.

I scowled.

He shrugged. "What? C'mon. You can't stand his touch. He's oblivious to your anxiety. He *causes* you anxiety. He makes condescending remarks. Wanting you to be everything in order to be a perfect wife while he has no intention of making his own changes?"

I blinked at him, feeling my RBF coming on. "Is Alisha so perfect?"

He opened his mouth to respond without a beat, but instead clamped it shut.

I rolled my eyes, savoring the warm cup in my hands. Explicit images of Alisha touching Daniel exploded in my thoughts like fireworks.

"How serious are you two?" he asked.

"He wanted to get engaged soon," I replied nervously, trying to swallow those words.

He harrumphed and muttered, "Shit."

What did he mean by that?

"I mean, congrats." Yeah, like that didn't sound critical and bitter. Not when his jawline hardened into a sharp knife edge or when his nostrils flared.

I fidgeted with the ruffled edge of the decorative couch pillow resting against my hip.

"Have you slept with him?"

My gaze shot up. "No. Obviously. Besides my touch aversion, we're not that close. I mean, we've been dating, talking, but nothing more."

"But you're getting engaged?" he pushed.

I shrugged. Breaking things off wouldn't seem final until I'd told my parents what I'd done.

Daniel ran a finger over the back of the couch. "You don't seem particularly excited about an impending engagement. Have you kissed him?" he asked, clenching his jaw in the slightest.

"No."

He sighed, as if relieved, or maybe agitated. "You're considering marrying a man you haven't even kissed?"

"Touch aversion," I grumbled.

"But not with your soon-to-be fiancé. Even *we* touched. A lot. Like, all the damn time."

"Yep," I gritted out, seething at the reminder that I grasped at straws with Yuvan, no matter how good we looked on paper. What better way to face that nugget of truth than having my ex shove it in my face?

He went on in a more tender tone, "He has no idea what you feel like, what you taste like?"

My skin flared hot remembering all those times Daniel had touched me, kissed me, made love to me. "We probably shouldn't be talking about my love life."

He held his tongue for a good five seconds. "Preeti. Your touch aversion is toward strangers and people whom you're not that close to. If you can't stand being touched by this guy, maybe you shouldn't be thinking about marrying him."

"No one really asked for your opinion."

"Why are you getting engaged to him?"

"Why do you care?" I retorted, my voice rising.

"Because I still care about you," he spat. "Even if I'm mad at you or don't understand why you do the things you do, I do care about you. I don't want you making a huge mistake like marrying someone because, what? Some random guy just came along and said, 'Hey, let's get married'?"

"That's not what happened."

"I know about your culture and family traditions. We dated a long time, remember? But I sort of expected something in the vicinity of what we had. Romance, love, touching, kissing, being comfortable enough to hold hands. Not clenching your teeth and balling your hands into fists every time he tries to hug you. What are you going to do when you have to make love? Does he even understand touch aversion?"

"Yeah, let's change the subject. Daniel, who are *you* dating?" I snapped. "Let's talk about Alisha." Oh my lord. I didn't want to hear him say that he'd been with someone else, that he was seriously dating her.

"Are you jealous?" He smirked, part playful, part baiting.

"No!" I rasped. *Stop torturing me.*

"Being petty?" He leaned toward me, brows cocked. Definitely baiting.

I jumped onto my haunches and leaned toward him, my skin blazing. "Hey! You started this whole mess about who's dating whom."

"I definitely wouldn't be considering marrying someone who couldn't stand my touch."

I groaned to keep from screaming. "I don't need your judgment. Especially not after an anxiety attack. I don't appreciate it being added to my list of areas where I fall short as a person."

"Hey. Hey," he said softly. "Wait a minute." He reached out to my hand, the one clutching the pillow between us in a death grip. "I don't mean that *you* are deficient or anything less than extraordinary, Pree." His fingers slipped in between mine as my hand relaxed.

"We can't act and talk like we used to." I glanced down at our interlocked fingers. His touch scorched and soothed, as chaotic a reaction as my warring feelings over him. I felt like a balloon being filled with air, stretched to the point of capacity with an inevitable explosion on the horizon.

"Bet he can't even get this close to you, can he?" he asked softly, running a thumb over the back of my hand.

When I didn't pull away, Daniel inched closer. My eyelids fluttered and my breath hitched. His closeness set my skin on fire, had my stomach tying into knots.

Daniel lifted my hand in between us and pressed our palms together. Mine was small and delicate; his large and protective.

"How's the anxiety?" he asked.

"Better," I replied, hypnotized by his touch.

"Even though we sort of just had a fight?"

I scowled.

He let our hands drop back to the couch.

"Please. No more about me tonight. Tell me what happened with your dad."

He held my hand and leaned his head back. Was it weird that I wanted to crawl onto his lap and lick his throat? Press myself against him and feel him between my legs?

No. Stop that.

He lowered his chin. "My dad can be an aggressive bull at

times. Okay, most times. All we do is butt heads. I tried talking to him. He won't listen, won't change. I do almost everything he wants, and I'm never good enough." He paused and glared at the wall ahead, past his desk, and added calmly, "I don't need to be here. I have dozens of firms trying to get me. I could even go out on my own."

I squeezed his hand. "Don't ever say that you're not good enough. Don't ever let someone else make you feel less than what you truly are, which is amazing and wonderful."

He swiped a thumb across my hand, sending lightning bolts straight to my core. "Thanks for listening. I know it can sound dumb: a grown man who feels inadequate in his father's eyes."

"It's not dumb. It's serious and has a huge impact on you. I wish your dad could see your worth. I wish he didn't make you feel less than worthy. I'd tell him myself, except he scares me."

He chuckled. "He has that effect on people. I finally told Jackson. He thinks I should leave if Dad won't back off. Brandy agrees. But my grandparents wouldn't be happy if they knew I was thinking of leaving."

"Don't leave…" I found myself saying.

He tilted his head toward me with imploring eyes, his question more of a whisper. "Why not?"

Because I want you to stay. "Your grandparents love having you here, and you shouldn't let your dad drive you away from the business. If that's what you want."

He shrugged. "I want the family business, but there's no resolution if Dad doesn't meet me halfway. At least I have my music. It's good therapy. I've played the hell out of that thing since I returned."

"Do you want to play now?"

"Yeah, actually. Might help both of us." He stood and went to the corner where the guitar rested against his desk and brought it back to the couch, tuning along the way. "Music helps me find my calm these days."

"Is that why you're so good at playing? You've been needing a lot of calm?"

He nodded slowly, as if my question had a loaded answer.

Daniel watched me as he played, his gaze intense and lingering, searching my soul for anything and everything. No one looked at me the way he did, like he saw so deep inside me that he could read my thoughts and emotions.

Music healed us as I closed my eyes and leaned my head back against the couch.

He sat beside me. He gave ample space if I wanted to move away; instead, I tilted against him, our arms crushed against each other, my head gently falling to his shoulder. I sighed, content. Daniel strummed and the apartment filled with soft notes.

"Thank you for playing for me," I said. "It really is the only thing that makes me feel better."

"Anything for you."

"You mean that?"

"Mm…are you about to ask me something I might regret?"

Every fiber of my being warned against this, and yet every fiber of my being yearned to keep him close to ward off the creepy-crawlies in my head. He was the breath I needed, the balm for my anxiety.

"Can you…sleep in the bed again?"

He looked down at me, searching my face, his nostrils flaring with a deep breath. He brushed his knuckles across my cheek. "Of course."

Chapter Seventeen

I woke up in Daniel's arms again, despite knowing for a fact that I'd resolved to sleep on the opposite side of the bed. My body just couldn't help itself, could it? Not when he was warm and welcoming and safe and stabilized my mental breakdown. I was sprawled against his right side so shamelessly, my right leg draped over his leg, my hand on his chest, the bedspread at our waists.

I carefully grabbed my phone from the nightstand and turned off the alarm so it didn't disturb this moment. Then I found myself returning to the scandalous draping of legs and arms over Daniel's very toned body.

He rumbled beneath me. Was that...laughter?

"Too good to get up, huh?" he asked, his voice gravelly and so sexy. Did I just about orgasm from his mere voice, or his gentle caress over my arm, or how he slightly leaned into me so that my legs were perfectly positioned for him?

I bit my lip to keep from moaning and then cleared my throat. "I didn't want the alarm to jolt you awake. Did you get any sleep?"

"Like old times. I was knocked out. So were you, by the sound of your snoring."

"I don't snore."

"Don't lie, now. You know you snore when you're exhausted. You probably woke yourself up yesterday with your own snoring."

Dang it! I had! "Snoring is a natural process for some people."

He chuckled. We lay there. Didn't move a muscle or anything. And I relaxed into him again. My eyes drifted closed and if I wasn't careful, I might fall back asleep.

"Are you still playing the sex text joke on your friends?" he asked.

"Yeah. They're just playing along."

"Didn't you say a picture in bed might persuade them?"

"I did, didn't I?" I bit my lip and turned on my phone camera. In dark mode, it made for the perfect nighttime bedroom postsex picture. I angled it one way and then another, trying to get the right angle. "Ready?" I asked when I was satisfied.

"Yep." Daniel closed his eyes like he was asleep and I took a few snaps.

"If that doesn't convince Liya, then I don't know what will."

"Here. Try this." He hooked his hand underneath my bent knee, the one already slightly draped over him, and pulled it higher.

I gasped at his touch, at the risqué and very open position, my gut spasming and my lady parts tingling with need. So much need. *Whatever you do, do not moan!*

The sound of his swallowing echoed through the room. His hand lingered on my leg as the inside of my thigh felt his readiness. I had to move, now.

But first, the perfect picture.

Now, get out of there! Get out of there before you kiss him, before you wrap your legs all the way around him and completely feel him, before you welcome him back into your body in the most euphoric way and become one coalesced piece of sexy flesh.

Crap. Was that a moan? Wait, *who* was moaning, though?

"Thanks for the picture," I muttered, breathless, and hurried out of bed, tripping over the entangled sheets around my waist. Oof! Face-plant.

"Are you okay? Did you fall?" Daniel asked in the semidark.

But there was enough light coming in through the blinds for him to know.

"I'm good!"

I gathered up my pride and went to the bathroom for my morning routine and to cool off. When I returned, Daniel was still in bed as I turned on the closet light and sifted through my clothes for the day's attire. He had his arm over his eyes, the sheets below his waist. I chewed on my nails as my gaze lingered on those taut, bulging muscles wrapped in a tight shirt, and lower to…um…other bulging things.

It took every ounce of reasoning and good sense to not crawl on top of him. I dressed in no time and just before I was out the door, I studied our boudoir picture a little too hard and ran a finger over the image. It was just like the old days, but imaginary.

I sent it to the girls in our group text. They probably wouldn't be awake for another couple of hours, but they were sure to freak out when they saw it.

And they did *not* disappoint come seven o'clock in the morning. There were way too many exclamation marks and emojis to keep up with. I had to gloss over all the replies because these girls were putting more sultry images in my head.

How much longer did we have? Two more weeks until he moved out?

All right. I could do this. No more sexy pictures. No more stupid getting-it-on jokes. No more touching.

*

I decided to sleep in the physicians' on-call room that night. I figured it was safer with the full moon overhead. Inconclusive scientific studies be damned; there wasn't one L&D staff member who hadn't seen the pull of the full moon send pregnant uteruses into chaos. But there was a lull around one in the morning after six deliveries in the past fourteen hours.

I sat on the bed with my textbooks and notebooks spread out in front of me. All of my infection research was ready, main points highlighted to be extracted during the presentation. My slide deck pattern had been meticulously chosen. Now. How to relay pages and pages of information into a few sentences and pictures per slide?

My phone pinged with a text.

Daniel: Hope you're doing better today.

I smiled at the message and then scolded myself for feeling this happiness.

Daniel: Are you at work?

Me: *Yeah. On call. What are you doing up so late?*

Daniel: The guys and Brandy were over for pizza, drinks, and the football game. They hung around late, and I can't sleep, so I did a little work. Still can't sleep. Brandy was in charge of decorating my new place, so I at least got my credit card back from her before she puts me in debt.

Me: *She had your card and free rein to use it? Too late.*

Daniel: Dead. Have time for a bite?

Me: *I can't leave.*

Daniel: I'm at the nurses' station.

Me: *Really?*

I jumped off the bed and rushed out the door, down the short hallway to the nurses' station, where I skidded to a stop. There was Daniel, leaning against the tall counter so that the fabric of his green T-shirt stretched across his biceps. When he saw me, he beamed, flashing those dimples, and lifted a plaid thermal tote. I cocked my chin to the side and smiled.

He met me past the nurses' station as I led him back to the on-call room, closing the door after him, hoping no one noticed. He set the food on the desk and looked around. "This isn't anything like *Grey's Anatomy*."

I laughed. "Yeah. There also aren't a bunch of people getting laid in here."

"That would be sort of gross."

"Housekeeping does change the sheets every morning. At least there's that." I plopped onto the bed. "Thanks for the food. I'm starving."

Daniel took out containers of cheese-stuffed pasta shells smothered in red sauce. "What are you working on?"

I took a container and inhaled the aromas of fresh Italian herbs and cheeses, my mouth watering. "My presentation on infectious disease. I wouldn't look at anything if you're faint of heart."

"Ah."

"I think this presentation might give me a much-needed edge to getting the job at my practice," I said around a warm, gooey, tart bite. "This is so good."

He sat across from me on the bed. "Thanks. Can I help with anything? I'm sort of a master presentation coordinator."

I nodded, shoveling another bite into my mouth. "How can I make it the best, most memorable, knock-some-socks-off presentation? There's so much information to relay, and slides are tiny."

He laughed. "Where is this going to be presented?"

"Hospital auditorium."

"So you'll have a large screen to display?"

"Yes. Why?"

"That'll determine colors, text size, and picture details. How long is your presentation?"

"Ten minutes."

"I'd suggest breaking down the information into four major sections across fifteen slides."

My mouth dropped. "Fifteen slides? Are you joking? I have at least fifty slides' worth of information."

Daniel watched me stoically. "Have you never given a slide presentation before in your life, or did no instructor critique you?" He took a big bite and waggled his brows.

"Okay, master presentation coordinator. Show me your ways."

Daniel very patiently and thoroughly helped me prepare the presentation. Everything from condensing the information into a powerful, poignant ten minutes with a strong finish, to the right design and color of the slide deck, to content layout.

Hours later, he yawned and rubbed the corners of his eyes, gradually leaning farther and farther back against the pillows between us until he was lying beside me.

"It's five in the morning, you party animal," I announced quietly.

He shifted, lifting his head a few inches above my lap. He pointed at a photo on the fifth slide and mumbled, "That picture of whatever the hell infection is pixelated. You can't use it." And then dropped his head onto my lap.

"Daniel?" I asked.

He didn't stir. He snored.

I went to carefully move him, but he had a heavy head. I didn't mind. My fingers traveled over his hair and tugged at a short twist. His hair was longer than it had been in school, but just as attractive. My thumb grazed over his cheek and down to his lower lip.

His mouth twitched into a lopsided smile. "Is this turning into *Grey's Anatomy*?"

I sucked in a breath and patted his chest. "Oh my god…"

Chapter Eighteen

Daniel left that morning before he actually fell asleep and before day shift arrived. Poor thing was dead tired and couldn't pull all-nighters anymore, which made him staying so late to help me extra sweet. My already long shift ended up being four hours longer covering for a resident's clinic hours. I didn't mind, though; just another six weeks of being chief medical resident and being overworked. I really hoped a job offer waited at the end of this tunnel.

I dropped by the corner pharmacy to pick up my new anxiety medication. The bottle was among many steps toward mental health, light in my hand but holding so much power.

I arrived home at noon. The blinds were open and the room bright in the warm, cozy glow of afternoon light. All I wanted was to shower and sleep a few hours in a real bed before practicing my presentation.

After taking off my shoes, I dragged my feet to the bathroom. I opened the door and yelped when I nearly slammed it against a half-naked Daniel.

He barely startled, wrapped in nothing but a towel low on his hips, a razor partway to his shaving-cream-covered face. His muscles flexed with every small movement in his frozen stature. He'd been nicely built back in the day, but had been a bit leaner, more of a cardio guy. Now? His biceps and triceps tightened as he returned to the mirror and kept shaving. Every play of his mesmerizing muscles ignited memories of his body gliding over mine.

The lines of his sides went in and out of shadowy contour as he twisted to catch the best light. His abs tightened with every breath and I wondered how solid they'd feel beneath my touch. My fingers twitched to reach out, but no. Nope. *Brain, we are not doing this. We are smarter than this!*

"Just gonna watch, huh?" he asked.

"I could've killed you!"

"Let's not get dramatic." He ran water over his razor and clanked it against the side of the sink, dislodging particles.

"What if, in your surprise, you'd accidentally cut your throat with that very sharp razor?"

"I'm guessing you've had one too many cut-and-go procedures lately?" He dabbed his face with a damp washcloth.

"Maybe?"

"At least you're a doctor and know how to fix me up."

"What are you doing here in the middle of the day?"

"I decided to work from home." He walked over to the shower and turned on the water. Then he clenched a hand over his towel and grinned. "Well...unless you want to join me?"

Eh? I stood immobile for a minute because...I mean...good lord! Seconds away from water and suds running down Daniel's glorious body.

His smirk teased even more as he slowly loosened the towel and oh my god, was I staring like a starstruck groupie? Yes. Yes, I was.

"You need to take a shower anyway, right?" he asked, stepping toward me until he was within reach. "Don't want to get the bed dirty."

He was close enough that I could actually run my hand over his defined abs, chiseled chest, and broad shoulders. I could almost feel the smooth skin of his back as I hugged him to me, smell the residual shaving cream as he leaned his head down to nuzzle my neck.

"No," I said firmly.

"No... you do want to get the bed dirty?" His eyebrow went up.

"Enjoy your shower. I'll wait until you finish."

"Ah. You know that I don't finish that fast." He winked and went back to the shower. This time, I expected him to whip off his towel without any shame, which was why I slammed the door closed and stood there like a buffoon. Staring at this slab of wood and knowing that on the other side was a very naked, very wet Daniel Thompson thinking of me while he... finished.

Okay. I pivoted on my heels, washed my hands in the kitchen sink, and busied myself by rinsing my water bottle and coffee tumbler, then cleaned out my backpack and organized the kitchen. Busy-work should keep my idle mind from getting ensnared in the Daniel Effect, where I forgot about reality and caved to carnal needs.

I waited patiently on the chair kitty-corner to the couch so I could see the door open.

"All yours, Doc," he announced, looking sort of smug.

When Daniel walked out, wrapped in that stupid towel with teasing water droplets sliding down his body, I had to pick up my jaw—and my dignity—from the floor and get to my own shower. Quickly. So that he wouldn't think I was in there reminiscing about anything.

Except, when I emerged, Daniel was walking around shirtless, with gray sweatpants on.

"Don't you have a shirt to put on?" I grumbled, walking around the couch but leaving plenty of space between us.

"I wonder if your boyfriend has you staring this hard when he's walking around shirtless." He sounded so cocky that I couldn't help but laugh. He craned his neck back and made a face that said, *Whhhaaatt?*

"You're so childish," I retorted on my way to the bedroom.

"Does this bother you? Me being half-naked? Because I don't think you can stare any harder without damaging your retinas."

"If I'm staring, it's at your armpits. Thought you had this oddly strong anti-shave policy for yourself."

He shrugged. "I now shave a couple new areas since the day. Nice and clean, you know?"

"Sure. Sure." Like his chest? It was so sleek.

"But if I recall, you used to like the smell of my armpits." He came at me, a mischievous promise lurking in his eyes.

I backed away. "Don't. I regret the day I told you that very weird thing."

He stretched up, all melodramatic, as my butt hit the back of the couch, my hands out to ward off whatever was coming. But there was no fighting it, not when over six feet of glorious muscles and wide chest and brawny shoulders easily overcame me. I laughed and faked disgust as he covered me with his giant arms, trying to plant my face in his armpit.

I pushed to no avail, screaming and dying with laughter. "Stop! That's so gross!"

"You used to love it, though!"

"Not like this!"

But there was something very strange about enjoying sniffing a man's armpits. Pheromones. There was a logical, scientific reason. And those stupid pheromones, or Daniel scent, or whatever, bombarded my senses and thrust me back to all those cuddles in bed surrounded by his smell and nothing else.

Since I couldn't fight him off, I closed my hands over my face and burrowed into his chest. He hugged me then, in all of our wild cackling over something so odd. But the truth was, Daniel smelled unerringly intoxicating and I wanted to cocoon myself in his embrace.

"What other very Pree things about you do I remember? Oh, yeah. This one." He reached down and touched the back of my knee.

I gasped, clutching his shoulder. "Daniel!"

He groaned. "Almost forgot the response to this one," he said as he gently rubbed the sensitive spot behind my knee, which sent lightning bolts of pleasure to my center.

Yeah, I know. It was a weird turn-on, one that he'd discovered during tickling sessions.

His expression went from playful to one of need, a war of emotions. "Your boyfriend probably wouldn't like me getting these sounds out of you."

I bit my lower lip. "I actually broke up with him."

His right brow quirked up. "Oh, yeah?" he asked, his fingertips brushing my skin in feathery touches that had me leaning into him.

"Yeah."

"So...no impending engagement?"

"No," I rasped.

"Should I..." He licked his lip in that slow, sensual way that had me wanting his kisses all over me. "Keep going?"

He didn't let up, stroking the sensitive skin while pulling my knee up as he slowly rose to a full stand. Oh, boy. I was about five strokes away from having my leg wrapped around his waist and quite possibly orgasming from behind-the-knee fondling. How was that even a thing?

"No!" I yelped, pushing against his chest while crawling up and away from him, hence over the back of the couch and falling onto the cushions.

I scrambled to draw my feet into myself and basically twirled around like a breakdancing turtle until my legs were off the couch and I was sitting upright. I jumped up, now having the safety of the couch between us. I held up a hand. "You can't do that."

He grinned. "But it *felt* good."

I tamped down a smile. Dang it! It had felt *so good* that my nerves were still lit.

Nevertheless, I marched into the bedroom and announced my nap time. Nope. Nope. Nope.

I mean... *what* was happening?

Chapter Nineteen

I woke up from a much-needed nap sprawled across the bed, content, until Laura and her loss crossed my thoughts. We'd discharged her earlier today, and I wouldn't see her again until her follow-up appointment at the clinic. I'd have to ask Dr. Wright if it was okay to send her a card with our condolences.

I scratched my back and opened sore eyes. I needed coffee. But first, I opened my new anxiety medication and downed a pill. Here's to hoping for the best.

Daniel worked quietly in the living room, hunched over his desk with earbuds in. He shouldn't sit that way. That was too much pressure on his neck, aggressive misalignment for his shoulders and back.

Not wanting to bother him, I started laundry, absentmindedly washing his clothes with mine, and decided to make sandwiches, a meal simplistic in skill but substantial. Let's see, what did we have? I opened the fridge door, realizing I'd never gone grocery shopping to stock the fridge. Daniel must've. We had three kinds of lettuce, all sorts of produce, sliced deli meat, seven types of cheese, condiments, sauces, juices, and so on.

"Hey, you want a sandwich?" I called out.

"That'd be great," Daniel called back.

Cool. I slapped some Black Forest ham and lettuce between two slices of healthy-looking nine-grain bread.

Daniel stretched as I moved around the kitchen and reached for a mug. Ugh. Everything was placed high because Liya was so freakishly tall.

From the corner of my eye, I could see Daniel lean back in his chair and watch me. He tapped a pencil against his chin. My arbitrary task of rearranging a few things to get mugs turned into an embarrassing struggle as my fingers accidentally pushed the mug farther back.

Daniel pushed back from his desk and stood, doing some side stretches as he approached. The extra-plush carpet hushed his footsteps as he walked to the counter. I ignored him, had to get a mug, make coffee, eat, get to practicing my presentation for Monday, and then figure out how in the world to break the news about Yuvan to my poor parents.

I reached up on the very tips of my toes and fumbled for a cup. Cold air hit my now exposed sliver of hip flesh. These pajama shorts were old and loose and this shirt was worn out and shorter than when I'd first bought it. How long had it been? Three, four years?

My hot-pink socks kept slipping on the wooden floor. I was about two seconds away from crawling onto the counter like the monkey-child my parents claimed I had been.

"Need some help?" Daniel asked.

I startled, except there was nowhere to go.

Daniel stood behind me, silent as ever—darn these noncreaky high-end floors. His chest grazed my back; his arm tickled mine as he reached up. He'd inadvertently trapped me between the counter and a hard body. I'd already been as far against the counter edge as possible.

I shouldn't feel glee in this, shouldn't enjoy his smell and closeness, shouldn't want him to press into me.

Daniel's arm slid against mine—that so, *so* indulgent sensation—as he gave me a mug while bringing down a few others. I grunted even as my gut clenched, throwing a mess of chaotic memories at me. His hands all over me as he bent me over, my giggles and sighs and moans. He'd felt euphoric against me.

Stop.

"Thanks," I said, breathless and on the losing end of this battle of the flesh.

Daniel moved toward the coffeemaker. "Sounds like you were trying for a while to get those mugs. I made fresh coffee, by the way."

"I need to rearrange the cabinets for shorter people."

"Or I could just help you out." He added cream to his coffee. His face was haggard, with thin lines beneath tired eyes.

On natural instinct, I cupped his face. For the briefest of moments, we both turned into pillars before he closed his eyes and leaned into my hand. I caressed his cheek with my thumb. He turned to kiss my palm.

"What's wrong?" I asked.

"You really want to know?"

"Daniel. You listened to my breakdown. You were there for me. Not to throw your lecture back at you, but if you're not talking to me, then are you talking to someone?"

I started to lower my hand but he kept it in place. "Wait. Just…can I hug you?"

I stepped toward him, closing the gap between us. His hands snaked around my waist and locked me in place, his head touching the side of mine as he inhaled.

"I shouldn't, but I really miss you."

My gulp was audible. My heart skipped a beat, and not in the panicked PVC way, but in the be-still-my-heart way. Fighting it felt as nonsensical and pointless as fighting an avalanche, even though I knew what it would do to my parents. I found myself confessing the same to him, albeit in a restrained way. "I…miss you, too. Is that what's bothering you?"

"Among a dozen other things."

"Tell me what's wrong," I whispered.

His fingers pressed into my shirt. "I just don't think I can handle my dad."

"Of course you can." I raked my nails through his hair.

"Constantly trying to do my best, and he's constantly squashing everything. I have a degree from Rice and a master's from Harvard. I've added my name to skylines. I've tackled real estate and made my own money. I do *not* need my father breathing down my neck and turning me into a yes-man to further his agenda while ignoring any talents of mine. Why did I even come back? Why didn't I start my own firm? I have the clout to do it.

"I'm not going to be that guy who works himself to the bone waiting for someone higher up to praise him while being walked all over. I wanted to give us another chance to work together because…well, I suppose because I wanted to please him despite everything. The business started as something he did for all of us, something he planned on sharing with me, and we had been proud of that. *I* had been proud of that. But I'm just never enough. I don't know what to do. Staying is going to kill me. Leaving will be the last straw for him."

"Sounds like you really want to branch out on your own, Daniel. Sounds like you need to."

"I do, but it's a betrayal."

I pulled back. "Could you possibly have two branches in your firm? Find a specialty that you excel in and spearhead that side? It would expand the family business, you wouldn't be competing, but you would be in a different division and have your say. Your dad would have to give you your space, though."

He mulled over my words. "That's an interesting proposition."

"Look at these frown lines." I brushed his forehead, unable to help myself. If we could be frozen in this position, without any worries from our families, I could stay like this forever and all time.

"It's not just his empire. He has…specific plans for me."

"Like what?" I chuckled. "Is he being Indian and planning out a wife for you, set number of kids with astrological signs, and a position in the community for you to step up to?"

He pulled back.

I grimaced. "Oh. I was joking. Wait, *does* he want you to marry someone? Alisha?"

"What? You thought only Indian parents arranged marriages?"

My heart sank. It shouldn't hurt, shouldn't feel like a hundred slashes to my soul, splashed with rubbing alcohol and crusted over with salt scabs. It shouldn't hurt after six years, after *I* was the one who initiated the breakup, after I refused to talk it out and ran. But these were the consequences of leaving Daniel. I should be happy for him. Alisha seemed like a good match. His parents certainly thought so.

His phone buzzed in his pocket and he backed away to check it. "Great. Dad wants to chat."

"Hopefully he's open to separate divisions."

"And if not?"

"We were both raised wanting to please our parents and making sure they're happy, mainly because what they want for us is typically what's best for us and they only want us to be great. But take it from me, don't do something that's going to mentally demolish you."

"Coming from someone who tried to marry a man who can't touch her."

"I know. I haven't told my parents. I don't know how." I stepped back and rested my left hip against the counter, facing him, and wrapped my hands around an empty mug as if it were filled with scalding liquid that warmed my fingertips. This anxiety medication clearly hadn't kicked in, because just the thought of breaking my parents' hearts had me wanting to peel my skin off.

"What's stopping you?"

I laughed at the irony. "Looks like neither of us can be adult enough to put our foot down about who we're going to marry."

"You got someone else in mind?" His brow went up, inquiring.

"No," I muttered.

"Coffee?" he asked and poured some for me.

"Thanks," I replied, thinking of his dad's plans for him and Alisha.

"Let me know if you want me to help you get anything else down. I forgot how short you are."

"I am not!"

"You are, a little." He pinched his thumb and finger together to exaggerate my shortness.

"I'm average."

He placed his hands on the counter behind me, gripping the edge, and leaned down to eye level. "Did you not see yourself struggling to get a cup? I mean, I don't mind pulling things down. Or giving you a boost up."

I shrugged, diverting my gaze to the stove, the fridge, the sink, anywhere except Daniel.

"You can look at me, you know," he said softly.

I paused, peering up from over the lip of my mug.

"You won't combust, I promise. I have a shirt on now."

"Think your looks are that outstanding?"

"Ouch." He laughed. "It doesn't have to be weird. We should be able to come home and relax. It's just a couple more weeks, right?"

I cleared my throat. "Yes. Good. Glad that we can do that." I slipped around him to the stove, moving his arm away with the full force of my side.

We walked around the counter and sat next to each other on the barstools.

He took a bite of sandwich. And almost choked.

I scrunched up my nose. "How bad is it?"

"It's good."

"You're not the best liar. It's okay. I know I can't cook."

"I mean, it's a sandwich. Not really cooking. Just assembling."

I gently slapped his shoulder. He feigned injury. "Ow!"

"What's wrong with it?" I asked, pouting and studying my own sandwich, trying to figure out the equation. How hard was it to make a good sandwich?

"It's just dry. Like…no mayo or dressing or cheese?"

"I forgot the cheese!" I yanked open the fridge and searched for sliced provolone.

"How do you forget cheese? You of all people?"

"I know! Cheese is the basic food group." I tossed him a slice and then doused my sandwich with ranch dressing and returned to the barstool beside him.

"Why are you sitting way over there?" he asked, taking the bottom of my barstool and dragging me closer.

I squeaked and grabbed his biceps. "What are you doing? Do you know how far this fall would be?"

Daniel held me up against him, his arm low around my waist. "I'd never let you fall. Thought you knew that."

I huffed and pushed away, my stomach doing all sorts of flips. "Eat your sandwich." My phone pinged and lit up with a text. I slid it across the counter closer to me and read the message. "Huh."

"What's up?"

"Your sister invited me to church tomorrow." I made a face, twisting my lips.

"*Our* church?"

"That's weird."

Daniel pulled out his phone and spent a few minutes texting with Brandy.

"What the actual hell?" he said and showed me his messages, looking more than a little annoyed.

Brandy: Oh yeah. Grandma was asking about Preeti and wanted me to invite her to lunch.

Daniel: Y'all having lunch without me? Cold!

Brandy: Well, they didn't want to make it awkward for you. Come if you want.

Daniel: This sounds like a setup. Out of nowhere?

Brandy: Not out of nowhere. Grandparents always ask about Preeti. I see her all the time, and they're always asking me to invite her over. She comes once in a while.

Daniel: Really?

Brandy: Surprise! Didn't want to hurt your feelings, but now you know.

"Oh, I never accept the invitation to go to church. Seems so intimate," I said nervously in response to his irritated expression.

"But hanging out with my grandparents isn't?" he asked, his tone sharp.

"Are you upset that we keep in touch?" I asked, biting the inside of my cheek.

"Nah. Just enjoying this sandwich," he replied with a hint of sarcasm, his jaw hardening.

"You don't have to eat it if it's that bad."

He placed a hand on his waist and leaned back to look at me, all dramatic-like. "No. You know what? I am mad. How the hell do you leave me without a word and then have the gall to hang out with my grandparents for the past six years?"

I froze midbite.

Daniel went rigid and snorted. "I stayed away from them, didn't move back for a few reasons. One, I wasn't ready to deal with my dad and this crap he's throwing at me now. Two, I wanted to branch out and accomplish things on my own without his help. Three, *you.*"

I swallowed down the bile bubbling up from my stomach, acidic and eroding my insides.

He laughed derisively, squishing the sandwich between his fingers before dropping it onto the plate. "No matter how badly I missed my grandparents and Brandy, I couldn't be in the same city where you lived because you'd crushed my heart, Pree. You devastated me."

I blinked back tears. His voicemails, the times he'd pounded on my front door, everything he did to get me to talk to him swirled through my head. Images of the pain on his face when we broke up, the way he tried to reach for me and make me stay and talk while I literally ran off were wraiths coming out of suppression and hitting my vision full force, no longer to be held back, denied, ignored, hidden.

"And turns out you were having meals with them all this time?" he spat.

Our knees touched when he fully twisted toward me. "I think I've waited long enough for an answer. Time's up."

My entire body quivered like a fever racked my bones. I had to face my cowardice and reveal to him how weak I'd been. I nodded, closed my eyes, and took a deep, shuddering breath.

Chapter Twenty

Daniel waited, tapping a finger anxiously on his lap. "Am I the only one who doesn't know why?"

"No. Most people don't know why. Including Brandy and your grandparents."

His heated gaze bored into me. "Does your boyfriend know? Did he ask about your past and why we broke up? Does some stranger who has nothing to do with me know when I don't?"

"Why are you fixated on him?"

He threw his hands up. "I thought we were forever and you left. And moved on. I'm sure he wanted to know and you told him. Maybe I should've just called *him* and asked." He groaned and rubbed the bridge of his nose. "Shit."

Pain shot through me like a dozen venom-tipped arrows. The initial cuts hurt, but it was the lingering poison that spread and destroyed. "How can you be this upset after six years?"

He froze, his hand still at the bridge of his nose, his eyes rising to meet mine. He slowly lowered his hand and spat, "You wanna know why? Is it that damn hard to see, to understand? Because I still have *feelings* for you."

My breath caught in my throat, my skin turning to ice. My

vision doubled behind hot tears and this thing called a heart that was pumping so chaotically fractured. My entire soul ached to tell him the same, but I knew my actions couldn't be forgiven. Daniel deserved better.

With our falling in love and caring for each other, I'd never expected to have my heart so full between Daniel and my parents, only to have it smolder to ashes because of hurting all three of them. If a broken heart was a decrepit, cracked organ sitting in my chest, then I was certainly rotting from the inside out. The black tar of a decayed heart, thick and suffocating, rose up in the back of my throat.

He went on after a beat, his voice trembling, his shadow falling over me. "Because I do. And I have no damn idea how you could leave me, someone who loved you and can touch you without you losing your crap, who can ease you off the ledge when you're depressed, and who you can talk to about almost anything. Your so-called boyfriend couldn't do any of that. We both know he doesn't even come close to me, but you still considered *marrying* him."

He heaved out a breath. "Why did you leave me? How could you break my heart the way you did and not even give me the decency of an explanation, a conversation, an email, even a damn text? Was I...not enough?"

The tears brimming at my eyes spilled over in cascading sheets. I swallowed hard, my throat raw, my breathing harsh, my chest aching.

"You were everything," I said, wanting to hold his hand but knowing I had no right. "I've missed you every day. Leaving you was the single worst decision of my life, and I regret it to the core of my being."

"Then why did you do it?"

My shoulders slumped. "Because many in my community and

family are cruel and ripped apart my parents for allowing me to date you. Because my own aunts tried to light an emotional fire to torch my parents and shoved us out of the community, the only link my parents have to their roots. People were hateful, and I couldn't stand how my parents just stood there and took it quietly, meekly, because they didn't want to cause trouble or didn't think they had a voice. They didn't think they could speak up to their elders, mainly my aunts."

Daniel went rigid in his chair and it was hard to read him. He asked in a tense voice, "So were you trying to save face?"

"No. It wasn't like that at all. I could care less about others." My words tumbled out now that the dam had been opened. "I couldn't take how my parents were being treated. When I spoke up, my aunts used it to nearly destroy them. I couldn't understand how some of my parents' so-called friends abandoned them. I couldn't bear how my actions devastated my parents. How, because of me, my mom had a heart attack and was hospitalized. *I* did that to her."

He let out a breath and closed his eyes.

"All the gossip and blame from the community, my aunts calling her a horrible mother, telling her she'd raised a slut, the bane of our family, the community pushing my dad out of his responsibilities, out of their entire social structure. It all crashed down on my mom, and I'm not saying she's a weak person, but she couldn't handle it. Physically. To see her crumple and literally fall from the stress...I couldn't keep being the reason for her suffering."

He had his elbow on the counter, his fingers rubbing his chin. "Shit. You think you're to blame for how others reacted? I'm sorry for what happened to your parents, and that must've been terrifying, but it's not your fault how others behave."

My tears fell even harder. "Of course it is! I'm supposed to protect my parents, and instead I brought so much pain no matter what I did. Being young and terrified and not knowing how to handle everything and what to do, how to do it without imploding…I just…did what I thought was best for my mom's health. And maybe I could've done better, or maybe you don't get it because it doesn't sound like such a horrible thing—"

The tenderness in his expression warped into stoicism. His words came fast and infuriated. "No, I *get it*. I'm a *Black man*. You think you're the first to walk away because someone didn't like the fact a person was dating outside of their race, much less a Black man? You can say it. You were surrounded by a bunch of racist assholes and were too concerned with what others thought to just stand your ground and make your own decision," he retorted. "It killed you to see your parents in pain, I get that, but what the actual shit? Ever think about the pain you caused me?"

"*Every day.*" I wiped my face, but these stupid tears wouldn't stop. "Between my mom being ill and my causing a rift with my parents and losing you, I cried every day for a year. My depression spiraled. I haven't felt whole since, like I'm walking around with my heart gouged out of my chest. I stood my ground. I spoke up. I tried to shut down the racism, the gossiping. I tried to defend my parents, myself, and you. Whatever I did and didn't do made everything worse. But I was terrified that my mom was going to die. My aunts didn't care who you were, just that they could use that to hurt my parents."

He snarled, "That's the thing. They *don't* care about you, either. Friends support you, not abandon you. Family tries to help you, not drag you. Community lifts you up, it doesn't drown you."

"I'm not defending them. I know I didn't break things off the right way. I didn't want to hurt you with the ugliness."

"Great job," he retorted. "Instead of telling me to my face six years ago, you just forced me to carry that heartbreak all this time. I can deal with racism; I have to all the time. But the pain of you running off and never telling me, never talking to me, that destroyed me." He gestured with his hands, aligned with palms facing each other, and jumped them from side to side with every word to drive home the point. "It was the pain you chose."

"I know. I'm sorry, and nothing I say will make up for it. I've had to live with myself over these decisions. I'm so, so sorry, Daniel," I sobbed. "But I didn't do it just because of that—" I stopped myself. He didn't need another stress added when it came to his father when he was trying so hard to work it out for the sake of their company. "You don't deserve to be treated that way."

He dragged a hand down his face in exasperation, his head shaking as he licked his bottom lip. "I'm going to face racism wherever I am. That's life when living while Black. But you could've told me the truth. We could've tried working it out. I could've been there for you. I...would've helped you to be stronger."

I hiccupped, knowing that we could've been together all this time had I just been the woman I am now back then. His dad's words echoed through my thoughts. I was *not* strong enough, good enough for him. "I thought I was sparing you, and I thought I was sparing my parents. But if our relationship was going to make me a target or was killing your parents, would you still choose me?"

"Yes! God damn, I did, Pree!"

I blinked. "Wha-what?"

He looked off into the corner and shook his head. "My parents have a very carefully sculpted plan for me. They want me to marry someone who...better matches our lifestyle. We're not that different."

"Your dad—" I bit my lower lip and stopped myself.

"My dad what?"

"He...didn't like me. He didn't think I was good enough."

"*And?* My dad doesn't like a lot of things, but he doesn't

determine my entire future. I'll be with whomever *I* choose. Because I am an *adult*. My parents aren't going to get exactly what they want in me; no parent gets that. Your parents…I thought they were strong and kind. I thought they'd want your happiness above anything else." He jumped off the barstool and paced the room.

"They do," I said through tight lips, abhorring how he might look down on my parents because they were meeker back then. I crawled off the barstool and stood there with fists balled. "They are nothing less than strong and kind, which was why they *never* told me to break up with you, why they *never* showed any emotion about any of it in front of me. They tried to shield me so that I could make my own decisions, but my mom having a heart attack was the final nail in the coffin. What was I supposed to do?" I asked quietly, my lips quivering.

Daniel's next words were daggers, sharp, double-edged blades meant to cut, but they were real, raw. They were *his* emotions and he had the right to express them. "You were supposed to love me," he said evenly. "You were supposed to trust in us."

My knees almost buckled, and my PVCs hit hard, knocking the breath from my lungs. I wanted to slip into a black hole and vanish as anxiety and panic caved in around me. He was right. I should've trusted in us, but it wasn't that simple seeing Mummie in the hospital, not knowing if she would make it or not. I'd seen patients suffer and pass because of heartbreak, and I'd shattered her heart.

"Things aren't always easy or black-and-white. There's a lot of gray," I said.

"And in all this gray, you chose a guy who can't even touch you, who will never understand you? That was better than me?" he gritted out. Slipping into his shoes, he swung back the front door and called back, "I need some air." Then he slammed the door behind him and left.

Chapter Twenty-One

Giving Daniel space wasn't easy. Not calling, not running after him, and checking my phone every five minutes for a text that never came. I put my frantic energy toward my presentation. Evening came. I typed and erased a dozen text messages. In the end, the only text I'd sent was to Brandy to decline her offer to go to church.

I went to bed around midnight, exhausted and depressed, but now I had medication in addition to my calming app. The *Alien* facehugger tried its hardest to attach itself, but I fought it and made it through the night, waking up every hour, my hand blindly searching the bed for Daniel.

It seemed that he'd slept on the couch.

The covers were pulled to my chin, my back to the door, when Daniel knocked and called out, "I'm opening the door. I need to get my suit."

I ignored him and glared at the filtered light seeping in through the closed blinds. It was easily seven in the morning, which meant I'd lazily stayed in bed way past my preferred wake-up time. I was curled into a fetal position, knowing that my cramps were at their apex and Crampus had fully descended.

Daniel had woken up before I had. While I'd only checked off my starting day on my period app, he'd showered and made breakfast. And what was I doing? Holding in my pee and my period.

While Daniel was in the walk-in closet taking his sweet time and humming a tune like he wasn't pissed at me, I went to the bathroom.

I got my day going, starting with a tampon and ibuprofen.

When I opened the bathroom door, my stoic face on, my intention to look unaffected went out the door when Brandy looked up from the living room chair and gave me a sly smile.

"Uh…hi, Brandy," I managed to say through my surprise.

Daniel was standing beside the couch. He looked over his shoulder at me and groaned.

"What are you doing here, Preeti?" she asked in a sing-song voice.

"Woman, I already told you that Preeti was living here," Daniel said.

I glared at him, but Daniel simply explained, "Brandy the super-sleuth was here the other night for the game and figured it out."

"How?" I asked.

Brandy clucked her tongue. "Girl, please. Plain as day that a woman is living here, and almost as obvious that it's you. Raspberry Rain shaving cream and pink razors. Women's gummy vitamins. An opened box of tampons. A stethoscope."

"Not to mention Brandy and Liya were in on this together," Daniel said.

"Yeah, yeah. That too. So. Are y'all…seeing each other again?"

"Definitely not back together, nor will we ever be," he told her without another glance at me as he fixed his tie. "Let's go."

Ouch. But I deserved that. And he was right. My actions had made sure of it.

"Wait a minute." She rose slowly with that ethereal grace she'd always possessed. Brandy Thompson had high-class style and always dressed to impress. For her church outing, she wore a sleeveless white silk blouse tucked into a crimson knee-length pencil skirt. Her matching red high-heeled shoes, or as I liked to call them, devil hooves, were in the foyer. She wore strands of pearls around her neck and wrist, paired perfectly with the pearl-white clutch on the chair arm.

Brandy twisted her ruby-stained lips. "You're living together and not talking? Not feeling anything?"

"I am feeling something right now," Daniel muttered. "How is it that my sister is still friends and hanging out with my ex, along with my grandparents, unbeknownst to me? Huh?"

That was a valid question. I often wondered why Brandy and her grandparents had been so nice to me after I'd broken the heart of their family favorite. I'd figured they'd hate me, or at the least want to keep their distance, expecting Daniel to move on with a new woman.

"I didn't take sides."

"Not even with all—" He stopped himself and took a breath. "Never mind. I'm here for another week or so, until my place is done. It's going to be ready early."

Our already borrowed time was going to be cut even shorter. Both relief and sadness trickled through me.

"Just don't tell anyone about this, Brandy," I pleaded. "No one has to know except us. The last thing we want is drama."

"Or gossip. Wouldn't want that," Daniel added dryly, his tie now perfected as he slipped on his vest. His three-piece suit was tailored and fitted in all the right places. Not baggy, not tight. The charcoal color paired with his dark gray tie with tiny white dots over a textured red-and-gray shirt.

"Of course not," Brandy conceded. "Why aren't you dressed?"

I glanced down at my pajamas, the nonsexy sweatpants variety. "I'm not going. Didn't you get my text last night?"

Brandy sauntered around the couch, took my elbow, and guided me into the bedroom, then sifted through my closet. "I see my brother's best suits are in here…"

The sound of clothes hangers clanking against one another filled the void as Daniel's shadow paced the living room.

"I'm one hundred percent sure Daniel would be upset having me at church, much less at your grandparents' place," I said as I made the bed and sat on the edge.

"He'll get over it."

"Why are we still friends?" I inquired.

"Are you kidding me? We were friends before you dated Daniel. Just because there's a rough patch in a relationship doesn't mean it should burn to ashes. You're a good friend and remarkable person. I don't understand why you never told me the real reason y'all broke up, but I'm not entitled to everything and your relationship with my brother isn't my business. Do I wish that you two stayed together? Yes. You made a great couple, and my grandparents wish the same."

"Just not your parents."

She waved them off. "They, like all parents, have certain expectations. My parents are especially detailed in what they want, but who is the perfect child? No one. Despite my brother's education, network, respect, community work, earnings, and so forth, they still expect more. They say it's to give us a high mark to aim for in order to live our best lives. As kids, you know, we feel like we fail miserably when we don't meet the mark, when in reality, we're pretty damn amazing."

"I do want to see your grandparents, but I don't want to step on Daniel's toes."

She pulled out one of two dresses that I owned. It was more of a springtime dress, meant for office get-togethers. Brandy laid it on the bed beside me with a cardigan and flats. "Ever notice that sometimes it's just fun to annoy him?"

"He's mad at me," I confessed.

"What now?"

"I told him why I broke up with him."

She stood back. "Inquiring minds want to know. You two were so in love."

"It had just gotten out of hand in my family."

"Because he's Black?" she asked tersely.

I blew out a breath and nodded. "I could deal with it, but my parents were destroyed by how my aunts tore them apart. My mom was hospitalized and I thought...she would die. Because of me. In some illogical, extreme, warped panic, I really thought it could happen. And how could I put Daniel through all the racism? He doesn't deserve it. So I had to let him go to protect him and my parents."

I'd rarely seen Brandy look as shocked and concerned as she did when she sat beside me. "Preeti. Oh my god, that is absolutely awful. I had no idea. Why didn't you ever tell me?"

"I don't know. It's difficult for me to express my thoughts. I kept it to myself. Only a few people knew about my mom. And the rest? Saying it aloud, especially now, it didn't seem like a good enough reason. But I was deathly afraid of what could've happened to my mom if I didn't leave Daniel behind."

She gave my hand a reassuring squeeze. "Honey, that wasn't on you. That's blood guilt on your aunts."

I stared at the partially open bedroom door. I couldn't see Daniel, but he was still out there. "The truth is, I'm a coward, and Daniel deserves better."

Brandy rose to her feet and pulled me up with her. "Now you have to come."

"Did you, uh, not hear a word I said?"

"Woman, I heard. You shouldn't be alone all day. Look at you. Besides, nothing like Grandma's pies to soothe your feels."

"I barely finished the last pie." I patted my stomach.

"What else are you going to do? Mope all day because y'all finally had the fight? That fight should've happened long ago. It's time to move forward."

"But my period literally just started half an hour ago. Crampus is upon me."

She snickered. "You better shut up with that. Now you really need good food and something to get you out of your head. Pack your tampons and let's go already."

"I can't believe I'm doing this," I muttered, but I got ready for church, much to Daniel's annoyance. Well, shoot. Crampus had alighted, igniting my hormones, so I was *just* as annoyed.

I started with the sexy Parisian underwear set because I needed to feel less miserable, and for some reason fancy underwear did the trick. It felt nice and cool against my irritated skin, as if telling Crampus to shove it. I wore what Brandy had picked out and ended with light makeup and hair down. Then I added the Parisian scarf, tied fashionably by Brandy because of course she knew how to wear a scarf.

Daniel, neither happy about me coming nor willing to wait for me to get ready, took his own car.

I rode with Brandy in her very sleek dark Lexus SUV. The car's leather interior and heated seats were so comfy, I could've fallen asleep. The drive was smooth and quiet and I absolutely understood why driving around lulled babies to sleep.

"It's not weird, right?" I asked nervously when we pulled into a large, packed parking lot in front of a grand two-story church with a towering steeple, surrounded by manicured lawns and winter-bitten magnolia trees.

We were running behind, thanks to me, and quickened our steps to get inside. But there was no hurrying past people when you were a Thompson. Everyone and their mama stopped Brandy to say hello and ask about Jackson and something about a gala, which, in turn, was her cue to introduce me.

The churchgoers offered a warm, vibrant welcome with so many handshakes. "Elbow bump?" I offered awkwardly. Ugh. Who said that? Apparently, people with touch aversion did.

"All right now," most said and agreed with a laugh, bumping elbows with mine like it was a dance.

"What is this newfangled greeting?" someone asked as Grandpa Thompson cut through the crowds at the entrance to the seating area, decked out in his finest dark gray suit with hat. "Elbow bumps replaced fist bumps?"

"Elbow bumps replaced handshakes for me years ago," I explained as Grandpa Thompson chuckled and drew me in for a big ol' hug. He was like a teddy bear. Next came Grandma Thompson with eyes full of happiness. She gave me a hug, rocking back and forth.

She stepped back and studied me. "My, my. Aren't you a sight for sore eyes, baby girl."

"I think you mean *Dr.* Baby Girl," Grandpa Thompson said.

In the next second, she was stopping everyone to introduce them to *the doctor*. Leave it to Brandy's grandparents to shower me with love and the sort of pride rivaled only by my parents. My cheeks hurt from grinning, but these minutes leading up to the start of church were exactly what the doctor ordered—joy. There was a sort of intense, grateful energy percolating in the air, loud and joyous singing and laughter to come if the pastor was as engaging and energetic as the last time I'd been here, years ago.

"Oh, lord, Grandma..." Brandy intervened. "You're one step away from introducing my friend as the doctor in the family."

Grandma Thompson waved off the remark. "She *should've* been the doctor in the family," she mumbled, but I caught every syllable.

With so many finely dressed people, it was safe to expect the onslaught of perfumes and colognes tangling in the air. Alas, the ibuprofen hadn't fully set in and my cramps were power-kicking my uterus to death.

"I should sit down," I told Brandy, suddenly very aware of exactly how large and touchy-feely this crowd had become. There were easily three hundred people, all chatting and laughing, hugging and shaking hands and bumping shoulders.

"Over here," she said and guided me away from her grandparents, who continued to eagerly show me off with a wave in my direction.

We spotted Daniel and his parents near the front, but before Brandy made a move for them, I clutched her arm. "Oh, no. I'm not sitting up there."

"We always sit up front."

"That's okay. You can sit with your family, no worries. I'll sit in the back."

"That would be rude of me. I brought you here; I'm not going to let you sit by yourself."

Up ahead, near the front pews, Daniel mixed into the crowd seamlessly, but when he moved, there was no denying where Daniel Thompson stood. Suddenly, everyone else became muted. All others blurred into endless brushstrokes of color and there was only him.

"Look at him any harder and you might actually pop a blood vessel in your head," Brandy whispered as she shimmied down an aisle not exactly in the back, but nowhere near the front, either.

Alisha Peterson was also hard to miss. She cut through the throngs to get to Daniel, nodding and smiling and greeting everyone on the way. Even his friends opened the circle to let her in. She was stunning. Suddenly, I felt so flat-chested and flat-butted and ineloquent and anything but glamorous.

She wore a snug knee-length gold-and-black dress with amazingly tall stilettos. How did she even stand up in those? She might as well have been walking on stilts. Her hair was black blending into brown and ending mid-back in perfect curls. Her jewelry was so bright that the diamonds sparkled even from this far. She stood with shoulders back and chin held just high enough. She was poised and elegant and...everything that Daniel should have. Apparently, he did have her. Because the way she rubbed his back and then leaned in for a cheek kiss and lingering hug was not the way friends did in passing.

I plopped down into my seat, my heart cracking all over the place. My throat was dry and raw, and not just from the chemicals in the air. Whatever good judgment I had told me not to even ask.

But Brandy noticed my stare. "That's Alisha, if you're wondering."

"I remember. She's gorgeous."

Brandy flicked a hand in her direction. "I guess. If you like that model look."

"Do I detect some shade?"

"Eh. She's nice. I guess she can't help how she looks, but if I catch Jackson checking out her backside one more time..."

"No!" I whispered. "He doesn't do that."

"All men do that."

I wasn't going to argue with her in the middle of church, but all men absolutely did *not* do that. Daniel didn't. My dad sure didn't. Yuvan, Rohan, Jay...just to name a few men who didn't.

Alisha had Daniel's dad eating out of her hand. Now, that looked like a woman he'd want for his son. Those cracks in my heart deepened. There was nothing as soul-crushing as seeing the love of your life moving on. Before I could think how that should be me beside him, I chastised myself and stopped. He deserved better. And I needed to find happiness and forgiveness in myself.

"What's the deal with her and Daniel?" I asked nonchalantly. Oh my lord. Who was I kidding! I needed the details.

"Alisha is touted as this brilliant businesswoman, and you know about our architecture firm? She was at Harvard right as Daniel was graduating. Her dad and my dad think it would be phenomenal if she and Daniel got married so that they could merge empires."

Those cracks in my heart? They exploded. One. By. One.

"Daniel is set to take over the firm and she would be great to assist on the business side. Alisha comes from money, too. Her mom and my mom are on the board for the organization that Grandma cofounded. Our families grew up together."

I gasped for air as subtly as possible while my vision grew blurry behind tears, watching Daniel's dad give Alisha a side hug the way fathers often did with their daughters. He must've thought of her as a daughter by now, having been that close to her family for so long. One didn't get more "in" than interwoven boards of directors and childhood friends.

"Dad is really pushing for them to get married," Brandy ended quietly, watching me from the corner of her eye.

"Oh," I breathed out. "That's lovely. She seems like the perfect match for Daniel and your family."

"If you sounded any less happy, you'd pass for a robot."

I shrugged. "It's best. Right? Your parents seem to love her. She fits right in."

"I just believe there's more than logistics and logic when you start thinking about someone as a spouse, you know? There has to be emotion, connection."

"Daniel's not into her?" Hadn't he been on dinner dates with her recently?

"They're friends. There's only one person he's ever loved. And it's not Alisha Peterson."

Daniel and his parents took their seats near the front, on the right side of the aisle, whereas Alisha sat to the left. He gave a short wave to someone down the row and happened to glance back. He caught me staring, but I couldn't look away, couldn't even blink. The funny thing? He seemed stuck, too. Like it took a great deal of effort for him to break his gaze until the service started.

I chewed on the inside of my cheek and tore my gaze away from Daniel and his apparent intended, my body numb and my head dizzy. I wanted to leave and drown my heartache in ice cream. Maybe try the new seasonal flavor from Blue Bell.

This was for the best. It really was. He would do better with someone who could keep up with him, who wouldn't disappoint him.

So, then…why did those exploding cracks in my heart fully detonate?

Chapter Twenty-Two

After church, Brandy and I helped with a bake sale so her grandparents and Daniel could take off to prepare lunch. We arrived at Grandpa Thompson's house a little before two. Brandy went to the backyard to help Jackson set up while I was content making my way through a house that felt like a second home. I lingered in the hallway just around the corner from the kitchen, where Daniel was covered in flour, side by side with his grandmother putting the finishing touches on a lemon chess pie. She was nearly a foot shorter than him, but she had no problem telling him how to do the job.

"Grandma," he said in a laughing, singsong sort of way, "why don't you sit down and rest and let me finish this, huh?"

"I just want to make sure it's perfect."

"We made it together, so…" He shrugged. "Can't get more perfect than that."

She laughed her sweet laugh. "Get the good napkins for me."

"What's all the fuss, though?"

"Aw, baby. You know Preeti is coming over."

He rolled his eyes. "Things are different now. We're not together, nor do we have plans to get back together. You know Dad wants me and Alisha—"

I winced at the thought.

She slapped his chest with the back of her hand. "Don't you go bringing that innocent woman into this mess. What your father wants is one thing and what you want is a completely different thing."

"If you're implying I want Preeti—"

"You act as if we did *not* notice you constantly looking over your shoulder at her during the entire service. Baby, who are you trying to fool? Pining over her like that. Now go set the table for six."

I pressed my lips together in amusement.

While she finished up with a pitcher of sweet iced tea and Grandpa Thompson piled a platter high with grilled vegetables, Daniel set the table.

I headed outside just as Daniel noticed me and ran to the sliding glass door, forcing me back inside and closing it behind him.

He scratched the back of his neck. "Hey."

"Are you acknowledging me now?"

"I needed space. And you went to church and now you're here."

"Do you want me to leave?" I tugged on the hem of my cardigan.

He planted his hands on his hips and craned his head back, gaping at the ceiling in thought. He worked his jaw. "No."

"Are you still mad at me?"

"Yeah," he responded quietly.

I touched his arm, my emotions less overwrought, clearer. He paused, looking at where my palm had landed on his forearm. "I know what I did was cowardly and not the best decision. I don't ever expect you to forgive me, but I am truly, so *profoundly* sorry for all the pain I caused."

"Are you that same person?" he asked through tight lips.

"I'd like to think I've grown since, become a stronger person."

"How would you handle the situation now?"

I replied without having to think about it. I faced the opinions of outsiders all the time, and it was draining. In the end, no one wanted my happiness more than my parents and myself, and Daniel would feel the same if we were still together. In the end, no one could fortify my mentality except me. I had to choose to be happy and believe that my choices were right.

"I'd communicate," I said simply. "Communicate with my parents, with you. Which means sitting down and working it out as a family. Communicate with the community, my aunts. Which means calling them out and ending their terror right away."

"Hmm," he grunted.

Daniel could've taken my words any number of ways in the consuming silence. Patronizing, pointless, agonizing, resentful, peaceful.

"Hurry up!" Brandy called from the backyard.

Jackson stood at the table and waved us over.

Daniel pulled his arm back so that my hand slid down his arm, wrist, and met his hand. His fingers slipped in between mine and gently squeezed. "Can't ruin a family meal, can we?"

My words came out in flutters, tingling my lips. "Let's be real. You were the only one who was going to ruin this lunch."

"Ouch." He flashed a fleeting smile, released my hand, and opened the door for me to step out first.

Grandpa Thompson planted his glass of tea near the head of the table with Grandma Thompson across from him. Beside him were Brandy and Jackson, while Daniel and I sat opposite them. The table was covered with butcher paper.

"Lunch is a little late and a little different today!" Grandpa Thompson announced as Jackson helped him empty a piping-hot pot of food onto the butcher paper. Crab legs, shrimp, sausage, corn on the cob, and potatoes, all smothered in red seasoning, poured out.

We applauded, because who didn't get excited at a seafood boil?

We ate peaceably, mainly because I didn't get pulled into the conversation and was too busy stuffing my face with this family-recipe seasoning. It was easy to sit back and enjoy the wave of joy that came from being with Brandy and her grandparents.

We could've been having these meals many times over with Daniel here, had we not split. By now, maybe he and I would have been married and having meals at our own house, starting new traditions.

Laughter filled the space like wind chimes and all the irritation, pain, and fighting faded away. In this bubble, nothing else mattered and we were like a family. No one was pissed at me or expected certain things from me. Daniel was at ease and enjoying his time, devoid of stress, cracking jokes.

Not once did I have to worry about him sitting too close and accidentally brushing against me, or which etiquette for my elders I'd overlooked, or dodging passive-aggressive remarks about my shortcomings. I'd only ever been this natural, this serene, with my parents and my girls. If it were possible to shove aside everything else, I'd keep to my small but mighty group.

Daniel told a story of trying to replicate his grandparents' cooking in New York and setting off fire alarms and putting an entire apartment complex on edge. The way he exaggerated the amount of smoke in the air, all in his nose and clothes and hair, burnt offerings to the food gods, I had to cover my face to keep from laughing too hard. I nearly had tears in my eyes.

He let out a final laugh and leaned back in his seat, draping an arm around the back of my chair. For a moment, neither one of us realized what we looked like—sitting close, laughing, acting like a couple.

But the pleased glances and giddy expressions came. Mainly from Grandma Thompson. And the second she hummed, "*Mm-hmm,*" Daniel cleared his throat and retracted his arm.

Oh, boy. Even if his grandparents hadn't already been on him for us to get back together, they would have been now.

Daniel rolled up his sleeves to his elbows, ready to get serious, exposing those muscular, sexy forearms. What was it about them?

I dunked crab into my bowl of melted butter with lemon and garlic, trying not to gawk at Daniel eating shrimp.

He deftly twisted off a head and drew out the juices. "What?" he mumbled.

"That's disgusting."

"No. It's delicious."

"Barbaric. It has eyes."

"You're not vegetarian. That crab had eyes, too."

"But not on my plate staring back at me and questioning if I ever had a soul while I eat its face."

"Sucking the head is the best part."

I stared at him, stunned but grateful that no one else was listening to our conversation. They were too busy eating and talking about the sermon and bake sale.

My face turned hot, my skin flushed, and a pleasant sensation tingled between my legs at the thought of his words referring to anything except food. The way he watched me, so intense and imploring, as if luring me into naughty thoughts while butter and juices dripped down his wrist.

He smirked and leaned toward me. "At least I think so. Gets all the juices flowing, flavor burst in your mouth, tongue action as it hits your taste buds."

I blew out a breath, refusing to show any effect he had on me. "You sound too into your shrimp. Maybe you need privacy."

He sucked another shrimp head with a slurp. "Can't wait for crawfish season. You might be open to, uh, trying head by then. Don't discount it until you've had it."

I clamped down a laugh, shooed out some immature thoughts, and gnawed on corn.

At the end of the meal, Grandma Thompson brought over a pie and set it in front of me. My eyes went big, taking in the sweet, luscious beauty.

She cut a slice for me first. "I know how much you love chess pie. I've been experimenting with chocolate and berries, but I think the lemon one tastes the best out of the variations. Try this, baby."

I took one delightful bite before my eyelids fluttered closed. I chewed with reverence as bliss swam across my tongue.

"You want a moment alone?" Daniel asked.

"You hush. This pie is a life-changing experience." To Grandma Thompson, I added, "Wow. That is pure perfection!"

Grandpa Thompson commented, "Didn't I tell you that she'd love it? Speaking of lemon, we need to make that lemon cake with cream cheese frosting your organization bake sale was raving about last month."

Chapter Twenty-Three

After dessert and coffee and enjoying each other's company, we all parted ways. And seeing that Daniel and I were headed to the same apartment, I went with him.

"While I appreciate it, you don't have to open every door for me like we're dating," I said when Daniel held his car door for me.

"And risk having Grandma throw her shoe at me?"

He hopped into the driver's seat and eased down the driveway, adding, "I have to drop by the new house to check on some things. It's on the way to the apartment."

"Okay." I kept my eyes set on the country drive ahead.

Although Daniel had seemed fine when we were with his family, he turned quiet now, leading me to believe that we were back to him being pre-church upset. Silence filled the air, suffocating me. I couldn't keep things to myself forever, and I hated knowing that I'd hurt him.

I steeled myself. "Listen. I know what I did caused you a lot of pain. And the guilt has eroded my confidence and trust and so many other aspects of my life. It made me feel unworthy of forgiveness. And I'm not asking you to forgive me. But I have to forgive myself. I can't hang on to my mistakes forever. I can't undo any of them. But I *have* learned, am continuing to learn, and this whole thing—how I hurt you, how I left, why I left, what I failed to do—has helped me to evolve. Even a little bit. Even if it's a little late. So you can hate me. It's fine, I understand. But I can't hate myself anymore."

He regarded me from the corner of his eye for a second, his focus still on the road. "I may be upset, but I could never hate you. I get it, but letting go of six years of pain, of six years of being without you, isn't something a person can heal from overnight."

"I understand," I said quietly.

We didn't speak for a long time, instead letting our words sink in. It wasn't until we rolled onto his new street that I sat up with interest. The place was almost as large as his parents' estate. He had his own private street leading up to his own private gate ahead of a long driveway.

The early evening sun shone across the incomplete land-scaping. We pulled up to an impressive white-and-cream granite house with black wrought-iron balconies. Opaque glass double front doors on a wraparound porch added a Southern touch. It all seemed vaguely familiar, even the circular driveway where Daniel parked.

"Gorgeous" was an understatement. "Glorious" was more like it. My mouth dropped. I tilted my head to the side and knew right then why this house looked so familiar.

"Do you want to come inside?" Daniel asked when he opened my door and offered a hand.

"Sure," I said as I took his hand and eased out of the car.

I looked all around, pivoting 360 degrees from the brilliant house to the thicket of trees around the property in a picturesque lot that instantly felt like home. Without warning, I was thrust back to college days of snuggling against Daniel as he drafted. The smell of pencil shavings and the scratch of lead against a drafting pad filled my senses while he shaded detailed oak trees. Those same trees surrounded us now.

Daniel unlocked the front door and showed me in first. "You can leave your shoes on. Workers are still coming and going."

I nodded and walked inside. I touched the eggshell walls and walked through arched entryways, trembling, my heart faltering. Instead of going to the living room to the right, I walked ahead into the study to the left. I knew this floor plan. I'd never been here before, but I knew every room.

"Daniel," I said and looked to him with tears in my eyes. "Is this *our* house?"

He stuffed his hands into his pockets, pressed his lips together, and nodded, pleased.

My heart quivered. Why had he done this? Was he rubbing this in my face? Showing me what we could've had all along and what he would have despite me?

"I don't know about you, but I think we came up with the perfect house," he said, his eyes wandering across the room and sweeping up to the ceiling.

I slid my shaking fingers across the glass walls. This was the study *I'd* designed. I wanted glass walls to scribble on, figure out problems, sketch, stick Post-its. On the far wall was a built-in bookcase. There would soon be a sofa in the middle of the room and a desk with a chair near the floor-to-ceiling windows that looked out over the backyard, at the glistening pool water (once the pool was filled). This was supposed to be where I came to study, to work, to read—a room all my own.

In college, I'd sat with Daniel, my back against his chest, as he drew and outlined everything to my specifications. We'd spent months designing our house, and here he went and built it for himself.

I wandered through the first floor: the living room, dining

area, the very large kitchen with two ovens and an indoor grill, and the wall-to-wall windows that opened the entire room to the backyard. Arching terraces would one day be covered in vines and flowers. There would be patio furniture and poolside lounge chairs.

Craning my head back, I could see a balcony that led to the main bedroom, allowing vaulted ceilings in this section of the first floor.

"Do you want to see the upstairs?" he asked, eager to show me with a beckoning smile.

My hands balled into fists.

"No." I did not want to see our perfect main bedroom with arched ceilings and grand windows, or the garden jacuzzi tub, or the waterfall shower big enough for four people with a bench on the side, finished in granite.

"Oh. Oh, okay," he said, sounding disappointed. "I have a few things to check on. You can walk around if you want."

I swerved away, listening to his footfalls fade. I touched the iron railing leading upstairs, imagining how he'd brought our dream to life. How could he do this?

"What do you think?" he asked on the way out of the living room.

"It's beautiful. Congratulations," I bit out and went to the main hallway.

Baffled, Daniel stood on the spot for a few seconds before coming after me. He gently took my wrist and pulled me back. "Wait. Is that all?"

I shrugged and averted my gaze in an effort to keep him from seeing the tears welling in my eyes.

He scoffed. "I know we just had a fight, but I expected more. Happiness, *joy* to see what we'd worked on come to life. Doesn't this mean anything to you?"

"Yes," I snapped, tears streaming down my face. "It means you're going to share *our* dream house with another woman."

"What in the hell are you talking about?" he asked. He frowned down at me, seemingly perplexed.

"This was supposed to be *our* home. We designed it together. But we're on separate paths and you're about to move on with Alisha. Why did you build this house? Why didn't you build your own? Or one with her?"

He cupped my face, swiping his thumbs across my wet cheeks. "Because this is my dream home."

"It's mine, too." I hiccupped. "And it's real now. Did you bring me here to rub it in my face? Make me look at what I could've had?"

"No. I was always going to build this house, and yes, every detail reminds me of you. It reminds me of all the good times we had."

"For Alisha to enjoy now?" I asked, hating that I was shaking in his arms.

"What are you talking about? Alisha?"

"Your parents want you two to get married, best for everyone's future. Good for you. Good for her."

"Why do you sound upset? You…don't want to get back with me."

"I don't want you marrying her, marrying anyone else."

"Who said I was marrying her?"

"Aren't you dating the woman your parents want for you?"

He scratched his chin and looked away sheepishly. "Um. No. It was one dinner."

I scowled. "You made it seem like you were dating."

"Because I was pissed at you. And you had a boyfriend. I thought you were moving on." He swallowed hard on those last words.

"You think I don't still love you?" I yelled, my lips trembling.

His hands landed on my waist, burning through my clothes

and searing an imprint into my flesh, forever marked by him. He peered so deeply into my eyes that I felt his presence in my head. He searched my face with intense, imploring eyes the color of chestnuts speckled with amber. He asked slowly, prodding with a hint of longing, "Do you still love me?"

"*Yes*," I croaked, my voice weak, hoarse. "I never stopped loving you and every time I see you or even think about you, it kills me. And everything is just so stupid and messed up. And you built this house." I gestured wildly around us. "I don't want another woman living in *our* house. I don't *want* to be with someone else. I don't want *you* to be with someone else."

Daniel leaned down, his gaze boring through me before dropping to my mouth. "Then do something about it," he growled.

His hand fell to my chin. His fingers fluttered down my throat, over the scarf. My breath hitched.

"He never made you feel the way I make you feel. He never understood you at all, why you react the way you do, why you struggle with certain issues. I don't even have to think about it. I already know. And I know right now that you want me."

He tilted his head, his lips a hair's width from mine, and paused. My breath escaped in quick, tortured pants, my hand lifting to stretch over his side. I closed my eyes as he moved a little lower.

I sucked in another breath as soon as his lips touched my jaw. My entire body was set on fire.

His mouth inched closer to my throat as he ran his tongue across my shivering flesh. I clutched his shirt, digging my nails into his back.

"Daniel..." I moaned, my other arm wrapping around his neck to pull him tight, to keep him close.

"I've missed the sound of my name on your lips." He gently pushed me against the wall, my gasp hitting his chin.

Just as he was about to kiss my lips for the first time in *years*... my stupid phone rang. I just about jumped out of my skin.

"Oh my god!" I blinked a good few times and slid out of his arms to clumsily fish through my purse. I had different ringtones for work, parents, and everyone else, so when the old-school Bollywood song that Papa had a band play for Mummie at their wedding came on, I almost flipped.

"I have to take this. One minute," I muttered to Daniel as I walked outside. I expected my lungs to continue burning for air between Daniel and anticipating a tongue-lashing from my parents. Surely Yuvan had told his parents, who then told my parents, and all hell was about to break loose.

Instead, Mummie wanted to know if I was coming for dinner this week. She could've texted, but if it wasn't on WhatsApp, she didn't like it.

"Yes. I'll be there. Thank you. Okay. Chat later," I told her and hung up.

"Who was that?" Daniel asked as he locked the house and unlocked the car.

"My mom. It's like she knows."

He grinned, but the smile slipped in an instant. "What are we doing here?"

I took a deep breath and exhaled. "I don't know. My head is clouded with so much. I just... can we pause for a little bit? I have my presentation tomorrow and I need to ace it. I haven't told my parents about breaking up with Yuvan."

"Yeah. Of course." He opened the door for me and we headed to the apartment.

"You'll do great on your presentation," he said once we were on the main road.

"Thanks to your help."

"Nah. It's all you."

Silence.

My pulse wouldn't calm down from that near kiss. I bit my lip and looked away, my mind tripping over itself with the urgent need to devour Daniel with kisses and seal our fate. Could it be... could he truly give me a second chance? While I could forgive myself, I wasn't sure that I could feel worthy of him again.

"How do you think your parents will handle the news about Yuvan?" he asked.

I chewed on my nail. "Not well. They really like him, and his parents and my parents are good friends. There's going to be bad blood and I already feel awful. I honestly haven't had time to think about it."

His hand landed on my knee in a comforting brush before returning to the wheel. "I think you're not giving them enough credit. They want what's best for you, and this guy isn't it. They're going to understand, and he needs to understand, too. I don't get some parents. Why would they allow a rift in their friendship? Sometimes things don't work out, and better to break it off now than when you're married. Don't think their reaction is your fault. Ever."

I nodded. "You're right."

He chuckled. "Look at that. Communication, huh?"

"Yeah, yeah."

He studied me during a brief red light. "How did this guy take the breakup?"

"Are you asking if I gave him a reason? Yes, I did. I learned. And he just walked off and left it alone. He got called for something at mandir and I left before he was free. He's texted a few times. A missed call."

"*Wow.* So this guy who was planning a future with you didn't even go after you? Some texts and a missed call is weak."

I agreed. Not to be dramatic, but had Yuvan felt any panic,

remorse, concern? Or did he think this was something I'd get over and crawl back to him?

When we reached the apartment, I went to the bathroom to wash up and do my business while Daniel went into the bedroom. I walked in minutes later, shrugging out of my cardigan with my fingers already on my dress zipper before realizing Daniel was still there. I froze.

He held eye contact and unbuttoned his vest, laying it over the jacket on the edge of the bed. Then he hooked a finger into his tie and undid the knot all the way, slowly pulling one end so that the rest slithered over his neck. It dropped to the bed. My gut tightened.

Then came the untucking of the shirt, the steady unbuttoning of his shirt until it came off. His lips curled into a smile, daring me to keep watching, provoking me to make a move.

I greedily took in the sight as he stripped off the undershirt. His body…good freaking lord. Then his fingers found his belt, then the zipper…

I snapped back to reality and spun toward the dresser, busying myself with removing my bracelet and watch and organizing bottles. But the thing about this dresser was that there was a big mirror in front of me. Daniel was watching me through the mirror, watching me watch him as he stepped out of his pants. And I was staring pretty hard. Speaking of which, he looked…quite ready.

He walked between me and the bed and pressed his chest to my back, his gaze meeting mine in the reflection of the dresser mirror. "Need help?"

His hands went up my arms and his forearm crossed my chest to untie the scarf. He plucked it gingerly out of its knot, and the silk against silk slid easily. He drew his arm back across my chest, taking the scarf with him, gliding it across my skin, leaving a trail of goose bumps in its wake, and set it on the dresser.

He slid his hand up my back, clasping the heavy metal coin attached to the top of the zipper, and effortlessly slid it down. The fabric filleted open to reveal the strip of my fancy, lacy Parisian bra. How many times had his lips trekked across my skin? Exploring every inch of me?

My grip on the small moisturizer bottle tightened. Just as his lips made contact with my shoulder, his tongue sliding down my shoulder blade, I jumped when a pop sounded.

"Oh, no!" I yelped, gripping my dress by mistake and stepping away. My hands, and the front of my slumped dress now gathered in my arms, were covered in a honey-tinged goop.

I ran to the bathroom, my dress half falling off.

Tinted SPF moisturizer in bronze-honey was a nightmare to get off my hands. I went through half a bottle of hand soap scrubbing away! And this dress? *Ruined* to crap. There was no way!

I stripped off the dress as quickly as possible and dunked the stained front of it into a sink full of water and soap and scrubbed. It just made the makeup smear across the cream-and-green fabric.

After at least twenty minutes of washing and rinsing and rewashing, I gave up. I marched out of the bathroom and tossed the dress into the hamper. I'd have to find time to take it to the dry cleaner's tomorrow, but I wasn't holding out much hope.

I turned off the living room lights and returned to the bedroom exhausted from an emotional day, only to find Daniel snug as a bug under the covers.

"What are you doing?" I asked. "It's early, still."

"It's been a long day with a lot of revelations, and I feel like resting." His gaze wandered down my body. "Since when do you walk around in your *Parisian* underwear?"

Oh, lord. I was standing in front of him half-naked, wasn't I? In lacy, not padded, sexy underwear from Paris. In front of a bed that was currently occupied by a shirtless, and perhaps pants-less, Daniel.

"What are you talking about? I always wear nice underwear," I asserted, even though my drawer of beige greatness begged to differ. I lifted my chin, pulled back my shoulders, and walked to the dresser as confidently and undeterred as possible, pushing aside that it was really cold in the room.

I fished around in a drawer for something to wear and...what was this? Sexy camisole with very short shorts in sapphire blue. Daniel's favorite color.

I slipped into the outfit, which didn't cover much more than my bra and panties had, cleared my throat, and got into bed while Daniel watched my every movement. The heat in his eyes was enough to ignite a fire, disintegrating the chill. A man hadn't looked at me with such hunger since—well, since Daniel. To be blatantly desired and appreciated by him felt nice, empowering, making me forget that I was dying by way of cramps and as bloated as a whale. The bedspread was tucked to my chin and my right hand felt for the edge of the bed. Two more inches over and I might as well sleep on the floor.

"So much room," Daniel teased. "Don't you want to move over?"

"No, thank you. I'm comfortable." I wasn't. I wanted to be closer to him, in his arms, smothered in his kisses, devoured by his touch. But I didn't deserve him.

He raised himself onto his elbow, his temple cradled in his hand. "I won't bite. Well, unless you want me to."

Butterflies thrashed against my insides at the thought of his lips on my body. I suddenly burst into laughter. "Remember what happened the last time you tried to bite me? I accidentally jumped and backhanded you." That had been an erotic rendezvous, until he nipped my hip.

He dropped his face into the pillow and groaned. "Mood killer."

"Heh." I wiggled deeper into the covers, grinning.

Chapter Twenty-Four

I didn't sleep well, not between the constant waking up and tossing and turning and being hyperaware of every movement. Plus, ya know, cramps, which came roaring to life. At some point, I must've hit REM and hard. Because the next thing I knew, in the miserable restlessness of the night, my alarm went off.

I barely registered blindly searching over the nightstand, grabbing the phone, hitting snooze, and passing out again. Until the phone's muffled alarm both rang and vibrated under my cheek.

First off, gross. There were tons of bacteria on any given cell phone surface.

Second, what was the pleasant heaviness pressed against my back? That smell of deodorant? The warmth of a heated body? The friction of a hand running up my side, along my arm tucked beneath my head, and searching out the noisy contraption?

The alarm turned off. The hand stayed on the bed beside my face. The delicious weight of a warm body stayed snug against my backside.

"You're going to be late, Doctor," a deep, gravelly voice muttered in my ear.

"Stop…" I moaned.

"I'm not doing anything," he said, and although he hadn't moved and was literally just lying against me half-asleep, I felt his hardness pressed against me.

"Oh!" I gasped and scurried out of bed. "Well, you have to stop doing *that* with your...*that*!" I grunted. Smooth. I didn't sound like a preteen who didn't know how to use words at all.

He chuckled. "I'm sorry. I didn't mean to."

"Control yourself!"

"It's not like I planned it. Stuff happens while a man sleeps."

"Yeah! Well," I grumbled, then announced, "I'm on my period. Take *that*, you morning enthusiast."

He laughed even harder, holding his hands up in surrender.

After a shower, I opened my laptop on the counter and practiced my presentation, ready to focus. I was going to knock them dead.

A short while later, Daniel emerged from the bedroom looking utterly adorable, rubbing sleepy eyes and walking to the bathroom in baggy sweatpants.

"What are you doing?" he asked when he emerged. He started a pot of coffee and leaned against the counter across from me.

"I didn't mean to disturb you. I'm practicing my presentation."

"Show me what ya got."

I crinkled my nose. "Really?"

"Yeah. I need to wake up anyway. And a few ten-minute practice sessions will do wonders. Helps to have a live audience."

"Putting together a visually stunning presentation might've been difficult, but presenting is my jam," I said and gave my presentation.

Daniel watched intently as he sipped coffee, his gaze so intense that I lost my train of thought once or twice but bounced back.

"Why are you watching me so hard?" I asked.

"Isn't an entire audience going to be hanging on your every word, attached to your every movement? Did I distract you?"

"A little."

"Good, I couldn't tell." He walked around the counter. "May I offer a few observations?"

I nodded, prepared for the worst. They taught us as interns to watch ourselves in the mirror or video-record to see what we were missing, but no one had time for that these days.

Daniel touched my hips. "You shift from foot to foot, like nervous energy. It's a little distracting."

"Oh. Never noticed that. Thanks."

He gently pushed my shoulders back. "You tend to slump when you have a lot of attention on you, as if maybe you're trying to make yourself a little smaller. Be big and bold. Own that stage."

I smiled. "Right."

He tilted my chin up a fraction with a knuckle. "Look authoritative, but also speak from your diaphragm. It'll come across as confidence and make your words clearer, louder in an auditorium."

He brushed a finger across my cheek. "Try not to touch your face or fidget with your notes or clicker. Keep the audience glued to your words, not your movements."

I gulped, trying to remain focused on my presentation and less concerned with the wonderful flutters his touch sent through me. My gaze darted away from his face. "Yep."

"And slow down your intro a bit. You sound rushed, which can come off as nervous."

"Thanks."

"One more thing?" He leaned down and pecked my temple. "Knock 'em dead, Dr. Patel."

I laughed. Daniel poured coffee into my mug and indulged me with one more practice session.

We had a quick breakfast of cereal and toast, and off to work I went.

I had meetings all morning. Afternoon came, and despite

my nerves and trembling voice with a small auditorium full of residents and physicians staring back at me, I presented my case study on infections.

There were a number of reasons I'd agreed to present. One, I might not like attention, but I loved presenting. Two, I volunteered not only to share my findings, but to showcase my strengths to my colleagues and potential future boss. Three, accolades. In a world where so many things went south and negativity was a suffocating cloud, being told you did something amazingly was a great balm.

My presentation was met with applause and the exchange of impressed nods between Dr. Wright and the other physicians.

If there were ever a mic-drop moment in my life, this would've been it.

The first person I told was Daniel.

✳

Since I had a short workday, Reema had invited me and Sana to her place to catch up. Our weekends were so warped with personal commitments that Monday night wine had to be it.

Sana fluttered around the living room helping Reema, excited for her upcoming trip to India. "I can't wait to meet this guy," she said, on cloud nine. It was wonderful to see her opening up and getting excited about things other than work and family.

I twirled my phone on the coffee table as Reema brought over ice cream and a tray of fresh homemade french fries. Because what was better than dipping hot, salty potato strips into a bowl of sweet, cold ice cream?

Sana had set up her giant tablet so we could video-chat with Liya. As soon as Liya popped up on-screen, she waved gleefully and raised a glass of wine.

"Meeting of the sisterhood can now commence!" she said.

"I have to confess something," I announced.

"What!" the girls said in unison.

"You getting it on with Daniel?" Liya asked as naturally as asking how my day was.

I bit into a fry. "Um. I was going to tell you about Yuvan. Remember him?"

Liya snorted. "Let's be real, shall we? You're just now mentioning having dated this guy, you're living with Daniel and sending us bedroom pics, and I bet Yuvan hasn't even gotten a kiss from you. Methinks you're not going to marry this guy. Boy, bye."

"You're right," I replied bluntly.

Everyone quieted, waiting for me to expand.

"He's nice and good on paper and all that, but he doesn't get me. I told him it wasn't going to work."

Silence. Sana and Reema sat on the edges of their seats and Liya had leaned so far into her screen that all I saw was her forehead.

"Well?" Sana demanded, surprisingly the first to slash through the quiet.

"He told me to calm down."

"Oh, hell no!" Liya said.

"Then he got pulled away by mandir duties and I left mandir afterward," I explained.

Liya rolled her eyes and dramatically threw herself against her couch.

"Are you okay?" Sana asked.

"I'm fine. I feel like the weight of the sun is off my shoulders," I confessed.

She smiled. "Then it was the right thing to do."

"Do your parents know?" Reema asked.

"No. Yuvan must not have told his parents, otherwise his mom would've called my mom right away and my mom would've chewed my ear off by now. Honestly? He hasn't said or done much other than a call I missed and some texts asking if I was okay and wondering when we could talk."

Liya shot me a dry look. "B-freaking-S. If I'd said that to Jay...well, he'd first want to know exactly what I meant, and then try to talk it out, and then give me space but also make sure I knew he was thinking of me and that I had no doubt he wanted to be with me."

"Wait a minute," Reema said. "Think about long term. If you leave Yuvan, and for good, solid reasons, how will this impact you and your parents? Talk to them first."

"Yeah," I agreed. "I was planning on telling my mom after I got my presentation out of the way. I just don't want to hurt them again. She got so sick before, and the gossip mill is harsh."

"Well, they can all cram it," Liya stated. "Seriously. Who the hell cares about them? They aren't one bit worried about your happiness."

I nodded. "I know. Heard my fois talking trash at mandir and I had to put a stop to it."

"Good! Let those biddies suffocate in the dumpster fires they create. They couldn't care less about you. It doesn't matter what you say or do, they'll hate on you for anything. And this time, Preeti"—Liya wagged a finger at me through the screen—"know it's not your fault and do the right thing."

Reema nodded. "I concur. No winning with that part of your family. But if you decide to let Yuvan go, make sure it's what's best for you in the long run, too. This is your life." Reema regarded me for a minute with understanding and empathy.

"I'm terrified of hurting my parents again," I said, tugging at the pillow beside me.

"Did you hurt them? Or did all those idiots butt their big noses in and give racist opinions that no one asked for?" Reema said.

"She's right, Preeti," Liya added. "You've never done anything to hurt your parents. You've made them proud since day one. Have you even asked if marrying Yuvan will make them happy if it makes you miserable? This whole thing isn't a matter of heart or reason or anything else. It's all muddled together. You want to be logical, but is it logical to be miserable the rest of your life? You don't want to hurt your parents, but won't they hurt if they know you're in pain?"

I tapped the pillow. "I know. I'm going to tell them this week when we have dinner."

"This Yuvan guy is done. Back to Daniel. Have you tried shower sex?" Liya asked so casually that I choked on my fry.

"No! I am *not* having sex with him."

"Ahaha! The sex text joke was a lie," she declared while Reema and Sana quieted their laughter.

"You all knew it was."

"Because shower sex is the *end all*," Liya added with a new energy and wild gestures.

I mentally went over the visual, tilting my head as my brain attempted to wrap itself around the logistics and physics. As sexy as it looked, especially in the movies where sudsy bodies writhed against each other with slick skin-on-skin contact, it seemed like an awfully dangerous adventure. Slippery floors and walls, angled tubs, annoying swaying shower curtains, water slapping us in the face and in the back of the head, trying not to drown in aforementioned water, trying to keep our eyes open in the aforementioned water, and, of course, the positioning.

It seemed like a lot of work, especially for the woman. Not slipping, standing up, staying balanced on one foot because the other leg had to angle out. And where did that one leg go? Was the woman supposed to practice yoga? Did the guy hold her up?

"You're going over all the ways it doesn't work, aren't you?" Liya asked.

"The physics of shower sex is not conducive to safety, nor is it romantic."

She groaned. "Until you try it. Then suddenly it's the hottest thing in the world."

"*Successfully* try it, you mean. I'm more likely to slip and break a bone. Then drown."

"One day, Preeti…and I'm sure Daniel would show you how it's done."

I sucked in a breath, suddenly bombarded with a hundred images of us naked, wet, covered in bubbles, and all over each other in a steamy shower. I could almost feel him touching me.

Liya regarded me and slowly grinned. "His naked body is all up in your thoughts, huh?"

I shook my head. Meanwhile Reema was laughing her butt off and Sana had the worst episode of blushing.

Liya went on, "It's all over your face! You're such an open book. Flushed cheeks. Wide eyes. Averted gaze. And you do this thing with your nose."

"What!"

"Yeah. Your nostrils get all big."

I frowned but had to laugh with her.

The girls went quiet all at once as Reema asked, "So, what's up with Daniel? Sex text jokes and fake bedroom pictures aside."

I sighed, attempting to be serious so that my girls could offer critical feedback. But when I spilled the beans, a collective scream erupted. Reema and Sana ambushed me with hugs, tackling me against the couch.

Yes. I was still in love with Daniel Thompson, perhaps more than ever.

Yes. I wanted to be with him, definitely more than ever.

Yes. I was determined to consider every angle and see where a second chance could lead us.

Chapter Twenty-Five

Now that the presentation was over, I could get back to job hunting, apartment searching, and figuring out how to break the news to my parents.

Daniel wasn't home yet, so I did my nightly thing and sat in bed, as snug as a bug cocooned in a blanket while searching job links. Around nine, the front door opened and closed and the lock clicked. A dim light from the living room seeped through beneath the bedroom door. It wasn't the thousand-watt overhead lights with their blinding intensity, but the mellow, low-level bulb from the corner lamp.

Daniel didn't make any noise. He didn't get his usual cup of water from the fridge or slide his keys across the counter or drop his messenger bag beside his desk. He was uncharacteristically quiet.

I threw off the covers and slipped out of bed. I quietly drew open the door and watched his broad frame drop to the couch. He threw his head back to rest against the couch and released a long, pent-up, frustrated sigh.

I frowned and pulled the door all the way open.

As I walked toward him, my toes digging into the plush carpet and my skin shivering in the sudden chill, he didn't seem to notice me. Not until I stood beside him and touched his shoulder.

Daniel startled and stared up at me as if he'd forgotten where he was. His brow creased with worry lines, his mouth turned down, but his eyes...they glistened with sadness, and my heart turned heavy and desolate.

"What's wrong?" I asked, taking another step to stand in front of him.

He groaned and his arm immediately went around my waist, pulling me closer so that I stood between his parted knees. Without a word, in the smoothest of motions, he drew me into him as he scooted to the edge of his seat and hugged me, his forehead against my chest.

Words tumbled up the back of my throat, and my hands hovered in the air above his shoulders, near his head. I froze at the unexpected intimacy, the touch, the feel of Daniel flush against my skin. His warmth seared through the thin fabric of my clothes.

As soon as he shuddered out a breath, I wanted nothing more than to comfort him.

It was the most natural thing in the world to become one with him, to hug him against my chest as the weight of his forehead pressed against my collarbone.

He didn't say anything for a long time. He didn't budge an inch or shift a centimeter as I ran my fingers over his hair.

I touched my cheek to the top of his head and whispered, "Daniel?"

He took a deep breath and muttered, "I love how you say my name."

Another minute of silence went by before he pulled back, just enough to look up at me. I continued to rub my fingertips through his hair just above his ears, massaging his scalp with my fingernails. His hands never left my waist.

I tilted my head to the side. My hair cascaded over his shoulders. "What happened?"

His chest inflated until he released. "My dad is so damn controlling. I keep saying I'm a grown man able to make my own decisions, yet here I am. Maybe it sounds stupid out loud."

"Maybe you just need to say it out loud to work through it?"

He shook his head. "I don't want you to worry about it."

"That's kinda how this works."

"What is *this*?"

I shrugged. "I'm not sure, but when you care about someone, you care about their problems."

He didn't say anything after that, and that was okay. Sometimes we needed to be held, and it was enough for now.

It didn't matter how long we stayed like this, motionless, silent. It didn't matter if my legs were aching or if my slightly bent back started to cramp. I wouldn't move. I didn't want to let him go.

"You should come to bed," I found myself saying. "Sleep might help."

"Are you sure?" he asked, his lips brushing the skin just below my collarbone, sending shivers across my skin.

"Yeah."

"Can you stay a little longer? Like this?"

"Of course," I replied and glanced down as he tilted back.

Our lips paused mere centimeters apart. He pressed his lips together and I knew exactly what he was thinking, because I was thinking the same thing.

I'd really missed Daniel. My body missed him, my soul, my entire being. I could tell by the way he fixated on my mouth that he wanted to kiss me, even as I gently cupped his face.

He arched upward and I expected to feel his lips press against mine. Instead, they gingerly kissed my neck. My breath was lost to me.

His hands slipped down the backs of my thighs and hooked behind my knees, brushing the right spots, pulling first my right knee up and onto the couch, then my left knee, until I was straddling him.

I clamped down on a moan. Opening for Daniel was as intoxicating as any high.

He settled me onto his lap as his lips moved up my neck to my jaw. I trembled from the sheer amount of exertion it took to control myself. My hips were aching to roll into him. My back was begging to arch into him. My mouth hungrily awaited his. My skin demanded to be free and flush against his.

My body screamed to continue, to see where this led because it knew without a doubt where we would go. But my logical reasoning stirred awake. *Do* not *do this on the heels of his anxieties.*

His breathing went from tranquil and level to a little faster, a little more abrupt as his lips met my neck, as his warm hands went up underneath my shirt and spanned my back.

I bit down a moan and tried to see through the fog inundating my thoughts. "Tell me what happened with your dad?"

Daniel groaned and leaned back. "How's my dad cock-blocking this right now?"

I smiled and slid off, sitting beside him while he kept a hand on my thigh.

He closed his eyes. "He has this idea of what he wants me to be. He always says it's the best for me, but it's really the best for him and his image."

"Parents have high expectations."

"Yours forcing you onto your not-really-a-boyfriend?"

"I'll find out tomorrow when I tell them."

"I don't think they will."

I shook my head. "Me either. Maybe this'll help you as much as it helps me?" I jumped up and grabbed the guitar from the corner. It was much heavier than it looked and definitely too large for my arms. I sat beside him on the couch as he dragged a hand down his face.

"Since when do you play?" he asked.

"Since ten seconds from now."

Daniel draped an arm over my shoulder as I got comfy against his side, the guitar on my lap, my fingers trying to strum. It was easy to glide fingers over the strings, but making music was another story.

He chuckled. "You've really improved."

I elbowed him, but he wrapped both arms around my waist to get a hold over my hands and moved my fingers through various keys and notes. All right, so it was much harder than it appeared to play, and coordination? I could use surgical instruments to repair tears, but I couldn't strum two areas on a guitar at once.

After several minutes of Daniel quietly laughing at me, I stretched my fingers. "How do you not have calluses?"

"I use a pick."

"Will a coaster work?" I leaned across the coffee table to grab one of the thin coasters, but he pulled me back against his chest and promised, "Not exactly the same thing."

He readjusted me in his arms so that my hands were at my sides while he played around me. "Let me show you something."

I picked up the tune right away. "Wow. That song was huge back in college."

"Funny, right? How we can hear a song that we haven't heard in forever and suddenly be singing every word and feeling everything we felt when we first heard it. Remember what we were doing when this song played?"

I bit my lower lip. "At a college party. It was too loud, too crowded, and people kept bumping into me. Ugh. I can't remember why I was there."

"Pretty sure Liya or Brandy made you go. But that was the first time we'd seen each other, at a party."

My head fell back against his. He pecked my temple, sending shivers through me, and ran a finger lightly up my goose-bumped skin. "You saw that I was uncomfortable and took me outside."

He wrapped an arm around my shoulders so that I was snug against his chest. "The relief on your face when I did that. It was like you'd held your breath the entire time until we got out of there."

And that was the first time Daniel had touched me out of nowhere, a hand to my lower back to usher me out and keep others from bumping into me. It wasn't in greeting or farewell. I hadn't minded that touch at all. It was the first of many, many touches to come.

He kept playing. I yawned.

"You should get some sleep," he suggested, shifting me away and putting the guitar back.

"What about you?"

"I can't sleep. Might as well get some work done."

I yawned again. "I'll stay up with you."

"No. Go to bed. Look at you."

"I can sleep here while you work. I heard the couch is very comfortable."

He shook his head, bent down, and scooped me into his arms without effort. "It's late and you have work in the morning, literally life-and-death decisions to make."

"I'm not an old woman. I can manage to stay up past ten," I argued as he lowered me gently onto the bed.

"We all know you hate staying up that late." He winked down at me, kissed my forehead, turned off the lights, and closed the door behind him.

＊

The next morning, I awoke to Daniel beside me. This time, he woke up with my alarm at five in the morning.

"Sorry," I muttered, turning the alarm off, shifting back toward him, and kissing his cheek before realizing what I'd done. I froze, wondering if I should apologize or pretend that we weren't slipping back into couple mode.

"It's okay. I wanted to get up at the butt crack of dawn," he mumbled, wrapping an arm around me and pulling me back into him.

"Are we snuggling?" I asked.

"Heh. I think so."

I melted against his side. "I was going to go for a run..."

"Okay." He pushed the covers off.

"What are you doing?"

"Let's go for a run." He sat up in bed and swung his legs over the edge.

"Really?"

"Yeah. Afterward, I'll make you the best frozen waffles you've ever had in your life."

I laughed. "You're slipping, chef."

Our run turned out to be more of a walk through the neighborhood while holding hands. It was dark and cool, but plenty of cars and pedestrians were out. I kept glancing at Daniel in search of any signs of how he was feeling about his father and their business and what I could do to help. In all this concern for him, the focus on finding work and an apartment took a back seat.

Chapter Twenty-Six

L ater that day at the clinic, Dr. Wright pulled me aside after my last patient. When she saw my look of confusion, she said, "I take it that you haven't checked your voicemail."

"No. It's been a full day. What happened?" I asked.

A grin cracked open across her face. "Congrats, Dr. Patel! We've extended an offer of full-time employment for you after residency is over."

My first instinct was to squeal, but I had to tamp that down quickly, considering Dr. Wright was my boss. I laughed instead, my body thrumming from racing heartbeats, and profusely thanked her. "This means so much. Thank you, thank you! I'm so honored to be a part of your practice, Dr. Wright. This is a dream come true. I love this place like a second home."

"It's my pleasure. We've enjoyed having you, watching you mature and take leadership roles, and how you handle patients, and your expertise is something we couldn't pass up. I hope you accept." She raised her hands. "No pressure. Not asking for a decision on the spot."

As much as I wanted to say yes, of course, and also there

weren't other offers, I nodded and took my time. Once I left an extremely thrilled boss, I listened to my voicemail and discussed the offer with HR.

Then I called my parents from the car. They'd canceled our weekly dinner because they had to head to Austin to check on my sick uncle.

The words spilled out of me like a geyser, my entire body shaking and tears spilling.

"Wait. Eh?" Mummie asked on speakerphone.

I beamed. "My clinic offered me the job! I repeat, I have a job! Your daughter will be a full-time, full-fledged, actual doctor after residency."

"Oh!" Mummie gasped, the phone muffled as she handed it to Papa. "Preeti got the job!"

"That's my beta! There was no doubt. Always making me proud," Papa said, his voice quavering as Mummie cried and mumbled every prayer she could remember. "So many years of hard work and dedication and tears and fears and heartaches come down to this. Preeti, you are amazing."

"Papa..." I mumbled, choking back sobs.

"We're going to tell everyone," Mummie said excitedly, her voice higher. "And we will do puja and offer the acceptance letter and your first paycheck to mandir, huh?"

"Of course," I said, understanding the importance of giving back the first of our fruits to God.

"We'll be back in town in a few days," Papa said. "Can we announce?"

"I haven't accepted yet."

"Why not?"

"Let me take a couple days to notify other places where I've interviewed," I explained, although no other practice appealed to me as much. But it was the professional thing to do, to not burn bridges, and just maybe someone else would want me and Dr. Wright's practice would up their offer.

"Okay. Okay. We'll tell everyone you got your first offer," he said.

We hung up shortly after, all three of us elated. In a matter of hours, through the sheer power of WhatsApp, every family member, friend, and acquaintance of my parents all over the world would be notified.

My parents were busy with my uncle, and I wanted to give them this moment of pride and joy. I would tell them about Yuvan later.

I giddily texted my girls in group chat, and was bombarded in return by a dozen exclamations.

I texted Daniel right after, notified all of my interviewers who had yet to decide, went to the hospital to check on a few patients, and then headed home through atrocious city traffic. But even Houston gridlock wasn't going to deflate my joy.

I walked through the front door, dropped my backpack, kicked off my shoes, and took my water bottle to the kitchen. Exhausted, exhilarated, humbled, proud, and everything in between.

It took a second while washing my water bottle to notice the bouquet of red and white roses, peppermint-striped carnations, and pink peonies tucked into a neat black box directly in front of me.

Mesmerized by the sheer beauty, I walked around the counter and touched the petals, taking in the soothing floral scent and marveling at the fanciness of a boxed arrangement for geometrically perfect blooms.

"Do you like them?" Daniel asked from the corner, his voice smooth and mellow. He was sitting in front of his desk, swiveling back and forth, watching me with the eraser end of his pencil to his chin.

"They're beautiful."

He stood and stretched, the hem of his shirt riding up to

expose a sliver of stomach, before walking toward me and hugging me from behind. The heat of his chest against my back had me melting into him, his arms around my waist, his chin on my shoulder as he kissed my neck. My breath hitched.

"Congrats on the job," he said in my ear. "I knew you'd get it. They're not stupid enough to let you go."

I closed my eyes and enjoyed a perfect moment. For the first time in a long time, I felt almost whole. The only piece missing was my parents' approval of Daniel.

"We should celebrate when you get a chance. A dinner, maybe? I know this cozy little restaurant downtown," he said, his voice low and gravelly, his lips brushing my skin with every word. "It could be a second first date?"

My gut drop-kicked me and I tensed.

He pulled back and cleared his throat. "Unless you don't want that?"

I turned to him, taking his hands in mine. "I never thought there would be a second chance for me."

He watched me quietly, thoughtfully.

"You forgive me?" I asked incredulously.

He pulled me into him, his hands caressing the skin above my pants, beneath my blouse. "Yeah. It's hard not to love you, Pree."

I blinked. "*Are* you still in love with me?" I dared to ask, holding my breath for either a heartbreaking stomp or a profound confession.

"Duh," he said with a chuckle.

I smiled. Oh my lord, my entire body flared hot as I pressed into Daniel. My thoughts wound around all the time we'd lost, all the pain I'd caused, all the regrets and unspoken words. I didn't want to let that happen ever again because this was good. Beyond good. Daniel was, right beside my parents and my girls, the best thing to have ever happened to me.

"We made mistakes. You owned up to yours, and love doesn't fail. We learned, we grew, we came around. Life is too short to stay mad. We're not kids anymore."

I wrapped my arms around his neck and hugged him tight, my heart swelling with so much love. "I would be honored to go on a second first date with you, Daniel."

He breathed into my hair, his embrace a little stronger. "I have a bottle of celebratory wine for you, too."

"Ew," I teased. "Why is it expected to celebrate with bitter drinks?"

His voice dropped when his lips brushed my ear. "Oh, I think there are lots of ways of celebrating."

I shivered against him. His fingers stroked my lower back, spurring a dizziness that made me want to crash into him. "Like what?"

He pulled away and I instantly missed his warmth. His hand glided down to mine, taking my fingers as he walked toward the bathroom before letting my hand fall from his. The inviting look in his eyes said more than words ever could, ignited by desire and fracturing the last of my attempts to keep myself from him.

If actions were more compelling than looks, then Daniel had that down, too. He peeled off his shirt, exposing the contours of his chest and abs to my eager, devouring gaze.

I ran a hand down the back of my neck, my skin turning hot.

He cocked his head toward the door and disappeared into the bathroom. The play of muscles on his bare back had my stomach tying in knots, like actual visceral knots.

The sound of water spraying in the shower behind a partially opened door captured my attention. I surrendered to smoldering images from our past as they infiltrated my thoughts. How my hands had curiously roamed over every muscle on Daniel's body in complete awe and gratitude for his beauty. His skin was a perfect shade of dark brown, nearly flawless, including moles here and there and scars from childhood antics and an ambiguous birthmark on his shoulder blade. His muscles were toned and hard and just…manly.

I'd loved how much larger than me he was. Taller, wider. He made me feel not small or insignificant but protected.

He was a room away. Naked.

I bit down on a moan.

I heeded his silent call and pushed the bathroom door open to the sound of cascading water.

I closed the door behind me.

His very sexy, very *naked* silhouette moved beyond the opaque shower curtain as he lathered up his neck and chest and back and abs and…

Oh my word.

I fanned myself. It was warm in here. Steam rose from the shower and fogged the mirror.

I stepped onto the lush lavender bathroom rug in front of the tub when Daniel turned away and faced the wall. He had his back to me. A beautiful, broad back. A back that suddenly stilled when my hand touched the shower curtain and pressed into him.

He tensed for a moment and wiped his face, or so I suspected from the movements of his silhouette. He turned his head to the side, as if checking out what I was doing. Then he relaxed against my touch. I lifted my other hand and pressed the curtain against his shoulder, feeling him through the thin barrier and running my hands down his back to his hips.

Daniel slowly turned toward me so that my hands glided over his hips and onto his abs. Yep. They were just as solid as I thought they'd be, with ridges and contours of cut muscle. My touch moved up as his silhouette seemed to look down at me while water sprayed his side. He sucked in a breath as I moved up across his abs to his chest, across his shoulders and down his arms.

My palm touched his as he raised his hand against the shower curtain. He slid our unified hands across the curtain while, with his other hand, he moved the curtain aside. The slick barrier escaped us. Our flesh touched. First just our fingers, then our palms, until he completely opened the curtain.

I gasped, partly shocked at the beauty of him. I expected to see him, had seen him before, but having Daniel Thompson right in front of me was no less stunning.

Iridescent sprays of water jumped from his skin and streamed down the side of his face and body. Trails of water dripped down *every* inch of him. My face flushed because I was staring. Yes. I was most definitely staring. And he was most certainly grinning.

"You just creep on every guy who showers at your place?" he asked, his voice low and raw.

"Sorry."

"Don't ever be sorry," he said as his gaze landed on my mouth. Water dripped from his lips as he spoke, until he finally licked droplets off. He breathed a little faster, a little harder, as steam spiraled up and around us.

Then he bent down and kissed me. Water dribbled down my skin, wetting my lips and my neck and my shirt. His hands squeezed around my waist and pressed me into his frame, soaking my white blouse to see-through dampness—something we both suddenly realized when he pulled back and glanced down. He moaned and my gut dropped. In fact, my knees actually buckled.

But Daniel deftly caught me in his arms and kept me pressed against him, his kisses searing my skin as they moved down my jaw and neck, where he muttered, "Bending over this tub is killing my back. Why don't you come in here?"

"But shower sex isn't logically—"

He cut off my sentence by hoisting me onto his hips. My legs automatically, naturally wrapped around him as he carefully closed the shower curtain and turned. My back hit the cold, wet tiled wall, eliciting another gasp and then a deep moan. *From me.*

In the back of my mind, my brain tried to throw out all the things that could potentially go wrong and endanger us. This wasn't some movie where shower scenes were staged to be erotic and doable and safe.

"Don't worry. I got you," he groaned, somehow reading my thoughts.

His hands moved up my sides, underneath my blouse, to peel off my wet clothes. My mind was hazy in an unprecedented euphoria as I rolled into him, my moans getting louder, faster, as his breathing turned ragged and urgent.

No man could ever shatter me the way Daniel Thompson did. And in this moment of physics-defying shower sex where one more touch threatened to push me over the edge, I knew that no other man would ever get this close to me.

✳

I shivered beneath the bedspread, my skin and body hyperaware of Daniel's lingering gaze. I clutched the covers to my chin while he lowered the sheets to his hips, exposing his bare torso to my greedy gaze. His muscles were cut, sinewy, beautifully etched into his frame as he shifted onto his side to face me.

"You still giggle out of control when you climax, huh?" he asked with a goofy grin.

I pulled the blankets to my eyes. I wanted to disappear. Who laughed like a maniac when they orgasmed? Me. Just me. There was something extremely...I dunno...ticklish about having all of my nerves on overdrive.

"It's cute," he said and tugged on the bedspread. "It lets me know that I can still get it done."

"I don't think there was ever a time when you couldn't get it done," I muttered against the covers.

"Are you still embarrassed?"

"No," I lied.

"Then why are you covering your face? We've had much more embarrassing things happen."

"Don't even start with that," I warned as I pulled the bedspread to my neck.

"Like that time I went down on you in your dorm room and your roommate came home and you kneed me in the face trying to get your shirt on. Do you remember that?"

"Stop! That was mortifying." Not the kneeing-him-in-the-face part, but having anyone walk in and see me trying to cover my crotch with my shirt and Daniel half-naked on the floor holding his face and laughing. And which roommate, of all people? Liya. Grinning like a fool as she said, "Get it, girl!"

He chuckled as I gently shoved him. "Or that time we tried hot wax and—"

"Stop," I said, covering his mouth with my hand as he laughed into my palm.

Chapter Twenty-Seven

There was a very rare bubble that I'd fallen into when Daniel and I had dated in college. It was a feeling of completeness, of not wanting more, of utter bliss and rightness. I hadn't felt that way since I left him. All it took was one kiss to slip back into that bubble. To feel safe and secure and whole and protected and *right*.

Even now as I walked around this magnificent house that he'd brought to life from the designs of our dreams, life felt complete. When I'd first seen the house, the surprise and pain of it all had prevented me from fully appreciating everything, but now? How could I not be in love with this home? How could I deny my love for a man who built our house? It was perfect.

Today, Brandy directed the furniture delivery guys this way and that as Daniel and I approved. Well, I shrugged or nodded. Interior design wasn't my forte, but everything Brandy had picked out looked very modern and chic.

The living room set was black and white. Mummie's warning chimed in my head of never having white in the house for fear of staining and the detection of the smallest speck of dust. No white counters or cabinets or rugs or carpets or furniture.

But here we were. Standing in a living room with white

furniture and white rugs and black wall art. And it worked beautifully.

"How much did all of this cost?" I asked, coming to stand beside Daniel. "Everything looks so expensive."

He stood with his arms crossed and a finger on his chin as he studied all of Brandy's purchases. "When you build a million-dollar house, you have to fill it accordingly. And my sister has expensive taste."

My jaw dropped. "*How* much?"

"The private road and land and building from scratch with imported marble and granite and metalwork?" He quirked a brow at me as if my question were serious.

"Did you have to get a loan?" I asked. I knew his family was worth a lot, but that didn't mean Daniel by himself had millions lying around.

"I don't get loans. I pay in full," he responded casually and then ran to the hallway to help a mover before he banged the dining table against the wall. He saved it just in time.

Before I could ask where in the world he was making millions from, he returned and asked, "This place is ready to move in this weekend."

I frowned.

"Some landscaping left, and the pool will get finished in the new year."

With forced enthusiasm, I said, "Congrats! You must be so excited to finally move in." Even if that meant he would be moving out of the apartment. What would we be then? Back to the days of trying to move on? Was this all a fling, or was it really a second chance for him, too?

"Thanks. It's nice to see this finally come to fruition. Sometimes I still can't believe that I can create a building from a sketch, you know? It's wild." He glanced around, admiring his beautiful work. "I'll be busy this weekend moving my things in and getting all the plastic off and washing sheets and all that fun stuff," he added dryly.

If he wanted me to help with that, I didn't mind.

"I was wondering if you wanted to..." he started, rubbing the back of his neck and watching me as if the words were lost to him. His cheeks flushed.

Move in with him?!

"If you'd like to attend a gala with me next Thursday?" he finished, hopeful, nervous.

"A gala?" I squeaked. Totally wasn't expecting that. Although the idea of moving in with Daniel was exciting and an affirmation of what he wanted, maybe I wasn't ready for such a bold move. "That sounds fancy." And important.

"It is. It's our winter gala to raise money and thank contributors. The entire family will be there, including my grandparents and Brandy."

Which meant his disapproving parents, too.

"I know you despise parties, but it would mean a lot to me if you came. Please say you'll come?" He pressed his hands together like he was begging me. How could anyone deny those puppy-dog eyes and that adorable pout?

I nipped his lower lip and he pulled me into him.

"You better stop that," he muttered. "Because there are four strangers and a sister in this house."

"Ugh. You better *both* stop," Brandy interjected, and Daniel and I pulled away. "Congrats on the job!"

"Aw. Thank you! I wanted to tell you myself." I eyed Daniel, who shrugged apologetically.

Brandy said, "Now Dr. Patel *has* to make her debut appearance as an officially employed physician, right? And what better place than a gala?"

My nerves turned jittery at the idea of being face-to-face with their dad. And parties just weren't my thing. I didn't enjoy the noise or forcing myself to converse or getting all dressed up. Parties required a lot of energy that I didn't have.

But Daniel was practically pleading. "It means that much to you if I attend?" I asked him.

He nodded. "It's the end-of-the-year fundraiser and it's work for me, networking and politics and all that fun stuff. But a huge event to show my face, and I can't imagine anyone else that I'd like to share it with. As, um, a couple?" he half stated, half asked.

We hadn't discussed what we were doing, where we were heading, or any goals. But at least we were on the same page. I beamed. "I'd love to go as a couple."

Daniel flashed that gorgeous smile and dimples and swept me into his arms. "Does this mean what I think it means?"

"That we're getting dressed up?" I joked.

He laughed. "That we're a couple."

I nodded into his chest, heat prickling my cheeks. You'd think I'd never fallen in love with Daniel before, yet here I was, feeling like a college kid finding first love.

He pecked my temple and pulled away. "Great! Awesome! Um…hey, Brandy, do you mind taking Preeti shopping for the gala and setting her up?"

Brandy's eyes lit up as she clapped. "Yay! Can I have the card?"

Daniel didn't bat an eyelash as he pulled out a card and handed it to her. Before Brandy could take it, he snatched it away and gave it to me. It was very pretty for a credit card.

I tentatively took the shimmering black card with shimmering silver font. It even felt expensive. "How fancy am I agreeing to?"

"Very. Black tie and gown."

"Shopping!" Brandy squealed.

✳

The following day, Liya arrived in Houston to see family, but of course she wouldn't leave without dropping by. She lounged around the apartment, admiring the bouquet and all hyped on my recent updates on job, Daniel, and gala.

"Woohoo!" Liya shrieked. "My girl has her dream job and her dream man *and* we're going on a real-deal shopping trip!"

"Oh, lord," I grumbled. The very thought of shopping had me spinning through traumatic flashbacks of being dragged all over Houston for Reema's wedding outfits with her and the bridesmaids. For weeks, I had nightmares of being left behind in clothing stores with bags upon bags of garments, the store lights flickering off as the employees forgot about me and locked me in, and waking up in a cold sweat.

"What's our budget? Because this is *the* gala of the year in Houston. Everyone who's anyone will be there! You need to look the part, woman!"

"I don't know. Daniel gave me his credit card and said there wasn't a limit, but of course I'm going to be mindful of every penny." I plucked out the card and held it up.

Liya's eyes went wide with an almost lustful gleam. "Is that an exclusive credit card?"

"I don't know."

"I mean…Preeti! Do you realize how elite that card in your hand is? I mean, I knew Daniel came from a well-off family, but damn. Trust him when he said you don't have to worry about price tags. I have some places in mind."

"Daniel asked Brandy to take me shopping." On my phone, I pulled up the list she'd sent me of stores I'd never heard of and turned the screen to Liya. She practically salivated.

"Please tell me that I can come with you guys, because these are invitation-only stores. What kind of money does Daniel really have?"

I shrugged. "Have no idea. Nor do I care, because I will still look at price tags."

"I'm pretty sure these places don't have price tags."

"That sounds illegal."

"It's an 'if you have to ask, you can't afford it' type of thing. Where they bring out expensive champagne and gourmet chocolates and caviar and all while you shop."

"Ew. Caviar?"

"Don't dismiss it until you've tried it."

I texted Brandy to ask if Liya could join us and she was more than happy to have her. "Great! Brandy's looking forward to spending time with you. She said you're going to die when you see some of these designer dresses."

Liya clapped her hands and beamed. "I wonder if Jay would be mad if I spent that much on a dress."

"Where are you going to wear it to? I can't spend more than fifty dollars on a gown that I will literally never wear again."

"Fifty? Try higher."

"A hundred?"

She jerked a thumb up to think even higher.

"Hundreds?"

"At least."

I groaned, feeling unease roll through me. Spending that much money made my eye twitch.

"And shoes! And a purse. I'm thinking a clutch with a strap because you'd probably forget you had a purse to begin with and lose it."

"What's wrong with the shoes I have?"

"Heels. You need high heels."

"Who on this planet started this high-heel trend? And then what sadist decided high heels were classy and to be expected?"

Liya placed a reassuring hand on my arm. "Calm down, granny. It's just for a few hours. You can break them in. We won't go too high, okay? Three, four inches max."

I slouched. "I'm done for. I'm going to look like a fool, like I definitely don't belong there."

"Do you not want to go?"

"Parties aren't on my fun list, but for Daniel, I'm happy to go. Make an effort, meet his friends and colleagues, be the... girlfriend."

Liya's eyes lit up. "Is that what this is? I knew it! He's introducing you to the heart of his social crowd. So they happen to be kind of elite, and pretty sure they're rich as hell, but this is your first and very public outing. There is no going back from this. The gala is a very big deal, and you'll have to deliver."

No pressure!

Liya took my hands and gently shook me loose. "Get out of your head. Yes, this is an important event, but it isn't the biggest thing you've accomplished in your life. You graduated high school early as a top student. You bulldozed through a leading college and made the dean's list at every turn. You aced the MCAT and got into your first-choice medical school and landed your second-choice residency.

"Girl, you went into medical school thinking you'd be a family doctor and ended up with L&D and surgical assist privileges and snagged your dream job. You are kickass all the way around, up, and down. Okay? *This* is just a fun party, a chance to get dressed up and blinged out, meet some high rollers, and play yourself up. You are *Dr.* Patel, not Ms. Patel. There may be a lot of money saturating the air at the gala and lots of well-mannered people who know the difference between caviars, but you are about intelligence. Intellect outplays wealth."

Yeah. She was right. I was an accomplished, smart woman. I

had lots to offer, and Liya knew exactly how to hype a woman up. "You know just what to say!"

Even as I dressed and we headed downstairs to meet Brandy, I couldn't keep from feeling a twinge of anxiety. But, thank goodness, I now had medication to keep me level just in case. A party shouldn't set me off, right?

When Brandy pulled up in a sleek black Bentley, Liya whistled and opened the driver's-side door. Brandy shimmied out in a form-fitting black-and-white abstract-detailed dress and gave Liya a hug.

"What is *this*?" Liya asked, bending over to check out the interior. "You leveled up in the last year!"

"Oh you know, make a little money and upgrade." She smoothed a hand over the top. "All right, let's get some shopping done!"

Liya snagged the very roomy back seat as I crawled into the front passenger seat. Wow. The leather interior and car smell had me wanting a new car myself. "Luxurious" wasn't an adequate word to describe how my butt felt in this cooled-down, posh seating. And here I thought her Lexus had been exquisite.

"I'm so glad you're going to the gala, Preeti," Brandy said and then looked at Liya through the rearview mirror. "And you're going to pass out when you see all the lovelies."

Liya wriggled her butt into the back seat and sighed. "I could fall asleep back here."

"You have my brother's credit card?" Brandy glanced at me.

"Yes. But I'm going to be conscientious about the price," I replied as she wove through traffic.

"Hard to be aware of the price when there are no price tags where we're going."

"Called it!" Liya said.

"That's no way to run a store. What about liability?" I asked.

"You worry too much. Listen, Daniel doesn't give out his card to everyone, okay? If he gave that card to me, I'd do exactly as he says: shop for the gala and not pay any mind to the cost. He knows what he's saying. And he knows that I'm taking you shopping, so you can bet he knows where we're going. The gala is elite, Preeti. You must come looking the same. Elite and extra."

The first place we pulled up to had a valet who took the car from us. All the shops were in the same vicinity, and many of them were in towering buildings. My feet hurt just anticipating all the steps I was about to get in.

Lights were strewn across windows, creating a vibrant, festive ambiance. The sidewalks were wide and clean with a few cafe tables and chairs. Men walked around in nice suits and women toted designer brands. I had no idea this section of the city even existed, but I imagined this was what Hollywood felt like.

A doorman with pristine white gloves opened the door for us and Brandy took us up to the fifth floor. Even the elevators, lined with decadent gold paint and glass, looked more expensive than my car.

The first store we entered was nothing like a department store. It was spread out, far from crowded with racks and sales items and messy displays where customers had thrown whatever they'd tried on and rejected.

A delicate woman with a high bun and manicured nails greeted us, offering to take Brandy's jacket. She returned with a platter of gold-rimmed flutes, a chilled bottle of champagne, caviar on ice with a gold spoon, and thin toast points. A saleswoman at our next stop offered wine and imported cheese. Liya went straight for that platter, despite having had enough champagne that I would've been tipsy by now if I'd kept up.

The women who worked in these stores sized me up and presented me with what they thought I would like, a marked change from my usual experience of silently shoving aside clothes on every rack myself and trying on a million things only to realize that clothes sucked in general. These women were pros. Ninety percent of what they brought out fit like a glove. The fabrics were smooth, sleek, lacy, heavy, light, toned down, sparkly...everything I could ever imagine. It was like the saying that you don't know what you're missing if you've never had it. Well, I'd never realized how nice something that wasn't sweats could feel. The right fabric in the right fit for the right style was actually comfortable yet exquisite.

I didn't have a particular color in mind until we were sitting on soft white chairs at our fifth store and a sparkling red slit of fabric caught my eye.

"The red one?" the saleswoman asked, following my hypnotized gaze. "Ah. That's a splendid choice." She brought over the gown almost reverently, holding it like a sacrificial offering.

Brandy and Liya glanced at each other with a nod and Brandy conceded, "That may be the one."

I tried on the dress, which fit perfectly. I'd never worn anything so comfortable and yet so gorgeous. The corset was folded fabric that fit snugly around my waist and breasts and climbed over one shoulder. It was crimson red, the color of blood, and absolutely decadent. While the fabric around the bust was smooth and shiny, the portion that fanned out from my hips shimmered like a million tiny sewn-in diamonds. There was a slit up one leg that ended halfway up my thigh.

When I emerged from the dressing room, Liya and Brandy went dead silent. Even in midsip, they froze.

"Wow," Brandy said.

"Damn," Liya reiterated. "How do you feel?"

I shrugged and spun a half circle. "Like a princess."

"Daniel won't be able to keep his hands off you looking like that," Liya commented.

In another hour, we'd found the right shoes and clutch. Just when I thought we were almost done...

We passed an über-ritzy store, one that put the already swanky others to shame, and Brandy clapped her hands and pulled me in. The place had floor-to-ceiling glass walls around glass cases displaying thousands of glimmering diamonds. The bling from these carats was so blinding I might need my sunglasses.

"Don't tell me this is one of those parties where I have to sign over my soul to rent out diamonds for a night?" I asked.

"No," Brandy promised. "Jackson and I are thinking about a wedding and all that, so I just want to get a feel for engagement rings. Not sure what looks best on these little fatties." She held up her hand.

"Oh, hush! Your fingers are perfect."

"I know exactly what would look ethereal on those fingers," the woman behind the counter said to both of us.

"Oh, not me. Just her." I jerked my chin toward Brandy.

But the woman had already pulled out a tray of dazzling rings and I couldn't help myself. I had never thought diamonds were pretty, but these diamonds were on a whole other level. I tried on a few rings for the heck of it, admiring the sparkle and feel and glamour against the golden tones of my hand.

While Brandy tried on a hundred rings, I tried on a dozen and Liya browsed. But I knew what I liked.

"Very nice selection," the woman behind the counter commented, eyeing the ring on my finger. "Just over three carats, round-cut, flawless-clarity engagement ring cushioned by smaller quarter-carat diamonds and sapphires along a platinum band. It comes with a matching wedding band with quarter-carat diamonds along the entire band. If you buy today, we can offer a special price of twenty thousand."

I nearly choked on the complimentary champagne. "For a ring set?"

She smiled. "No. That price is just for the engagement ring."

I quickly but carefully took the ring off and placed it back on the cushioned tray.

"You like it, though?" Brandy asked, studying it as if she might go for it herself.

"It's gorgeous," I confessed.

"And it feels right? Not too big or heavy?"

"Definitely too big for work, but if I wanted a forever ring, that would be it." For a woman not considering an engagement ring, I seemed to have stumbled across the perfect one.

Chapter Twenty-Eight

Before I knew it, Daniel was all moved into his new house and he had yet to ask me to move in with him. Which was fine. We could take it slow, but one thing I knew for sure was we would be appearing at the gala as a couple. My inner college self wanted to squeal, while my guilt-ridden self slowly faded away.

Over the past few days, Daniel had met me at the hospital for daily afternoon coffee breaks while he went over the new wing with the CEO. Life finally felt like it was on track again—well, at least it would be once I told my parents.

This weekend I would tell them, when I could see them in person again. I had been avoiding their calls. They left a few voicemails, mainly saying that they wanted to see me, since I'd missed mandir, and talk about my future. I assumed they meant work, since they hadn't mentioned Yuvan. I'd texted them to let them know I was doing well but was busy, hoping to catch up as soon as possible. I knew pushing it off would make it harder, but I wanted the stress of the gala over first. A couple more days wouldn't hurt.

When Thursday night came around, Reema and Sana came over to "fix me up" while Liya watched on video call.

"Dayum." Reema whistled.

"What! Let me see! Turn the phone, Sana," Liya said.

"Oh! Sorry!" Sana turned her phone to me, as stunned as Reema, while Liya nodded appreciatively. "Now that's what's up."

I grinned at my reflection, eager for Daniel to see me, and actually excited about meeting his circle.

Reema went to work on my makeup and hair while Sana and Liya chatted and commented.

"Daniel will be taking you home tonight," Sana declared.

We gaped at her before bursting into laughter.

"Done!" Reema said. "And just a little glimmer..." She patted highlighter on my cheekbones, nose, and clavicle.

The girls oohed and ahhed as I checked my reflection. The blood-red dress shimmered with metallic strands, covering one shoulder, snug at the bust, and flowing from the waist down. My hair was subtle in long waves and actually left down. It felt weird not to have a hair tie nearby.

My makeup was on the natural side, but Reema went with red lipstick to match the dress.

"Um. Are you sure that I don't look like a clown? I've never done red lipstick before."

"You look stunning!" Reema argued.

"Don't take it off!" Liya warned.

"At least it's not nude."

"At least it's not just ChapStick," Liya added.

My phone pinged with a text. "Daniel had to get to the gala early. He's sending a car for me to meet him there."

"That's our cue! Go get 'em. Remember, those rich people at the gala are about money and prestige and blah blah blah, but you are amazing and intelligent and you're going to wow them," Reema coached.

Reema and Sana hugged me on their way out.

I stuffed my phone, credit card and cash, keys, and lipstick into this tiny clutch purse and flung the studded metallic strap over one shoulder. It wasn't even big enough for a water bottle! Forget about emergency tampons or ibuprofen or hand sanitizer.

I took the elevator and walked extra carefully to the lobby, wobbling a bit in these heels and clutching the railing the entire way. I expected an Uber, not a sleek SUV with a driver in a suit holding the door open.

"Thank you," I said to the driver. He nodded, made sure my entire dress was inside the car, and closed the door before hopping into the driver's seat.

We arrived in twenty minutes, and I'd found my calm before the driver opened my door. I thanked him again and steeled myself for whatever was to come.

The hall was grand and glittering with lights, bustling with conversation, and smelled of money. The front doors automatically slid open. The next set of doors was propped open, inviting me in with subtle sounds of clinking glasses and classical music.

I stood at the top of a majestic staircase, controlling my shaking, although it didn't help that so many people were watching me.

Everyone was so poised and elegant, dripping with expensive clothes and jewels, cultured elegance. The way they stood, chins high, full of swagger. Even in the way they held champagne flutes, they looked posh.

I searched for Brandy, but everyone blurred together. Until my sights landed on Daniel near the balcony doors. He was staring so hard he might've actually calcified into a statue, even as Jackson slapped his chest with the back of his hand. Jackson grinned up at me before being pulled away by someone.

Daniel trained his eyes on me as if no one else existed.

If there was ever such a thing as a Cinderella moment, this was it.

With a few breaths, I walked down several steps to meet him halfway up the stairs.

"Can't say you've never stopped a room dead in its tracks," Daniel commented, closing the distance but pausing two steps below me. He filled the heck out of his tuxedo.

"You look stunning," he added and kissed the back of my hand.

My cheeks heated to insurmountable levels. "Thank you. You look pretty good yourself."

His eyes stayed on my mouth and I smiled. "What?"

He scratched the back of his neck. "Just…'stunning' isn't a strong enough word. I usually see you with your nose in a book, in slacks, pajamas. Gowns suit you, too."

"I feel beautiful in this dress, to be honest."

"I've seen you at your best and your most vulnerable. In this moment, Pree? I see all of you, and you've never been more radiant."

My insides convulsed into intense, delightful knots. "So I'm like a princess?"

"A queen." He offered his elbow.

My face flushed. No one had ever called me a queen, unless queen of medical presentations counted. I took his elbow and we descended the stairs. "Does everyone stare at every new arrival?"

"Only when staring is warranted," he replied.

I forced myself to keep my posture pristine and my chin high instead of cowering, reminding myself that I was here for Daniel.

"Every inch of me just wants to take you home right this second," he whispered close to my ear.

"Well, you can't. It took a long time to squeeze into this dress."

"And it would take less than ten seconds for me to get you out of it."

"You are so full of it."

"But you'd be full of me."

"Stop that," I muttered.

He grinned. "Does that bother you?"

"Yes."

"Or does it turn you on?"

I gently slapped his chest with the back of my hand, catching sight of the one person I hoped to evade. "Your parents are watching us, you know. Your dad doesn't look too happy about me being here."

"Please excuse him and don't give him another thought. Come with me. I have something for you," he added as we escaped the perilously smooth stairs. How I managed not to slip was beyond me.

"Daniel. Knock it off."

He laughed. "It's an actual gift. It'll go perfectly with this dress, which is just…damn, Pree." He leaned back and appreciated my backside while leading me to a balcony outside. I most definitely put in a little extra strut for him, which had him biting his lower lip.

We left behind the soft noises of the gala, partially cut off by the open doors and replaced by the bustle from the city below. I relished the chilly breeze, willing my nerves to settle.

"Not that I'm complaining, but why did we come out here?"

"Fresh air. I don't want you to feel overwhelmed with the amount of people. And in case we get separated for any reason and you need to recharge, the balcony is always a quiet, nearly empty area."

"That's very thoughtful."

"How are you doing so far?"

I laughed. "I'm fine. I'm excited to meet your friends and get to know what happens at this event."

He smiled warmly. "Good. I didn't want you to feel pressured. There'll be a lot of talk about money and fundraising tonight. Please don't be intimidated."

I blew out a breath. "I'll try. This event looks much fancier than even the physician parties I've been to. Some were meant for fundraising or asking for grants, but not quite a gala. How much are these people worth, anyway?"

"At least a million each, to lowball."

"Yeah. I can handle a million. It's when we get into billionaire territory that I might get wobbly," I teased.

He smiled reassuringly, his dimples deepening. "Thank you for being here. It means a lot. To finally have you meet my colleagues. Lots of board members and charity organizers. The annual gala is meant to allocate funds to the right places, but it requires a lot of politics. Thank god it only happens once a year."

"Of course I'd be here."

Daniel pulled out a blue satin pouch from inside his jacket, presenting a glimmering drop Y necklace with a blue-jeweled cluster clip in the middle. "This is for you."

I gasped. "You shouldn't have."

"But I wanted to. Here, let me." He held up the necklace, smooth and flexible in his palm, catching all the light.

I turned from him and lifted my hair over one shoulder so he could drape the necklace around my neck. It lay cold on my skin and slid down between my breasts. He clasped it and left his hand on my shoulder, kissing the back of my neck.

I turned toward him and touched the necklace. It shimmered against the darkness of my skin. The necklace came together a couple of inches below my collarbone, clasped with the cluster of blue gems, and the rest disappeared beneath the bodice of my dress.

"I love it," I said, smiling up at him. "But this looks expensive, and feels heavy. Don't tell me this is real."

"Is it so bad if it's real?"

"Daniel..."

He chuckled. "Yeah. It's real. Real platinum, real diamonds, real sapphires."

"No."

"Yes. You can't dictate my gifts for you. I wanted to congratulate you for getting through residency as a chief resident and landing your dream job. It's an amazing achievement."

"You know I'm a total penny-pinching, keep-track-of-all-gifts-and-monetary-items type of Indian. This is too much."

He stuffed his hands into his pockets and raised his chin. "Why?"

I stuttered over my words. "N-Need I remind you of the ledger? I was taught to keep an account of every gift so I could return one of similar value. How much will my next gift to you cost?"

He laughed. "No way in hell I'm telling you."

"Daniel..."

"Pree..."

"I saw something similar to this when Brandy took me shopping, and it was well over three grand. I will end you if you spent that much."

"I guess end me, then." He shrugged like *No biggie.*

I sighed. There was no winning with Daniel when it came to gifts; we'd had the ledger argument many times in college. "Thank you for the gift."

"And before you say anything about me buying you something—"

"Oh, boy," I interjected. "Are you about to give me the learn-how-to-accept-gifts lecture?"

"No."

I tilted my head and called his bluff.

He took my hands in his and ran a thumb across the backs.

"Please accept my gifts with no weird, negative connotations. Forget the damn ledger."

I eyed him skeptically. "All this time you could've been living in a hotel and it really wouldn't have made a dent, would it?"

"No," he replied, glancing down at our interlocked fingers, "but then I wouldn't have had the excuse to be around you. And none of this would've happened."

"Why did you keep all this from me in the past?"

He took a deep breath and exhaled. I'd never seen him look so nervous. "This is all glamour on the surface and cutthroat underneath. It's stressful, and I didn't want to subject you to that, I guess. These people have been around this environment for years, decades, generations even. They know what to say, how to be coy and plot, and I couldn't throw you into this. You were untouched by all of it, and you had enough on your plate with med school."

"So you lied to protect me?"

"Partly. And partly because…other girlfriends had been aware of my family's money and either took advantage of it or freaked out. Pree, I should've never lied to you. Do you forgive me?"

"Of course."

Daniel brought my knuckles to his lips and kissed them. I released a shaky breath. I'd known from early on that Daniel's family and some of his friends were well-off, I'd just never really cared, which was why I never pried. It didn't matter if he was rich or poor. I'd grown up poor and I hated when someone judged me for it. I respected Daniel for himself, not his money.

"Ready?" he asked.

"Yes. Let's network and raise funds and have a great time."

Daniel sighed in relief, placed a hand on my lower back, and brought me inside.

But as I walked into a sea of diamonds and gold, I'd never felt so out of place.

We mingled as Daniel introduced me to so many people that I couldn't keep track. I smiled and brought my chief resident energy backed by my physician confidence, and even incited some laughs. Things seemed to go well until I spotted Alisha.

She appeared from across the room. She fit in so seamlessly with her tall, curvy body in a high-end gown, dripping from head to toe with splendid jewelry she'd presumably bought with her own money. No wonder Mr. Thompson had told me that I wasn't good enough for Daniel when there was someone like Alisha.

Chapter Twenty-Nine

"Your dad doesn't look happy," I told Daniel.

Mr. Thompson made a beeline for us, cutting through conversations, to ask Daniel, "Have you seen Alisha?"

Daniel followed my gaze and jerked his chin to the left, toward where Alisha conversed in a small group at the opposite side of the room. The air around us turned thick with tension and restrained energy.

Mr. Thompson finally looked to me. "How did you get in here? This isn't the place for someone of your status."

"*Dad*," Daniel growled.

"Well, have a drink and eat while you're here. Best money can buy. You should meet Alisha on your way out. Very highly regarded and impressive young woman. Alisha is the woman Daniel is getting engaged to."

My chest went numb.

Daniel clenched his jaw, moving between me and his father. "What are you doing?"

Mr. Thompson kept his composure. "What are you doing with her?"

Daniel looked to me. "I'm so sorry for this. Give me a moment?"

My lips twitched, the most I could manage as they walked away with heated words.

I found myself engulfed in a staggering room full of rich strangers who seemed to glance my way, their heads full of questions and assumptions about what had just transpired. This was like college parties all over again. But elite. And way more awkward. I didn't belong here with them, and their pretentious glances made sure I knew it. But I wasn't going to cower or sit in a corner.

In the near distance, Brandy drank a chilled glass of champagne. Before she had a chance to see me, Jackson said something in her ear and off they went. I followed.

They left the main ballroom and disappeared into a smaller banquet room at the end of a long, deserted hallway. I stopped myself from entering as soon as I spotted Mr. Thompson. He and his wife were in the middle of a heated argument while Brandy tried to console Daniel on the other side of the room.

The thought of them fighting because of me tore at my insides.

"That boy has lost his senses!" Mr. Thompson bellowed.

"Shh…" Mrs. Thompson hushed him. "You need to take a moment to yourself. Do *not* go at our boy the way you did years ago. I'm not losing my son again, not over this."

"Then over what? Am I the only one who has any sense left? Huh? Ruining his future for what? Some girl who has no clue. You should be more upset, Helen. Who's going to continue on with the tradition of your organization? Alisha is already a member. Her mother is a board member. She's perfect to carry it on."

"And she will. Maybe not married to Daniel, but she will."

"That girl was supposed to leave him alone after I had a talk with her. She was supposed to go her separate way so he could live his best life."

"*What?*" Daniel barked, storming across the room. "What did you say?"

"Whoa!" Brandy said, jumping toward Daniel to keep him from advancing on their father, but Daniel moved her to the side. She bit her nail and clamped down on her words.

"What did you say?" Daniel repeated. "Did you tell Preeti to stay away from me?"

Oh, no. Daniel was never supposed to find out about this. Tentacles of dread sprouted around my brain.

Mr. Thompson replied, "I sure did."

"What did you do?"

"I did what any concerned father would do. You wouldn't listen to me, so I went to Preeti and told her to stay away from you. I explained what you two being together would really mean, because, as I had suspected, she had absolutely no clue. And you need a wife who has a clue, not just about life but about *our* way of life, our business, our organizations, our families. To her, you're just a relationship. She wasn't looking past you. She wasn't looking at the future, or at your family or her family. You two were living in a moment and it was ready to shake the foundation of everything I'd set out to do for you."

"Wow." Daniel seethed. "That's low, Dad. I mean, hit-a-man-while-he's-down low."

"You had no idea? You never wondered why she broke up with you?"

"Of course Preeti wouldn't tell me that my own father was a reason for her leaving."

I swallowed hard, my hand clenching at my side. The last thing I wanted was to be the reason why Daniel stopped talking to his father. Family peace was important. He had too much riding on them hashing things out.

"She kept that to herself all these years to protect you, to keep from dividing us. And *that's* not the type of woman you want me to be with?" Daniel snapped.

"Listen here—"

"No. You listen. For once. Stop talking. Stop pushing your narrative and your selfish wants and just listen to me, your only son, the person you claim you built a life for, the child you claim you want to take over your empire. You drove away the love of my life. And no, it wasn't a fleeting relationship. It was real and pure and wonderful because Preeti is real and pure and wonderful. All these years I've been mad at her for leaving without a word, when the truth is that she couldn't tell me because she wouldn't have wanted to come between us.

"But here's the thing: I *wish to the lord* that she had told me, because I would've been able to help her realize that it was you. You're the one who drove us apart. You always have. Nothing is ever good enough for you. Nothing is ever worthy of your praise or a simple 'good job.' Nothing is ever right unless it's done exactly your way. But I'm not your sheep. I'm a grown man who's already proven myself out there on my own, and whether you want to acknowledge it or not is irrelevant. You can deny the truth, but you cannot erase the truth.

"My truth is this: I am a capable, successful man who's made a name for myself. And yes, that's partly due to you and this family, but it's also due to my own intelligence and skill and hard work that I've poured out for years. My other truth is that my love for Preeti is undying. Even when I was mad at her all these years for leaving the way she did, I never hated her. One second in her presence and there is no one else. Least of all Alisha."

Mr. Thompson's nostrils flared out as he said, "If you choose her again, if you leave now, then don't expect a third chance at becoming a partner in this company. Don't even *think* about returning to be any part of it!"

"Daddy," Brandy tried to intervene.

"Stay out of this, Brandy!" he snapped back.

"*Oh!*" She shook her head, ignited but silenced.

Daniel paced the room, his head down, muttering before he said, "Do you value love and loyalty so little? Would you easily give up Mom to get a higher footing in the world? I'd rather be poor and living with Preeti in some one-bedroom apartment and working at my own one-man firm than sell her out."

"I built this all for you!"

"I appreciate everything you've done, and I'll always love and respect you, but I have my say in who I marry. If you can't accept that, then that's too bad. And I'm heartbroken that this is what tears us apart. But I'll never regret going after Preeti."

"You need to decide, right here, right now. You want that girl, or do you want this family and this business?"

Daniel rubbed his chin, nodding. "All right. All right then."

He took Brandy to the windows and talked with her in muted tones. He handed her the black card and she hugged him. She hugged him so tight, she might've never let go, and I knew right there he'd made a devastating decision.

"Where are they?" someone said from behind me. A woman pressed a hand against her earpiece. "I'm down the back hallway. Let me know if you find Mr. Thompson first. The presentations are about to start and he has the keynote speech."

I stepped backward, away from the room as the woman walked past me and spotted them. She exclaimed, "There you are, sir! We're all ready to begin."

Tears blurred my vision as I got turned around in these stupid halls. By the time I made it back into the main ballroom, everyone had taken their seats. Their glares bored into me, as if they could tell something was wrong. I was the anomaly barely holding herself together, the spectacle of the night.

I walked toward the staircase, to the edge of the crowd, the exit in sight. I desperately needed fresh air, even as my cell phone vibrated in my clutch.

The brightly lit ballroom was lined in an iridescent sort of haze, the kind that I often saw before the onset of an anxiety attack. My body thrummed with both heat and cold as goose bumps prickled my skin. My bones ached. My ribs felt like sharp knives threatening to rupture my heart. But the worst part was yet to come. The part where my head pulsed with gnawing trepidation, pushing my tenuous control to the edge.

As I gathered the skirt of my gown to avoid tripping, I spotted Mr. Thompson taking the stage with Alisha at his side. And then there was Daniel to the left of the stage, glaring at his father, who beckoned him with an inviting wave of his hand.

Daniel's mother rubbed his back, his grandmother held his hand, and Brandy was speaking urgently with Jackson.

Now wasn't the time or the place to ask Daniel to chat. He had pressing matters at hand and he needed to finish work. But as I climbed the last of the steps, he looked up and saw me. I forced a smile and waved, holding my phone in my hand. If nothing else, maybe he would think I had a work call so he could go on with business as he needed to without worrying about me.

Outside, chilly, refreshing air cooled the perspiration on my forehead as I gulped much-needed deep breaths in the quiet.

Daniel was an adult who could make sound decisions. He'd never been impetuous. He thought things through with a level head. With his ambition and expertise and network, he would do just fine without the family business. Yet it tore me apart to know that his family ties would be severed if he chose me.

Part of me wondered if Daniel would choose his family. After all, we'd been together again for only a short while. I was a proven flight risk, and we hadn't discussed our futures. But Daniel had said it himself, that love never fails. So I had to trust in our love, too.

I checked my phone. I couldn't ignore the slew of messages, not when they came at me from everyone. Yuvan, my parents, Reema, Sana, Liya...

> **Reema**: Everyone is looking for you. Your mom is in the hospital. She knows about Daniel. Everyone does. You need to get there now.

Horrendous thoughts formed in the recesses of my mind. I couldn't scrape them out of my skull. I couldn't crawl out of my skin. I couldn't stop the onslaught of dread as it fought against my medication.

The *Alien* facehugger.

It was back.

Chapter Thirty

I'd taken a cab to the hospital, leaving a message for Daniel in hopes that my departure wouldn't interfere with the importance of to-night and what he needed to get done. I would explain to him later.

The messages had initially poured in with concern, my parents asking how I was and checking in, since I hadn't attended mandir. I'd listened to those early ones before.

Over the course of today, they'd turned into slashes of dis-appointment about my interactions with my fois, tempered with pleas regarding my decision to leave Yuvan.

To add to how pissed off our parents were, Yuvan had seen me having coffee dates with Daniel. Had he told my parents?

Damage control. I could repair this. I had to. Maybe things wouldn't be spiraling out of control had I just had the conversa-tion with my parents and been woman enough to talk to everyone with clear intentions. Not grappling in the aftermath. I'd wanted to believe that there was too much going on at once: job interviews, apartment hunting, presentations, work, gala, anxiety, depression. And maybe that was true. But the fact remained that I was making the same mistake twice by allowing excuses to hinder communication.

I cursed my gown when I crawled out of the cab and hurried through the hospital. Mummie was in room 436 in the labyrinth of a medical floor.

Someone walked out of her room, closing the door behind him, and dropped his head to read his phone.

"Yuvan?"

"Preeti," he nearly shouted and came for me, arms wide before I staggered away.

I muttered, "Oh, no."

"Right. No touching. You look…amazing," he said, sounding confused, maybe at my attire or maybe at having thrown a compliment at a time like this.

"What the hell?"

"What?"

I seethed, not at all expecting to see him, "What are you doing here?"

"Your parents are supposed to be my future in-laws. Of course we're going to be here for them."

"*Were*," I corrected, walking past him.

When I opened the door to my mom's little hospital room, I didn't expect to find Yuvan's parents, too. Or a collective gasp at my appearance. I saw it in their eyes, accusations of me running around partying and having the time of my secret life with another man while my mother suffered. Not to worry…the loathing was mutual. I hated myself for it, too.

Papa lifted his arm for me to go to him. I immediately attached myself to his side and hugged him, my hand reaching out to hold Mummie's where she lay in bed.

"What happened?" I said, kissing her forehead.

"You happened," Yuvan's mother replied from across the bed, looking pissed.

"Ma," Yuvan rebuked, but neither of his parents was having it.

"Can you excuse us?" I asked as politely as possible, but with severe annoyance.

"Don't be rude, beta," Papa said softly.

"I'm not. It's okay to ask people to leave the room. We need privacy," I calmly replied.

"We're staying," Yuvan's mother said.

"This is *my* mom. I'm asking you to give us a minute."

"You want a minute now? Who do you think has been sitting with her all evening in the hospital? Where have you been?"

"Ma, stop," Yuvan said and gently ushered his parents out, despite their arguments to stay.

I sat on Mummie's bed, my shoulders slumping and curling over her. "I'm so sorry," I sobbed.

"Beta, for what?" she asked, running her hand over my head.

"What I did. I messed everything up again. I kept it from you. Everyone else knew before I came to you." I hiccupped, remembering how, last time, I had avoided my parents instead of talking with them, instead of supporting them and allowing them to support me, instead of sticking to their side and creating a unified front. Maybe if I'd done that, then we could've withstood the storm and Mummie would've never been hospitalized. I should've been stronger before, proactive, instead of allowing anyone else to fracture us.

She sat up in bed and I adjusted her pillows, raised the top portion of her bed so she could lean back.

"I've never said this before, beta, but I'm disappointed in you."

I clenched my eyes, holding back tears, and nodded.

"I'm disappointed that you didn't tell me what you were feeling, that you had doubts about marrying Yuvan, that you broke off the relationship, that you were still in love with Daniel, that you've been *seeing* him. I'm disappointed that you didn't talk to us but avoided us. We're the last people in the world who you should feel that you can't turn to. I had to hear the truth, again, from someone else. And if they know, everyone knows."

"I'm sorry I did this to you."

"What are you doing with your life?" she asked, rubbing my head.

"I don't know. I thought I knew. Do you hate me?" I mumbled.

She *tsk*ed. "No. Never, beta, never."

A few minutes went by as I gathered myself, surprised to look up to see that Mummie was crying. Nothing broke my heart faster than seeing her suffer.

I cleared my throat. "What did the doctor say? Is it like last time I put you in the hospital?"

"*Preeti*," she said in a seldom-used commanding tone. "*You* did not hospitalize me last time or this time."

"Yes, I did. It was because of me being with Daniel."

"It was because of others. You've always done good things."

I shook my head. That was hard to believe when Mummie was sickly and pale in a hospital gown with tubes poking into her.

Yuvan knocked and popped his head in. "Your fois are on their way up."

"What? *Why* are they here?" I demanded.

"Beta, they're my sisters," Papa said.

It took everything inside me not to lose my temper. "They're conniving little witches who tormented you and Mummie. I'm not allowing them inside."

"Don't argue. It's extremely rude to prevent them from coming," Mummie said, despite all they'd done to her. "You must always respect your elders, and sometimes that means holding your tongue."

I let out a rough sigh and excused myself. I wouldn't be able to hold my tongue around them. In the hallway, I had no choice but to wait with Yuvan as his parents walked back inside, his mother giving me that sharp look.

"Your mom hates me," I muttered, although who could blame her?

"She's upset," he replied.

"You're not?"

"I am, but I'm not going to lash out."

"You're too calm."

"You just need extra time to get over Daniel, but does that mean you never will? Does that mean you should put your life on hold or end what we could have? You have to move forward, and I'll be there. What you feel for him will fade as you find happiness with me."

Did he seriously want us to work out? Did he seriously think that I could force myself to get over Daniel like it was a matter of choice?

Yuvan looked past me and I expected my fois to parade around the corner as if they gave a crap. Daniel was the last person I expected to see.

There was no ignoring or missing Daniel Thompson. Not with that tall, wide frame, that commanding posture. Definitely not in a tux.

"What are you doing here?" I asked him, his long, fast strides bringing him into my space in a matter of seconds. The tendrils of anxiety rose up behind me in a near physical, overpowering entity, growing larger and harsher.

He barely looked at Yuvan, his concern only for me. "Liya texted me. Are you all right?"

"An emergency with my mom. It's happening again," I replied, my words rotten little bites on my tongue. I avoided thinking about what his father had said, what Daniel had decided.

"Then let me be here for you. It doesn't have to be like last time," he implored, taking my hands into his.

Yuvan watched from my side in a bitter silence. Because one, it was obvious Daniel and I had been at the same fancy-shmancy party. Two, Daniel was touching me and I didn't abhor it. And three, there was obviously no comparison between the two of them. Daniel would take the cake every single time.

A small horde of relatives rounded the corner from the elevators. Clucking tongues wagged. We were hard to miss in these glimmering outfits.

Had the gala mishap and my relatives' arrival not happened, I would've been moved to tears by Daniel showing up. But the facehugger came from behind. It punctured my thoughts from the back of my skull, inciting a throbbing headache.

Realization crested on Daniel's features, maybe not of everything that was happening in that secluded, closed-off room behind me, but definitely of the thing that was perceptible only to him. The torment no one else saw. The anguish most people would never know.

He kept a soft hold on my hand. "Breathe. Don't go there. Stay with me, Preeti."

"You should leave, but she needs to be here," Yuvan told Daniel.

That wasn't what Daniel meant at all.

Daniel ignored him, never losing his calm or his concentration on me, and said, "I see it on your face. Don't let go, okay? Just...we'll discuss whatever we need to discuss, but right now? Stay focused, calm."

"Did you come to save me?" I asked.

He leaned down to meet my gaze. "I will *always* come to save you."

The fois were *tsk*ing and glaring and openly muttering about my filth, about Daniel, in front of me, directing pity at Yuvan, taking my elbow and pulling me away from Daniel, telling him that he needed to go, igniting his concern and anger, evoking my rage. All in a blur of movement.

I released his hands, my face hardening. "It's time I saved myself."

I had never seen red, but I was about to. The hallway spun and I let them drag me into the room, leaving my lifeline to sanity in the hallway. Yuvan followed and closed the door.

I spun to face the accusatory, staggering stares as my fois went into a spiel, demanding to know why Daniel was here when they should've inquired about my mom's health, or at least greeted literally anyone else.

"Sharam nathi?" Kanti Foi hissed with an aggravated hand gesture as if I couldn't get common sense into my brain.

"What's going on?" Papa asked.

"That *man* is here," she snapped, as if Daniel's presence caused her personal harm. "What is he doing here? Weren't you shamed enough when we discovered you two before? Yuvan... you cannot marry someone as wretched as my niece." She turned to his parents and pleaded, "What a mistake it would be. I kept my mouth closed to be polite, but she has a history of being with men, *American* men. She is an immoral girl, sullied by another, and still prancing around with him. The indecency."

Yuvan stepped between me and his parents, surprising us all with his next words. "We are *not* going there." Then he said to my fois, "Whatever you misunderstood is between us, not you."

"*Beta!*" his mom chastised.

"No. This is not what we're doing, not here, not right now," he responded, his voice low and even, yet irate.

"Were you with him? Dressed like this?" Jiya Foi jumped in, dismissing Yuvan. "Running around with him? While this poor boy is waiting for you? While your mother is—"

"*Don't* talk about my mother," I growled. That red lurking in my peripheral vision? It came rushing toward me, an undertow of rage and anxiety mixing into one hideous conglomerate of a monster. The facehugger was like an annoying cockroach in comparison, and this evolving anxiety monster was tearing through my medication like an alien emerging from its pod.

"Beta…" Papa scolded, but I wasn't hearing it.

"Why are you here?" I demanded, stepping around Yuvan. "I told you many times, and actually not very long ago, to stay away from my parents."

"Preeti, you should calm down," Yuvan whispered to me. "They're your elders."

I shook my head. "Mm-mm…Nope. This is where you're all wrong. We can't let crap like this slide just because they're older. Everyone has to evolve; they have to deal with their consequences."

"Preeti. You need to sit down and be quiet now," Kanti Foi said.

"No. This time, *you're* going to listen and learn and then *you* get out and don't come near my parents again."

She gasped, stunned, playing up her offended nature like a master thespian.

"You are the vilest women I've ever encountered. I used to look up to you, used to be so happy when you came around. But I was blind. You've spent your entire lives tearing down my dad, and spend your energy trying to ruin my mom. You've dragged them for so long and so far, hoping they'd be miserable, hoping people would believe your pathetic lies and turn on them. Telling every auntie and uncle that my parents were horrible people and raised a slut. Guess what? You never broke us, and you never will."

My voice rose, heated. "Take a step back and realize that *everyone* sees the monstrosity of your ugliness. *Everyone* rolls their eyes when you open your mouth. *Everyone* talks about you behind your back when you act so pious. And before you come in here and point fingers at me without knowing anything, remember that the God you worship so hard watches everything you do.

Say what you will here, but remember, one day it's going to be you and Him and you cannot manipulate or lie your way out of *that* conversation. And yes! I had a relationship with Daniel! Yes! I had sex with him! *Don't* talk about him again."

"You're defending him?" Jiya Foi pointed at me. "You bring shame to our entire family, you selfish child!"

"Because I had sex with a man I was in love with for years? For being in a healthy, loving relationship with a man who respected me and my family? With someone who treated me like a queen, better than you've ever been treated? Before you say anything, what do you think your daughter does when she goes on vacations and work trips with her fiancé?"

"Don't you dare talk ill of my daughter!" Kanti Foi yelled.

"Why? Because you can talk nonsense about me and be a hypocrite over her? Everyone knows they've been having sex since high school. I've caught her! My dad has overheard her! But guess what? We're not heartless, cruel people to slander her and tear her apart and tell everyone. My dad told you discreetly and you turned it around on him. No, what you really have an issue with is Daniel being Black."

"It's not right," she snapped. "What you do reflects on all of us."

"It's called *racism*. You are a *racist*. You are a hypocritical, defaming, racist liar. You are everything my parents are not. Are your shoulders not burdened by the amount of sins you've amassed? You come in here because you saw Daniel outside and run your petty mouths. You haven't said hello to anyone. You haven't asked my mom how she is. You didn't come here to make sure she was okay. You came here for lip service and to drag her again."

I clenched my fists so hard that my nails nearly broke skin. Red inundated my vision. My breathing was fast, hard, sharp. "You almost killed her last time. You will *not* get near her again. You won't break us, but you will get out."

Kanti Foi looked to Papa with crocodile tears streaming down her face. Yuvan and his parents stood against the wall in shock.

I didn't care if I razed every rule of etiquette to the ground, or if ashes of charred relationships floated around us. There were more important things than being polite and respectful of my elders.

This was okay.

Everything would be *okay*.

"You're going to let her talk to us like that?" Kanti Foi demanded of her younger brother.

I clasped my hands together and bowed my head to my parents, tears fighting their way to my eyes. "I'm sorry, Papa and Mummie. Please forgive me for losing my temper. But I care more for you and protecting you than about etiquette. The only thing I regret is not saying this six years ago."

"But you've said this often to my sisters since, haven't you?" Papa asked.

I swallowed hard and nodded. I'd stood up to my aunts countless times without my parents knowing. Of course, my aunts had probably complained to them, but my parents never told me, never scolded me.

The quiet and stillness in the room was thick enough to slice with a knife. Mummie gripped Papa's hand. He reached out with his other hand and took mine.

He said to his sisters, "I guess we're too meek to say such things because we want to keep the peace, despite how often you try to destroy it. But you toy with us like it's a game. I'm supposed to protect my wife and child first. I've failed at that, haven't I?"

Tears flooded down my cheeks. I never meant for him to feel bad, never implied that he hadn't protected us.

He brought me into his chest and I managed not to bawl my sore little eyes out.

"I suppose we start now," he told the fois in a hard tone. "Don't go after my wife or my daughter again. *Get out.*"

I let out a trembling breath, the tentacles of anxiety and rage retreating the tiniest bit. I hugged Papa, then marched to the door, swinging it open, my glare hot. My aunts stormed out, revolted, chins high in the air, with looks that could kill. I shoved the door after them, but the hospital rooms had door-closing mechanisms that prevented slamming. It smoothly, quietly closed.

Whatever.

My stare washed over Yuvan's parents, whose stunned expressions hadn't worn off, and landed on my mom.

"Are you all right, Mummie?" I asked, rushing to her side. "I didn't mean to upset you."

She nodded as I wiped her tears. We held each other in silence.

A minute later, the doctor knocked and entered, giving us a moment for Yuvan to take his parents out and clear the room.

The doctor spoke to my parents with a tablet in hand. "According to your records, Mrs. Patel, you're a fairly healthy woman. When we saw you six years ago, you'd had a minor heart attack from stress. This time, it was an anxiety attack. Not as serious as last time, but certainly something we need to keep on top of. I'm prescribing some medications to control the symptoms. Take this medicine to help you relax and sleep tonight."

He held up one packet of meds, then another, explaining, "This one for blood pressure, which you'll need to take regularly until your primary care physician says otherwise, and this one for anxiety to take now and tomorrow and when you feel another attack coming on. These are a few to hold you over tonight and tomorrow until you can pick up the prescriptions from your pharmacy. As always, check in with your primary care physician. We're getting discharge papers ready."

"Thank you," I told him as he nodded and walked out. "That means we can go home now," I told Mummie.

"Anxiety?" Papa asked when the doctor left. "Such an awful thing to have."

"Don't tell anyone," Mummie muttered as he helped her change.

My hands clenched and unclenched at my sides. It was time to give up the stigma. It was time to own up to our health issues and take care of ourselves, because the lord knew no one else was going to do it for us.

I squeezed her hands. "This isn't something to be embarrassed about, Mummie."

"No one must know that I have something wrong with my brain."

I shook my head. "Don't think that. It's okay. We'll make an appointment with our doctors and get the right medicine. It's better to take care of ourselves than ignore a problem because we're embarrassed or think it makes us less. Who decided these things were shameful?"

"What do you mean *our* doctors?"

I gave her a reassuring smile. "We have a lot to talk about. I'll even sit with you during a therapy session if you want…the way Daniel sat with me." Daniel being there for me had alleviated a lot of stress, and I could do that for my mom.

She furrowed her brows as realization dawned on her.

"I'll let you get dressed. I'll be right back," I told her.

"Pree? Are you all right?" Daniel asked as soon as I stepped into the hallway. His hand ran down my arm to take my fingers.

I wanted nothing more than to be held by him, but I pulled back, my brain still incredibly, irritatingly full from tonight. "You should return to the gala and get what you need done."

"You know that's *not* what's important for me right now. Don't push me away."

I bit my lip. "I need time, and I need to take care of my mom."

The movement of his throat as he swallowed, the flare of his nostrils, the look of panic in his eyes, the shifting of his feet. I'd only ever seen Daniel as strong, intelligent, a man who knew what he wanted, calculated. Right now? I'd never thought desperation was a thing he knew about.

"All right," he finally said and stepped back. "But I'm here, okay?"

"I may need time, but I'm not going to run."

Papa opened the door behind me. "Daniel?"

"Mr. Patel. Hi. I hope things are all right. How is Mrs. Patel?" Daniel asked.

"She'll be okay," Papa replied. "What are you doing here?"

"I came to check on Preeti and Mrs. Patel. Is there anything I can do?"

Papa gave me a curious look. "Would you like to see her?"

"Papa," I objected.

"I would love to," Daniel said, "but not at the expense of furthering her stress or bothering you or Preeti."

Papa said to me, "Beta. Can you get the paperwork and ask the nurse to send the prescription to the pharmacy near the house instead of the usual one at the grocery store? That way I can pick it up in a quick trip in the morning."

"Of course," I replied.

"And a wheelchair. We're almost ready to go."

"Okay." I walked toward the nurses' station and frowned at Daniel, who walked into the room with Papa.

Chapter Thirty-One

That night, I went home with my parents and settled Mummie into bed.

"Are you sure you don't want something to eat or drink?" I asked her.

She shook her head and closed her eyes. Her meds had kicked in.

"Good night. I'm going to crash in my room. Let me know if you need anything. I'm right here."

"Thank you, beta," Mummie mumbled as she fell asleep. Papa sat beside her and ran a hand over her head.

I closed their bedroom door, went to my room, and fished through my dresser for something to change into. It wasn't unusual for me to leave clothes behind or sleep over once in a while at my parents' house. My childhood bedroom and bathroom were just as I'd left them.

Pulling out an old college T-shirt and shorts, I struggled out of my gown, removed my jewelry, and laid everything reverently on the bed. It all had to go back.

I took a long, hot shower, but it reminded me of Daniel. I touched my fingertips to the smooth, cold tiles, remembering all too vividly when I had my bare back pushed against the apartment shower as Daniel devoured me with kisses.

Water pounded down on me from overhead like a million tiny knives, my skin hypersensitive and burning beneath the soaring-hot temperature. Water masked my tears, the shower drowning my sobs as anxiety reached across the expanse of my mind and took its hold.

Somehow managing to get out and dressed, I took my anti-anxiety medicine and reached out for the ibuprofen PM. I stopped myself, my eyelids heavy and puffy. No. I needed healthier ways to cope. I had to stop using these meds as a crutch, and the anxiety medication itself made me drowsy enough.

I crawled into bed, remembering way more of tonight than I wanted. I didn't want to remember anything, to think of anything. I just wanted a head full of nothing as I turned on my calming app.

My insides were on fire from the embers of disillusion, stoked to flames by grief until the searing blaze burned from the inside out. It was a crippling pain that had me bowed over until I curled into a ball and dry-heaved.

The great thing about my anxiety medication was that it actually worked. Between the meds and exhaustion, I was out in a matter of minutes. The claustrophobic thoughts and memories and pains and realities came to a halt as I fell asleep.

And I slept for a *very* long time.

※

The first thing I did in the morning was check on my parents. Then I called into work, sent Daniel and my girls a quick text to let them know how Mummie was doing, and drove to the corner pharmacy. I returned home and placed Mummie's meds on the counter, along with a few other items.

"What's all this?" Papa asked.

"You're almost out of milk. I can make some cha for you."

He gave a soft smile. Yeah. Making cha was pretty easy; even I could do it, although mine wasn't the best. Nonetheless, he always drank it and made me feel like a star chef.

"And some snacks. A lot of chocolate," I added, pulling treats out of the grocery bag and displaying them on the counter for quick access, my hands trembling until I balled them into fists.

"What's wrong, beta?" he asked as he pulled out the cha saucepan, the one with a little pour spout designed for spill-free transfers.

A startled, incredulous laugh left my lips. "What *isn't* wrong?"

"Your mummie will be okay." Papa rubbed my back and tears stung my eyes, my lips quivering before I cleared my throat and poured milk, water, loose Indian black tea, sugar, mint, and cha masala into the saucepan. I could barely see the rise of bubbles and darkening liquid from behind this veil of tears.

"What do you need to tell me?" he asked.

"It can wait." My hand shook as I placed the strainer over a porcelain cup, preparing it for the pour.

Papa turned down the gas and took my hands in his until I was forced to face him. "Life is too short to keep holding back. Is that how we raised you?"

"Um. *Yes.*"

"Oh...well, then that was our doing and things have to change. You can tell us anything. You can tell me if you don't want to stress Mummie, but we know what's on your mind."

I bit my lower lip. "I never wanted to hurt you or disappoint you."

He pressed his lips together and nodded. His eyes glistened and, dang it, now my tears fell! He pulled me into him and hugged me as I quietly bawled against him.

He said, "It wasn't an ideal situation. We always envisioned you would keep close to us and your roots. The only thing left was marrying a man of the same religion to fit into our family and community. Someone who could take the lead at mandir and know how to prepare for all the observances and raise children to one day do the same. Someone who makes you happy and takes care of you."

"Yuvan isn't that person," I mumbled. "He doesn't understand me, Papa. I tried to like him, but he gets upset because of my touch aversion, thinks I should be the perfect cook and maid, doesn't plan on helping with the household work, thinks what the fois do is dismissible, doesn't seem to care about what happened with Liya, and his mom—ugh. I can't with her, either. When they look at me, all they see are shortcomings. I'm never going to be that perfect, religious, obedient, drama-free wife and daughter-in-law."

He ran his hand down the back of my head the way he often had when I was a kid and needed comforting.

"Are you upset?" I asked.

"No. I need you to be your best, and Yuvan isn't going to help you be your best."

"I broke it off with Yuvan a couple of weeks ago and couldn't tell you. If I had, none of this with Mummie would've happened."

He pulled me into him. "This isn't your fault."

Of course it was. I pressed my forehead into his shoulder and muttered, "I still love Daniel."

He sighed into my hair. "I know. It's not hard to see. And we know why you love him."

"What do you mean?"

"Daniel is a good man, kind. Educated and able to take care of you. He loves you and treats you well. After you stopped seeing him years ago, he called us. He was worried."

I pulled back. "Really?"

Papa nodded. "What happened between you two was between you two, so I didn't tell him everything. I didn't know everything. I told him that was for you to discuss with him. You wouldn't talk to us about him. But Daniel and I had many chats, sometimes about you, sometimes about your mummie, sometimes about Harvard and architecture. I wanted to know who this man was."

I shook my head, trying to understand. "Wait. What did you tell him about Mummie? And why didn't you ever tell me about this?"

He pressed his lips tight and his gaze flitted to the counter. It was his telltale sign of regret, and it broke my heart. Not just because he'd kept this from me, even though I didn't know if it would've made a difference back then. I knew now that I hadn't been ready for all of this then. But my heart broke seeing my dad show remorse, because that meant he felt it deeply.

He replied, "I told him that Mummie was sick, but not why. He visited her at the hospital."

"What? H-how?" I stuttered. "I never saw him."

"He didn't want to use the situation to push you into a corner."

I blinked back tears, my chest aching. I remembered spending as much time with Mummie as possible when she was admitted, and then when she was sent home. I remembered stressing out over her health and then over her medical bills. I tried to take them over, to pay little by little, but Papa said they were taken care of. I looked Papa in the eye and asked, "Did Daniel pay for Mummie's hospital visit? Is that why the balance was suddenly zero?"

"It was an anonymous donation, but my guess is that yes, Daniel paid."

Tears streamed down my face and Papa gently wiped them away, pulling me back into his chest. "Shh. Don't cry."

"All I had to do was talk to him, to talk to you."

He didn't respond, which was an affirmative answer in itself.

"I keep messing up."

"We all make mistakes. Including myself. I didn't speak up, either, at the time."

"I'm sorry that I can't be the perfect daughter."

"Never apologize for being who you are, huh?" He pulled me back as I wiped my cheeks. "You are the perfect daughter because you are you."

✳

"Do you want to come out and talk to Yuvan and his parents?" Papa asked later that day, closing my bedroom door behind me.

"Not particularly. I just want them to go away so I can take care of Mummie," I replied, folding laundry. I had to clean the house, go grocery shopping, make dinner...

"You have to speak with them soon. Yuvan, well, he wants to keep the engagement."

Eh? I made a skeptical face.

Papa sat beside me on the bed.

"Because he doesn't listen," I mumbled.

Even though my shirt was big and my sweatpants loose, the clothes felt too tight.

My mind was full. Cramped, really. My brain throbbed against the hardness of my skull with each pounding, inundating thought.

Papa said in a stern voice, "You have to move forward."

"What?"

He released a long-pent-up breath. The nervous energy between us thickened, shimmied into a tangible existence. "I want you to think about yourself and what you want, what you need.

No parent wants to sit around and watch their child shrivel from sadness. We want the best for you and that is all we've ever desired. We want you to have an easy, stress-free, happy life where you want for nothing and are filled with joy. If you're happy, then so are we." Papa watched me, an expression full of longing and understanding and something that I recognized as pain because I was in pain, too. "Do you want me to tell you to suck it up and do the right thing?"

I froze.

"Because that's what I'm telling you to do. The right thing is being with the one who you love and who loves you and makes you better, happy, fulfilled."

"Do-do you mean be with Daniel?"

He replied in a soothing voice, "Yes. Because I'm your father. I know when my daughter is sad, when she isn't herself, when she's having struggles." He watched me carefully. "I know when her heart's breaking. And her heart has been breaking since she left her only true love."

Tears stung my eyes as I cursed them. *Don't fall. Don't cry.*

He touched my hand, which sat shaking on my lap. "I know my daughter. I might not have carried you in my belly, but I lulled you to sleep at night, I cradled you when you were sick, I held you when you fell, I wiped your tears. I know the sound, the look of pain in you. And it has not gone away since you left him. *Six years*, Preeti. Six years you denied yourself Daniel and suffered, and for six years we let you. What do you want?"

"Daniel." I wanted to be with Daniel, to love him forever, to marry him, to have my family whole. I bit the inside of my cheek to keep from bawling.

"What kind of a father am I to let you hurt, and for so long?"

Oh, there went the tears down my cheeks. "Papa..."

There was a deafening quiet consuming us, the kind that

thrummed and rang deep in my ears. My mind went blank and my entire being dove into keeping my emotions together.

I stared at our hands. They turned into ambiguous blobs of color as tears flooded my cheeks. I froze into place to keep from convulsing and bawling. But when Papa wrapped an arm around me and drew my shoulder into him, the ugly-crying started.

"Shh, shh," he cooed.

I clenched my fists in my lap and struggled to grasp on to some sort of control. I hated crying. I really did. There was no sense of authority over my own body. While pain could last for years, crying was swift, albeit brutal. The passage of time warped. Maybe I'd cried for seconds or minutes or hours. All I knew was that there was no one other than me and my parents in this moment. The rest of the world didn't exist. Maybe that was why crying felt as wonderful as it was miserable.

When my sobs subsided, when my heaving stopped, when I managed to move, I pulled away and desperately wiped my tears with the tissue Papa handed me.

With a final dab below my tender eyes, I sucked in a shaking breath and finally looked at Papa. His eyes glistened and a light shade of pink crossed his cheeks. It pained me to see him like this, to see him as anything but joyful.

"What do you want to do about the guests in our living room?" he asked.

I shook off the trepidation and emotions. "I'm going to tell them what they already know but apparently won't accept."

"That's my Preeti. But, as your Papa, I'll speak to Yuvan and his parents."

"No. Thank you, but this is my mess, isn't it?"

"I will never leave you to suffer or stand alone, beta."

I nodded.

He dragged in a long breath before releasing it. "Besides, it's my duty as the parent to let Yuvan and his parents know. You don't face them by yourself."

I opened my mouth to protest, but he went on, "And with us here, they won't turn their anger toward you, or lash out at you. They'll come for us."

I swallowed hard. "That's exactly what I don't want to happen. You don't deserve for anyone to be mad at you."

He patted my head. It was his sense of duty, to deflect harm from me by absorbing it himself.

Mummie knocked and entered the room. "Challo, beta. Company is waiting."

Words tumbled over one another on my tongue, fighting to form a coherent sentence. I prepared to break the news to her. But with Papa's presence behind me, I knew that no storm could take me down, and that included the torrential downpour of my poor mother's distraught dreams.

My hands shook like unstable rocks in an earthquake, with uncertainty, not knowing if the ground would open up and swallow me whole or if this was just a minor tremor.

"Mummie. I have to tell you something, something that I should've told you weeks ago," I began.

She blinked a few times, her expression warm. "It's okay," she said before I could explain. "I know. We discussed this morning after you made cha," she clarified, her eyes shimmering.

"Are you upset?" I gulped.

She gave a slight shake of her head.

"Are you sure?"

She took both of my hands into hers and squeezed. "I only want what's best for you."

I clenched my eyes for a second, then nodded. "Are you disappointed in me?"

Mummie slid her hand down the side of my head, caressing my

hair with that motherly, tender affection, and kissed my forehead. We were both blinking away tears as she said, "You, my beta, will never be a disappointment. How can you be? Look at you." She hiccupped on those last words.

"Mummie..." I hugged her tight and never wanted to let go.

Chapter Thirty-Two

Yuvan and his parents stood when we entered the living room. Even though we all knew this was coming, it wasn't any less nerve-racking.

"Let them talk. We'll discuss in our room. Come," Papa said to Yuvan's parents. They followed my dad, leaving us in silence.

I swallowed hard, my throat as raw as my emotions. "I appreciate you intervening at the hospital with your mom, but what are you doing here?" I asked Yuvan.

"Trying to salvage us," he replied.

"I don't know any part of what I've said or done that makes you think that's possible. Not that it matters, but you had weeks to make a real effort. Why now?"

"Oh, boy," he interjected, looking skyward and running a hand over his gelled hair. "No. Don't do this."

"It's not fair to you if we get married. You know this isn't what you want in a fiancée or wife. You're grasping at straws."

"Hell," he muttered. "Because of *him*?"

"Because of me. I don't want us to be together, and it wouldn't work well even if I did. I'm in love with Daniel. I always have been and always will be, no matter how far I am from him, no matter how much time has elapsed."

"Preeti, you're ruining your life."

"Now you're the one who needs to stop," I said indignantly.

He blew out a harsh breath. "Life with me would be simple, easy. We already have the same community, our families are friends, there's nothing to adjust to. Our path would be set. How are your parents going to handle you walking away?"

"Oh. See? You're forgetting the part where we're incompatible."

His face hardened. "You're throwing everything away for *him*!"

"You need to lower your voice or get out."

My heart ached and my stomach seemed to literally plummet. All of my adrenaline began sinking. My head felt light and buzzy. I grasped the back of the chair beside me. Yuvan immediately came to me, his hand touching my back, and I froze.

"I'm sorry," he said slowly and pulled back. There was such a depth of wretchedness and despair in his tone and on his face. His pain was almost tangible. I *felt* it.

I stood up, fighting the light-headedness. "I'm okay."

Behind me, arguing escalated in my parents' bedroom, and I wasn't about to have that. "They can't be here or ever do that," I growled, taking a step toward my parents' room.

"Let me at least do this," Yuvan said. "I'll speak to them and let your mom rest."

He quickly walked into the room and removed a pair of irate parents. "Calm down, *please*. We can't worry Preeti's mom right now."

His mother said to me, "Beta, don't make this mistake. We forgive you for what happened."

My eyebrows shot up. Yuvan shook his head and lifted an apologetic hand between us.

Yuvan's father spoke to Papa. "How can you let your daughter make this mistake? You're her father. You must reason with her. Make her understand. She is a child acting like a child."

"I'm right here," I piped up. "We don't work."

And here came the backlash I'd expected. His father said, "You were defiled by another man and yet we still supported Yuvan because he wanted you. We supported you both, despite what people said about you."

"Papa," Yuvan intervened.

But his father went on, "This is an embarrassment! I told you not to pursue her! I told you she would break your heart and you said, 'No, Papa. Preeti is a good woman.' That we shouldn't let our mistakes define us. Well, look at this situation now."

"*Hey!*" I spoke up. "You do not get to undermine me or speak about me like that. I am not some piece of property that you can dictate my worth based solely on your opinion. You will not demean me as a person. And you will not speak to my parents in anger. You have something to say, you say it to me."

Everyone gawked in my direction. I might've finally found my voice, and it came out booming.

"This was never going to work. We all know this. Right now, I need you all to leave and let my mom rest. When we see each other again, you're going to be civil and kind. You can go now."

I glanced at my parents on instinct to silently apologize, but instead they offered supportive, encouraging bows of the head. For once, I wasn't questioning how my actions reflected on my parents but saw them handing me the reins. It was both loving and empowering, and I absolutely believed we were coming out of this stronger than ever.

※

Later that night, the girls came over with their parents and Jay and Rohan. Liya and Reema's moms unpacked home-cooked meals into the fridge. When the moms herded into Mummie's room to look after her and the guys took to filling the living room, I took the girls to my room and unloaded what had happened earlier today.

"*Damn*, Preeti. You did it like that?" Liya asked, leaning against the dresser.

"I had to channel my inner Liya," I told her.

Sana entered my room with two large pizzas, and we all sat in a semi-circle on the floor. She handed me a paper plate first. "I was going to get tacos, but I know how mad you get about soggy food."

I blinked at her and then laughed for the first time since yesterday afternoon. "I guess I do get really mad at soggy tortillas, don't I?"

"Like She-Hulk. Remember the first time we all ordered fried avocado tacos from Torchy's and by the time they delivered, your tortilla was soggy and fell apart and you just about threw the table over and refused to ever order tacos again that you couldn't eat right away?"

"I'm embarrassed that happened." I pulled up a cheesy slice of veggie pizza on thin crust.

"Where's the hot sauce and ranch?" Liya asked, digging around the second bag.

"Thanks for driving all the way down. You didn't have to," I told Liya.

"Like hell I didn't have to. I moved to Dallas. I didn't abandon my friends."

"Did you drive this morning?"

"I drove last night. Stayed with Jay."

"Your parents told my parents not to come to the hospital until they knew if your mom had to stay," Reema explained. "I told Liya not to go until we had the green light. Which was the only reason I wasn't there last night."

"Don't worry," I promised. "It was crowded anyway."

"Would've liked to have been there to buffer the situation."

"Maybe you would've snapped, too," Sana told her around a bite. "I think I would have."

"Really? Sweet, innocent Sana losing her shit?" Liya asked.

"I lost it over Mukesh and your dad, and I'd lose it over Preeti, too," she said firmly.

Liya smiled and nudged Sana's shoulder with hers. "My baby is growing up."

"Thanks for coming over, y'all." I yawned.

Liya dunked a slice of pizza into a tub of mixed sauces. "We need to get you out of sweats."

"Nope. Do you think the guys want to eat?"

"Eh." Reema shrugged. "They're adults. They can get food if they want. Your parents, however, will have enough food to last for days. My mom will be back tomorrow with idli sambar."

Ah. The fluffiest of comfort foods.

My phone screen lit up. I didn't bother checking who it was. Everyone I needed around me was already here. And Daniel? Well, things with him felt weird, off-kilter. I needed to figure out how to tell him about overhearing the conversation at the gala, ask him what his decision was, and if there was a future for us. First, I needed time to calm down for myself.

The girls spent the night, and as we tucked ourselves in, Liya put her phone on speaker. "You need to listen to this. Don't argue."

"Eh?" My head hit the pillow, my eyes fluttering closed as a moment went by in silence.

Then the soft strumming chords of a guitar came on. The song. My song.

Tears slipped down my cheeks as Daniel wordlessly played on speakerphone.

✳

Early the next morning, I stepped over all the sleeping bodies in my room and swung open the door, heading to the bathroom when I noticed someone sitting in the living room. I swerved back and gasped. "What are you doing here?"

Daniel offered a comforting smile from the couch.

"Ah, beta. You're awake," Papa said, handing Daniel a cup of cha.

"Thank you, sir," Daniel said as he took the drink and placed it beside a plate of Parle-G biscuits and mathiya snacks.

"What in the world..." I muttered.

He jumped to his feet and crossed the room to meet me in the hallway. "I came to check on you and your mom."

"So you just came to my parents' house?"

"You weren't answering your phone or replying to texts."

"I invited him," Papa said. "You two have things to discuss."

I crossed my arms and eyed Papa, who sat back in his recliner like this was a show for him to watch. I told Daniel, "My mom is better. Thank you, and thank you for last night, for playing music, for being patient as I sort through things."

He ran a hand down my arm and took my hand into his. "Are you all right?"

"I'm getting there. I'm exhausted."

He caressed my cheek with his free hand. "Do you want to talk?"

"I have a lot to say, things to ask. I just...my head is pounding and groggy, and I feel really sick and gross. Can we please promise to talk later?" In fact, nausea rolled through my stomach. Devouring copious amounts of junk food last night hadn't been the best idea.

He pressed his lips together, a flash of disappointment and worry crossing his face. "Of course. I'm not going anywhere." He met my eyes. "Are you?"

I squeezed his hand. "No."

✳

"You've been moping for two days," Reema said that evening. She kept checking her phone. In fact, all the girls kept checking their phones. Mine was under a pillow somewhere.

"It's Saturday night and all of your friends are here. Beta, get out of the house," Mummie ordered. She looked refreshed and relaxed and not at all worried.

"I was thinking I'd move back in and help take care of you."

For the first time ever, she said, "Don't move back home. I'm okay."

Papa poked his head out from around the corner. "You want to move back in?" Hearts practically sparkled in his eyes.

"No. We're not moving backward," Mummie said. "Challo." She took my hand and led me to my room, plucked my fanciest dress out of the closet, and tossed it onto the bed.

"What's this?"

"Put it on," she demanded.

"Why?"

"Life is short. We're not going to feel bad the entire time. Put on the lengha, feel good about yourself, be extravagant or ridiculous, and move on. Then we get back to living."

"Is this some psychology thing you heard about from the auntie squad?"

"Yes. Works very well. Let's go. We'll do it, too."

I groaned but went along with this…whatever this was. In half an hour, the girls had left and my parents and I were all dressed in our Indian best, staring at our reflections in the dresser mirror in some weird therapy exercise.

Mummie had a shimmering pink-and-green sari wrapped around her. Papa wore a matching sherwani. And I was decked out in the pink-and-pistachio lengha that I'd worn to Reema's reception.

"I feel ridiculous."

Mummie squeezed my shoulder. "But you look radiant. Sometimes we need to shower, dress up nice, and look our best to feel better on the inside."

"What now?" I touched the beadwork of tiny pearls against the light pink fabric of my skirt.

"Go, beta," she said simply and kissed my forehead.

"Huh? Go where?"

"Don't argue with your sick mother." She held up my phone, placed it on the dresser, and left me alone in my room.

Daniel: Can we chat? I won't bother you at your parents' house. Come to my place tonight?

Chapter Thirty-Three

I couldn't believe my parents had kicked me out of the house. They didn't even let me change back into sweats. But they were right. I had to talk to Daniel.

First, courage. And tacos. Because, as I stared at my reflection, at my beautiful lengha contrasting with the horrendous dark circles under my eyes and frizzy hair, I knew that I couldn't lose him again. We were headed for a long night, and I needed energy.

Drive-through tacos were hands down the best comfort food. It was impossible not to inhale two crispy tacos, a small queso blanco with warm tortilla chips, and a medium Big Red. I pushed my seat back as far as it would go and enjoyed how safe and normal Tex-Mex made me feel. I sipped my soda, contemplating my next move as people walked in and out of the restaurant.

As the last crunch of taco echoed through the car, I reminisced about all the things Daniel and I had been through. He'd always been the one, the only one. From that first touch, my heart knew it couldn't live without him.

His dad had given him an ultimatum, and that was his decision. But as far as mine? I couldn't be that coward anymore, that little submissive girl who shied away from conflict and drama. It had already destroyed me before. It wasn't going to destroy me again. His dad had once told me that living for ourselves was selfish, but I'd learned the hard way that trying to live for everyone else was destructive.

I dragged in a deep, sobering, and shaky breath and finally looked at my phone again.

Time to woman up and get my man.

✳

It was dark by the time I reached Daniel's place. Ugh. All the Tex-Mex in the world wasn't going to ease my nerves. All the Big Red in Texas wasn't going to calm my jitters. I knew exactly what had to be said, and I wasn't letting Daniel get away without a fight. If he wanted me *and* his family business, we'd find a way.

I blew out a breath.

The porch lights were on and the living room lights flickered. I gathered my thoughts, and then gathered my skirt in my hand as Daniel jogged out to help me from the car. He was dressed awfully nice in a suit. Maybe he'd been at another fundraiser.

"Thanks," I mumbled, my hands already trembling.

"Wow. You look amazing."

"My parents made me get out of sweats."

His hands landed on my hips. He rubbed the exposed skin at my sides between the cropped top and the flowing skirt. I stepped away.

"Wait," he said, pulling me back into him. "I'm not letting you go that easily."

My words spilled out, otherwise they would never come. "Your dad hates me. I know because he told me to leave you years ago and he feels the same now. He said that I wouldn't fit into your elite world, and maybe he was right. At least back then. I don't know your world, but if you want me in it, I'll be the best gala girlfriend anyone has ever seen. If you want me organizing events, I can do that, too. If you want me to get into politics and networking, well, I'm not great in that area, but I can act like I am. And I don't mean changing myself to fit your lifestyle, but I'm more than prepared to be in your world because, no offense, if I can save lives when everyone is yelling and panicking and blood and guts and organs are spilling out, then I can handle some rich people. I don't want you or your parents to think I'm deficient because our worlds are different."

"Where's this coming from?" he asked.

"I was terrified that your dad was right six years ago when he told me that I was holding you back. I don't think I'm holding you back now."

He shook his head. "Of course not. We support each other, not restrict each other."

I clutched his shirt at his sides, fidgeting with the fabric in my fists, desperate to have him near and never let go. "I overheard you and your dad arguing at the gala. He wanted you to choose between me and your empire."

"Oh, shit. I'm sorry you heard that. You know my dad is bullheaded, even though that doesn't diminish any hurt he caused you. But we have to be better than the people who try to tear us apart. We have to speak our minds and work around it. We can't allow them to manipulate us. We have to be a united front."

"I'd hate to be the reason that you and your parents drift apart."

He cupped my face. "You wouldn't be the reason. Dad would be. Do you get that?"

I nodded.

He leaned his head back for a second. "My answer has always been *you*. It was you six years ago and it's you now."

My lips quivered.

"Hey. Hey. What's all this?" he asked, brushing my tears aside.

"I'm happy to hear you say that."

He pulled me against his chest. "Did you think I wouldn't?"

"I was ready to fight for you."

He chuckled and kissed my temple. "You always had me, Pree."

"You're jobless now?"

He muttered into my hair, "I'd already made plans to start my own firm. That day you gave me advice on asking Dad to let me lead a separate division? It didn't go over well. And that's when I knew that things would never change. I made diverging plans. I spent a lot of money investing in real estate and the stock market after grad school, and the risk paid off. I have the funds to start my own firm with my own money."

I clutched the back of his shirt.

"My mom and grandparents and Brandy are on my side. I don't know what's going to happen with my dad. But I do know that my grandparents and sister adore you. That I love you more than anyone I've ever loved."

"Don't let your grandparents hear you say that," I muttered against his chest.

He rubbed my arms and then said, "Let's get inside and talk."

"I'd like that."

He gently took my wrist and led me inside. I slipped off my sandals in the foyer and followed him to the living room with the vaulted ceiling and romantic arched windows.

The house was dimly lit by candles, a dozen large and small colorful flames casting shadows across the elegant simplicity of the black-and-white décor. It wasn't until now that it fully hit me. My life was finally whole again. I had Daniel and my parents. I had my dream job, and Daniel had built our dream house. My heart couldn't be any fuller. I couldn't want anything more, except a hundred lifetimes with Daniel.

"Were you expecting a romantic night, or are you a fan of candles now?" I teased.

He chuckled. "Funny. I was trying to set a mood for us to get some calm going."

"Because you anticipated some fighting?"

He nodded. "I talked to your dad a bit at the hospital. He told me about what went down between you and your aunts. He asked me to come over to his house and we had a long talk."

Daniel picked up a remote control and pointed it at the blinds covering the floor-to-ceiling glass that made up the entirety of the back wall. The blinds hummed quietly and stretched open.

"Wait," I said, turning to him, away from the windows. "Before you tell me what you guys discussed, I need to say something."

"What is it, Pree?" he asked gently, his gaze flitting to the windows and then back to me as the hum of the motorized blinds stopped.

I swallowed. "I made mistakes, but I learned from them. And I will never hurt you again, will never repeat my mistakes. I've loved you for so long that I can't imagine not loving you. It's impossible. Not only that; my parents like you. They respect you and admire you."

He grinned. "I already know. I mean, I *am* me."

I laughed and then paused, biting my lip. "I don't want to lose any more time with you."

"I don't, either."

I took both of his hands in mine and looked down at them. "I used to be scared and nervous in medical school and residency about trying new things, knowing that lives changed in my hands. And the only way I could get over that was to dive in. That helped me to take control. That helped me to take the lead and be confident and sound and assured that what I was doing was the best course of action. I was scared of being chief resident, too, but I dove in, and all these things made me stronger."

I paused again and searched his dark brown eyes, which twinkled with the reflections of the backyard lights. "So I'm diving into this moment with my all."

He narrowed his eyes as a smile crept across his face. "What are you saying?"

"Daniel?" My heart was spasming and my hands were getting clammy, but I kept my voice composed.

"Yes?"

"Do you really, truly forgive me?"

"I do. You know I do," he replied in a guttural voice, peering down at me with the moon and stars sparkling in those chestnut eyes.

"Daniel?"

He closed the small expanse between us and leaned into my ear. "Yes?" he whispered before pulling back.

My breath came out in short, fast bursts. "Will you marry me?"

His eyes went wide and I didn't think I'd ever heard him stutter before. "Are—are you proposing?"

I gasped for air. "You want me to get on one knee? I'll romance the crap out of you, Daniel."

He laughed, grinning so hard his cheeks had to hurt. He swept me into a hug and cast a hundred gentle kisses all over my face.

"Is that a yesh?" I asked, smooshed against him.

"Yes. Of course! Nothing would make me happier than to be Mr. Dr. Patel," he said in that low, sultry voice that made his chest rumble.

I laughed. "The name suits you."

"But you have an extraordinary way of ruining surprises," he added.

"What surprise is that?"

"This," he whispered in my ear, his hands on my hips as he turned me around.

I gasped. The bright patio lights and strings upon strings of large fairy lights created a bright canopy around pillars of pink and white peony and rose bouquets.

My breath hitched at some very familiar and smiling faces beneath that canopy. Brandy and Jackson, Daniel's grandparents, Reema and Rohan, Liya and Jay, Sana, and in front of them all, my parents. Everyone was dressed to the nines, with Mummie and Papa still wearing their Indian best.

Daniel took my hand and walked to the opened doors. "It's pretty standard across most cultures to ask a woman's father before proposing. I wanted your parents to be a part of this, and I thought you'd want them to be as well."

"*What?*" I pushed out.

"I'd been thinking about this since grad school. I didn't take my chance then. And when I got into the fight with my parents at the gala, I asked Brandy to help me make this happen, because I wasn't going to let this chance fall through the cracks again. No one can put together an elegant event faster than my little sister. But you beat me to the question."

My breath caught in my throat as he walked around me.

Daniel got down on one knee, between me and our loved ones. He looked up at me with a faithful twinkle in his eyes as the lights glimmered all around like some magical fairy tale. Behind our friends and family, beneath the canopy of fairy lights, stretched a long table set with floral arrangements and plates and flutes on a shimmering gold tablecloth.

Daniel took my hand as Liya, Reema, Sana, and Brandy whipped out their phones to take pictures and videos. And my dad. He was probably WhatsApping this entire thing.

"Oh my god," I whispered. Even though we had technically already been engaged for all of three minutes, I somehow felt more nervous now than I had been a moment ago asking him for his hand. I looked a hot mess. My eyes were swollen, my hair barely combed, my outfit stained with salsa.

I smiled down at Daniel as he took his turn to speak. "I knew that you were someone extraordinary and special and imperfectly perfect for me when I pulled you out of that party in college. I'd never met someone who was so incredibly brilliant and wonderful. Someone who makes my heart pound with just one thought. Someone who makes everything feel better with just one touch. Someone who understands and accepts me for me and not what the business insiders or elite social circuit say.

"I'd lived years before you and things were fine. But then I met you and every facet of the world opened up and came to life. So, when we went through a time without each other, part of me died, stayed dead until I saw you again." His eyes glistened, and crap if I wasn't about to cry in front of everyone.

"You are the breath that I need to live. You are the blood in my veins. The glimmer of radiance that my day so desperately needs. I built this house for you, for us, for our future. There is no living here without you."

He held up a red-and-gold box. "This is my eternal devotion to you, a promise made in front of you, your parents, my family, and our friends that I will always love you and cherish you and take care of you. I will always be here to protect you and save you, even when you're saving yourself. Your parents call you their princess. With their blessing, you'd be my queen."

He flipped open the box and I almost passed out upon seeing a very familiar ring. "Oh my god! Daniel..."

He grinned sheepishly as I shot a look to Brandy and Liya, who each gave me a thumbs-up. Oh! Those plotting women!

Daniel pulled out a platinum ring with a large diamond and smaller sapphires down the sides, which perfectly matched the drop Y necklace he'd given me at the gala.

"Dr. Patel…"

I laughed. "Oh my lord."

"Will you do me the exceptional honor of marrying me?"

I could barely breathe, could barely string together a coherent sentence. I glanced beyond him at my parents, the lights of my life. In the ethereal glow, they beamed with happiness and approval and nodded with joy as Mummie wiped her tears.

"Yes! Oh my lord, yes!" I exclaimed.

He slipped the ring onto my finger.

Everyone erupted into a cacophony of applause and cheers as Daniel sprang up, picked me up off my feet in a giant embrace, and spun me. He laughed against my neck as everyone rushed us.

When my parents came to congratulate us, Mummie held an aarti tray for a shortened version of an engagement ceremony/blessing. And that was when I lost it. I hugged her so tight and wept into her rose-scented hair.

We cried for a good couple of minutes as Papa patted my head, his own eyes glistening. Then Grandma and Grandpa Thompson took their turns, their laughter like music fluttering through the air. Then the girls came over, screaming and ambushing me with unadulterated joy while the guys congratulated us both. My heart was full, brimming. I had everyone I needed right here.

After an exciting dinner complete with decadent desserts and drinks, Daniel and I sat on the top steps of the back patio, my head against his shoulder, our fingers intertwined as we watched everyone eat and drink and fill the night with laughter at the table before us. My parents chatted and laughed up a storm with Daniel's grandparents as if they were already one family.

Daniel kissed my head. "What are you thinking?"

"I'm completely in love with this moment. But don't forget that I proposed first."

He chuckled. "You're so modern."

"Is this the ring from the gala shopping trip with Brandy? When she told me to try on rings while I was there because she wanted to give Jackson an idea for her engagement ring?"

"Yep."

"Think you're slick, huh?"

"Yep."

I bit my lip. "I wish that I hadn't wasted so many years without you."

"We don't live in the past, Pree."

I stood and pulled him up with me. I draped my arms over his shoulders and moved in a side-to-side sway. Soft music played through the speakers. The breeze tossed petals through the air; the candle flames flickered; the canopy of strung lights shimmered overhead.

"Huh," he said.

"What?"

He brushed my wayward hair aside. "Just thinking that you're glowing like an angel, hair flowing, clothes glimmering. You're absolutely the most beautiful woman in existence. I would trade all the riches in the world for you. We made mistakes, and we fought through them. But now? We chose *right*."

Acknowledgments

This book was hard, y'all. It took a year to formulate. It took months to write. It took another month to completely rewrite because I might've had a meltdown about some aspects of the story. This book drained me and revived me and it was the wildest ride, one that I never anticipated. Through it all, it took a team to see it come to life.

My husband, who supported my decisions with unrelenting logic and understanding, was the calm I needed. He kept me from drowning. Stop loving me so hard (just kidding, don't ever stop!). My corner fighter of an agent, Katelyn, who essentially said, "Tag me in, I got this," is irreplaceable. You're the solid, unbreakable foundation beneath my feet. Kind and understanding at all times, ferocious when the need arises, and woke AF. I mean…dang, Katelyn. How did I ever deserve you? <insert ugly-crying here>

My 2020 PoC Debut group, who listened to my ever-flowing worries, thank you for offering wise words and being there because y'all just GET IT. Thank you to my small but fierce group of writer friends for creating a fortress of solitude to celebrate and commiserate.

Where would I be without my WhatsApp Wifey? We may live half a world apart, but it's been an honor sharing the highs and lows. You get all the donuts!

Thank you to my editor, Madeleine, who may not have expected me but definitely poured sweat and tears and maybe even blood into this story. Thank you for listening and understanding and supporting Preeti and Daniel's story and providing essential insight. Plus, comments that had me LOLing so hard that my dogs were concerned for me.

Thank you to the entire Forever team for taking a chance with Preeti and Daniel.

Endless, countless thanks to all of the readers out there. You have inspired me, raised me up, and brought me to tears with your love and your want for more of my stories. I hope that you've enjoyed!

READING GROUP GUIDE

QUESTIONS FOR READERS

1. The opening pages of *First Love, Take Two* begin with Preeti at work and quickly reveal several issues she has to juggle at once. What are these issues and what sort of impact do they have on Preeti throughout the book? Discuss how these areas build on one another and whether you've found yourself in a similar situation.

2. Preeti had several reasons for leaving Daniel. What are they and were they valid? Why or why not? Were the reasons or consequences amplified by her age at the time? Discuss what you might've done if you were Preeti.

3. Daniel has his own burdens. What are they and how deeply do they affect him?

4. There's obviously tension and attraction between Preeti and Daniel from the start, which only intensify. Why do you think Preeti fights them for so long? Why is there such a slow burn?

5. Why does Preeti stall in telling her parents the truth about Yuvan and Daniel? Is her delay understandable?

6. Why does it take Preeti so long to seek medical help for anxiety and depression? Discuss the dissonance between reality and perceptions of and social stigma around mental health. Do you think Preeti should've sought treatment earlier? How would you react in her shoes?

7. What role does racism and anti-Blackness play in the story? Discuss various ways the characters could've responded to racist tactics and the possible outcomes. Have you faced similar issues or seen them? If so, how did you respond?

8. Family, friends, and community play an integral role for both Preeti and Daniel. Discuss the importance and effects each group has on them as individuals and as a couple. Do you find these areas affect you as a person, couple, or family as well? If so, how?

9. There are toxic people close to both Preeti and Daniel. Who are they and how do they impact Preeti and Daniel? Discuss how we can or can't avoid toxicity in our own lives.

10. On both sides, a sense of duty clashes with the pursuit of happiness. What are these expectations and how have they shaped Preeti and Daniel as individuals and as a couple? Have you faced similar decisions?

11. Consider how much you've grown as a person in the past five, ten, fifteen, or more years. What type of growth have you seen in Preeti and Daniel from the time they first dated to the conclusion of their story? Which qualities do you hope they continue developing?

12. Yuvan gave Preeti space when she asked for it. Do you believe Yuvan acted appropriately, or should there have been more urgency in his actions? Discuss what you would've expected his response to be and whether that would have made an impact on the ending.

13. How docs the Houston setting play a role in the story?

14. Food is prominently displayed throughout the story. How is this meaningful?

15. There's an ensemble of colorful, passionate characters in the story. Who is your favorite character and why? Which character do you most relate to and why?

Q & A WITH
SAJNI PATEL

Q: In a book that's supposed to be about romance, why did you bring up racism?

A: Racism is reality. It's in every culture and society and country. It impacts decisions, creates hostility, and brings out the absolute worst in people. Several people in Preeti's community, particularly her aunts, express very common beliefs that erupted during colonialism that white is superior, and black, whether Black folks or Indians with darker skin, is to be abhorred. It's mind-boggling that anyone can think this way. What does skin color have to do with anything? And how can the Indian community, knowing we'd once been enslaved and colonized and hated for our skin color, knowing that we fought through such a mental assault, use it against others?

The book is set in Texas and in the United States, particularly in the South, racism is rampant. It is a deep-seated weapon choking out acceptance and basic humanity.

Racism needed to be addressed in this story. Even the slightest hint of racism should be snuffed out, reevaluated, and replaced with an ever-evolving retraining of what many of us have been taught, whether directly or indirectly.

Q: Why doesn't Preeti just leave her community?

A: That's a loaded question. It seems to project an easy answer: If it's toxic, leave. But it's not that simple. When your identity and culture and religion and sense of belonging are tightly woven into the community, leaving can have lifelong effects. While Preeti isn't very involved in her community, her parents are. Leaving would mean having a gaping hole at the intersection of family and culture. The Indian community, particularly at a mandir, is the beating heart of life, second only to the home. One doesn't just attend service and detach. It's socializing, cultural and religious festivities, a connection to roots. Preeti's parents aren't going to leave it because of a few toxic people. They stood their ground for their place and their right to worship and associate. When it means that much to her parents, Preeti isn't going to simply walk away. Some things are worth fighting for.

The entire community isn't problematic. Preeti has friends and her mom has an auntie squad. The good is worth saving, and the good is worth supporting, worth expanding to fight against the bad.

Q: Why was it a pivotal moment when Preeti sought medical help for her mental illness and asked Daniel to support her?

A: There are stigmas in the medical field, within Preeti's family, and in society at large that view mental illness as something to be ashamed of, a taboo, too wretched to even discuss. Preeti never felt free to discuss her mental health and felt it reduced her as a doctor and as a daughter, as a person in general. She dealt with anxiety and depression quietly, locked away in a mental war zone. Daniel had seen this in her and instead of walking away or not understanding, he helped her deal with it. He played music for her, introduced her to calming apps, listened to her, held her in silence, and gently encouraged her to seek help, all without judging her. So when Preeti makes a decision to seek help, she makes the decision to take care of herself first. She's spent her life and career taking care of others. Asking Daniel to sit with her through her first therapy session was an incredible moment of vulnerability, which in itself required a sense of strength and trust.

Q: Why did Daniel keep his financial information private?

A: Daniel had lied to Preeti on several occasions while they were dating about his financial situation because he didn't want her to be intimidated or take advantage or feel uncomfortable. Daniel comes from an architectural empire worth millions. He's been exploited in the past, hurt. Maybe he didn't necessarily think Preeti would react in a negative way, but he wanted to keep that political, cutthroat, materialistic environment out of their relationship and was willing to lie to her in order to do so.

Q: Preeti left Daniel for various heartbreaking reasons. Should Daniel have let her go once he found out why she left him?

A: Another loaded question. Preeti ultimately chose her parents' health and well-being over her own happiness, and she was afraid to tell Daniel because she didn't want to hurt him. However, true love is strong and we all make mistakes. But do we learn and grow from those errors? Daniel and Preeti recognized that she made mistakes and that she would handle things differently now. Daniel also recognized that Preeti was terrified of her mother dying because of the stress and attacks from her aunts. Preeti grew, and Daniel saw that. In the end, Preeti had a chance to show how she's changed.

Q: How does Preeti's inner circle of strong women support her?

A: Preeti has a small but ferocious set of friends. Reema is described as being the "mama duck." She's the oldest, recently married, and fits into the community just fine. She's often the voice of reason and lends a listening ear. Liya is strong, opinionated, and has gone through a horrible ordeal with the community. She understands how it feels to be shoved out and ripped apart by gossip. Sana is the youngest, quiet and traditional. She offers the view of seeing the other side of things to round out the group. These women will make sure they're there for Preeti. They text and video-chat and have girls' nights to make sure each woman is seen and heard. Family is important, but so is a strong network of friends.

Q: Why did you write Preeti's aunts as such horrible people? And why did it take so long for Preeti to stand up to them?

A: Regardless of their culture, people can be horrible with or without a reason. Preeti's aunts have a long history of trying to damage Preeti's parents and will try to do so despite the costs. I've known people like this and wanted to bring them to light on the page so we can perhaps reflect on whether we know these types of people, whether we stand up to them, or whether we *are* them.

In traditional South Asian communities and families, one doesn't disrespect one's elders. It's considered extremely rude and disgraceful, a poor reflection on the child and the parents. Preeti adores her parents too much to bring them shame or any pain. This becomes problematic quickly. It gives elders all the rights and a platform to say or do whatever they want with little recourse or backlash. Society changes quickly and what was considered acceptable even five years ago may not be acceptable now. Removing the ability to safely correct or question or discuss with someone who shows toxic behavior strips the younger person of a voice. They are a victim with hands tied behind their back to such practices. We should have respect for elders, but also for younger people—for everyone, really. It should be mutual.

The other thing we see is Preeti's parents' belief that the older generation must discuss, dispute, and settle issues among themselves, leaving the children out of their mess. This is a two-sided coin. Parents want to alleviate the burden and carry things out in a diplomatic manner, and if it gets ugly, the situation won't spill onto the children and create feuds. It also keeps parents apprised of issues. On the other side of the coin is that it takes away the child's opportunity to stand up for themselves.

Q: Which characters did you enjoy developing the most?

A: I thoroughly loved writing Grandma and Grandpa Thompson, as they remind me so much of people in my life. But the characters I enjoyed developing the most were Preeti's parents. They remind me so much of my own. They're imperfect, but they want to repay every deed with a kind act, keep the peace no matter the personal cost, and love Preeti with their entire souls. The three of them have a remarkable relationship, even if Preeti finds it difficult to tell them certain things. Also, writing Preeti's parents was such a breath of fresh air after writing Liya's parents, particularly her father, in the preceding book, *The Trouble with Hating You*.

Q: Why is it important for Preeti to take her mom's hand in the hospital when she's diagnosed with anxiety?

A: Since Preeti has silently suffered from anxiety due to social stigma, she doesn't want her mother to endure that same stigma, to feel ashamed or inferior, the way Preeti has felt. Preeti is a physician, and she wants her mother to know anxiety can be treated and patients can live full, happy lives.

Additionally, the Indian culture often teaches that the younger generation should always care for the older generation, especially in regard to children caring for their parents. Preeti has a deep love for her parents, so her desire to comfort them is natural.

She also just wants to be there for her mom so her mother doesn't feel alone and to make sure that her mom is healthy and thriving. Anxiety and stress have placed her mother in the hospital twice, and Preeti knows this could've been avoided had they taken other steps.

Q: In the end, Preeti chooses herself first and then other things align. Why was this important and how did it lead to her making other decisions?

A: Preeti needs to take care of herself for once instead of trying to appease others. While it makes her happy to see her parents happy, the route she was taking wasn't conducive to good mental health. She has to learn to take a stand for herself first, for her mentality and happiness, and that enables her to be stronger when she has to make choices. She has to learn that loving herself and making decisions pertaining to her happiness are nothing to feel shame over, and once she accepts herself and makes strides for her own well-being, future choices begin to revolve around that.

Eager for more romance by Sajni Patel?
Don't miss Liya's story,

The Trouble with Hating You

Available now!

About the Author

Sajni Patel was born in vibrant India and raised in the heart of Texas, surrounded by a lot of delicious food and plenty of diversity. She draws on her personal experiences, cultural expectations, and Southern flair to create worlds that center on strong Indian women. Once in MMA, she's now all about puppies and rainbows and tortured-love stories. She currently lives in Austin, where she not-so-secretly watches Matthew McConaughey from afar during UT football games. Queso is her weakness, and thanks to her family's cooking, Indian/Tex-Mex cuisine is a real thing. She's a die-hard Marvel Comics fan, a lover of chocolates from around the world, and is always wrapped up in a story.